Praise for the novels of Robert Littell

"Besides being hugely entertaining, *The Company* is a serious look at how our nation exercised power, for good and ill, in the second half of the twentieth century."
—Patrick Anderson, *The Washington Post Book World*

"*The Company* reads like a breeze. . . . Guaranteed to suck you right back into the Alice-in-Wonderland world of spy vs. spy . . . a ripping good yarn—entertaining, chilling, insightful."
—Andrew Nagorski, *Newsweek*

"Since his Cold War classic, *The Defection of A.J. Lewinter,* Littell has been steadily creating his own subgenre, the counter-thriller, witty and highly original tales that play off the clichés of the Cold War thriller and subvert them."
—Joseph Finder, *The Washington Post*

"*The Sisters* is so clever, so outrageous and cynical that your breath is taken away. . . . We're seduced by the game of who's controlling whom . . . and by his amusingly quirky characters. . . . Ultimately, we are hooked by the story, which it is not much of an exaggeration to call the plot of plots."
—Christopher Lehmann-Haupt, *The New York Times*

Connoisseurs of the literary spy thriller have elevated Robert Littell to the genre's highest ranks along with John le Carré, Len Deighton, and Graham Greene. Littell's novels include the *New York Times* bestseller *The Company* (rights sold in eleven countries, film rights sold to Columbia Pictures), *The Defection of A.J. Lewinter, The Once and Future Spy, The Amateur, The Sisters, The October Circle, The Revolutionist, An Agent in Place, Mother Russia,* and *The Visiting Professor.* His novels have been published in eleven languages. A former *Newsweek* journalist, Littell is an American currently living in France.

THE DEBRIEFING

A NOVEL

ROBERT LITTELL

PENGUIN BOOKS

For Mel Bernstein, Ernest Finch, and Jim Riouff,
who started me out on the not-so-beaten path

PENGUIN BOOKS
Published by the Penguin Group
Penguin Group (USA) Inc., 375 Hudson Street, New York, New York 10014, U.S.A.
Penguin Group (Canada), 90 Eglinton Avenue East, Suite 700, Toronto,
Ontario, Canada M4P 2Y3 (a division of Pearson Penguin Canada Inc.)
Penguin Books Ltd, 80 Strand, London WC2R 0RL, England
Penguin Ireland, 25 St Stephen's Green, Dublin 2, Ireland (a division of Penguin Books Ltd)
Penguin Group (Australia), 250 Camberwell Road, Camberwell,
Victoria 3124, Australia (a division of Pearson Australia Group Pty Ltd)
Penguin Books India Pvt Ltd, 11 Community Centre, Panchsheel Park, New Delhi – 110 017, India
Penguin Group (NZ), 67 Apollo Drive, Rosedale, North Shore 0632,
New Zealand (a division of Pearson New Zealand Ltd)
Penguin Books (South Africa) (Pty) Ltd, 24 Sturdee Avenue,
Rosebank, Johannesburg 2196, South Africa

Penguin Books Ltd, Registered Offices: 80 Strand, London WC2R 0RL, England

First published in the United States of America by Harper & Row, Publishers, Inc. 1979
Published by The Overlook Press, Peter Mayer Publishers, Inc. 2004
Reprinted by arrangement with The Overlook Press, Peter Mayer Publishers, Inc.
Published in Penguin Books 2008

1 3 5 7 9 10 8 6 4 2

Grateful acknowledgment is made for permission to reprint lines of poetry from
The Complete Poetry of Osip Emilevich Mandelstam translated by
Burton Raffel and Alla Burago. Copyright © 1973
by State University of New York Press. Reprinted by permission
of the State University of New York Press, Albany, New York.

THE LIBRARY OF CONGRESS HAS CATALOGED THE HARDCOVER EDITION AS FOLLOWS:
Littell, Robert.
The debriefing / Robert Littell.
p. cm.
ISBN 978-0-14-311440-6
I. Title.
PZ4.L772Dc 1979 813'.5"4   78-22442

Printed in the United States of America

"Debrief? That means you will ask me questions. But I have no answers. I don't know secrets.... How long will this debriefing take?"

"It's already started. It will end when we know more about you than God."

CHAPTER

1

He seems at loose ends, half-hearted, polite but distant, vaguely disreputable with his crosscurrents of thick wavy hair spilling off in several directions, vaguely sinister behind his steel-rimmed eyeglasses that trap the light at odd angles and turn into tarnished mirrors. He stares vacantly over the shoulders of people and tends to become aware of their voices when they stop talking. He has trouble swallowing, digesting, defecating. And remembering; especially remembering. His mind wanders; sometimes he gets where he's going with no memory of the trip. Sleep is out of the question. The few times he has managed to doze off, he woke up screaming—though he was never certain which of the recent events in his life he was screaming about.

"Aksenov broke a leg," the duty officer is saying. "The report neglected to specify which one." His upper lip curls into a suggestion of a sneer. "Walked in front of a taxi, so it seems, so it seems. You're the only warm body on the courier list I could find."

Oleg Kulakov stares past the pinned-up sleeve of the duty officer's blouse at the wall calendar with the photograph of the girl driving a shiny new tractor; something in the girl's smile— its unrestrained quality; she doesn't stint for the photographer—reminds him of Nadia before she . . .

"The calendar's on the wrong month," Kulakov says, cutting

3

off the thought before it becomes painful. "We're not January. What we are is February."

The duty officer glances at the wall without interest, then turns back to Kulakov. "I'm sorry about you losing the weekend," he says. "We'll make it up to you. In any case, you'll be back by Sunday night. There's a military flight from Cairo to Moscow. Going, you'll fly Aeroflot and stop over in Athens for six hours. The embassy people will hold your hand between planes."

The pulse beats in Kulakov's ear; he feels suddenly faint and presses his knees against the duty officer's desk to steady himself. For an instant he is afraid he will black out. *Going, I'll hold over in Athens for six hours! Going where?* "Going where?" he asks the duty officer, a fussy man who has obviously missed several promotions along the way. He has the same rank as Kulakov—they are both majors—but the duty officer is at least ten years older. Judging from his medals and the missing left arm, he must have been a war hero in his day. Oddly, Kulakov has never set eyes on him before. "Where is it I'm going?"

"You haven't been listening," complains the duty officer, who wears a small plastic plate over his medals, with his name, "Gamov." He brushes dandruff from his left shoulder with an impatient gesture. "Aksenov has a broken leg. You're the only one on the courier list I could get hold of on a moment's notice. Someone has to deliver this pouch to Cairo by tonight. You're elected. By one vote. Mine."

Kulakov tries to concentrate on the mechanics of the assignment, but his head is spinning; he is dizzy with possibilities. "Of course I'll go," he says quickly. "I'm glad to fill in. Aksenov is an old comrade. He'd do the same for me."

Kulakov is instantly sorry he spoke; to his own ear, he sounds too eager. He is sure his voice will give him away, will prompt the duty officer to look up at him suspiciously, to search out the memorandum he, Kulakov, has seen with his own eyes ordering his name stricken from the courier list. But Gamov is bending

4

over his blotter, stamping and signing Kulakov's orders, which will serve as an exit visa. He deftly folds the single sheet of paper with his one hand and slides it into a brown envelope stamped "Courier Service." For some reason Kulakov focuses on the duty officer's fingers; they are long and thin and graceful, feminine even—the fingers of a woman on the hands of a man.

"Your travel documents," Gamov says, offering Kulakov the envelope. "Your flight leaves Moscow in"—he studies his watch, which he wears on the inside of his wrist—"an hour and a quarter."

Kulakov slips the envelope into the breast pocket of his civilian jacket, starts for the door in a daze.

"Ho, Kulakov, not so fast," the duty officer calls. Kulakov turns back and stares at him, his heart pounding. Any second now he'll wake up screaming!

"The pouch," the duty officer reminds him. "You forgot the pouch."

"Yes, of course, the pouch." Kulakov smiles weakly.

Shaking his head, the duty officer squats before an old office safe. Shielding the dial from Kulakov with his body, he carefully spins the knob. The heavy door clicks open, swings back. Gamov rummages in the shadowy interior and extracts a worn leather diplomatic pouch. Kulakov, who has been a diplomatic courier for twenty-eight years, hefts it, locks the thin linked bracelet around his left wrist, sets the destruct mechanism, then stoops and deposits the key in a compartment sewn into the inside of his shoe. Straightening, he reaches across the desk and signs in triplicate the receipt acknowledging that he, and not Major Gamov, is now in possession of one sealed diplomatic pouch, the contents of which he vows to protect with his life.

As Kulakov leaves, Gamov stares after him in a peculiar way. His upper lip curls into a suggestion of a sneer as he absently turns toward the wall, tears off January and throws it away.

The driver, who doubles as an embassy heavy because of a

budget squeeze, keeps glancing at Kulakov in the rear-view mirror to catch his reaction. "So our Soviet adviser tells the Egyptian general staff—"

"I spent two years in Cairo," interrupts the pale second secretary sitting next to the driver. He nervously grinds out his American cigarette in the ashtray, which is already overflowing. "Give me Athens anytime."

They are speeding along the coast road in a Mercedes toward the Athens embassy. Another Mercedes, with two embassy heavies, follows right behind them.

"So our Soviet adviser tells the Egyptian general staff," the driver begins again, casting an annoyed look at the pale second secretary, " 'The trick is to do as we did with Napoleon. You let the Jews penetrate deep into the country until their supply lines are very long and yours are very short. Then, when they're inside the trap, you sit back and wait for winter!' " The driver observes Kulakov's failure to react in the rear-view mirror. "You wait for winter," he explains. "Get it? *There is no winter in Egypt!*"

"It's an old joke," snaps the pale second secretary. "Everyone's heard it. Here—" He twists in his seat belt toward Kulakov, stares at him for an instant before he catches himself staring and finishes what he started to say. "You'll get a glimpse of the Acropolis any second now."

The car turns inland up a broad avenue and Kulakov sees the Acropolis in the distance through the front window. It glistens in the cold sunlight, bleached laundry drying on an ancient skyline. He inches to his right to get a better look at it, and casually rests his fingertips on the door handle.

"I've been here fourteen months," the pale second secretary remarks—he is uneasy with silence and tries to fill it—"and I never get tired of looking at it."

"One ruin is the same as the next," grunts the driver.

Kulakov's fingers tighten around the door handle. He wonders if he'll have the nerve to do it.

6

In a curiously detached way, he has been wondering ever since he walked out of the duty office. The old janitor was in the corridor, standing on a step ladder changing light bulbs in the ceiling. Kulakov didn't trust himself to look up at him. Instead he gripped his ankle as he passed—his way of saying goodbye. Outside, a Ministry of Defense Moskvich was waiting to take him to Moscow Airport. Kulakov settled into the back seat, expecting at any moment to hear the car radio burst into life and a voice blurt: "The diplomatic courier Kulakov must not be permitted to leave the country." But there was no voice, only the droning of traffic and the running comments of the driver, a cranky civilian who thought that pedestrians had been put on earth by God to torture the lucky few who found themselves behind steering wheels.

At the airport, Kulakov was ushered into a small lounge set aside for ministry personnel, along with two colonels and an inspector general, all on their way for one reason or another to Cairo. His papers were carefully checked by an unsmiling frontier officer, who studied his passport photograph, and then his face, for a nerve-racking moment. When the flight was finally called, Kulakov mingled with the other passengers and headed for the gate. Trying to breathe normally, suppressing a last-second urge to turn and run, he passed the control point and then the two armed soldiers who stood on either side of the boarding ramp. Inside the plane, Kulakov sucked in a lungful of stale air and sank into a seat in the first-class section on the aisle next to the inspector general, a red-faced bureaucrat who demanded ice and poured himself a stiff vodka from a small flask without offering one to his neighbor. No matter. Kulakov's stomach was in no condition for vodka.

The plane taxied to the end of the runway—and then abruptly stopped. Through the small, scratched oval window, Kulakov saw several limousines approaching at high speed. He slumped in his seat, breathing with so much difficulty that the stewardess bent over him and asked if anything was wrong. No, nothing was wrong, he muttered, and he turned his head and watched the limousines pull up with a squeal of brakes, saw the crew open the plane door and let down a portable ladder. Outside, a tall, immaculately dressed man in his early fifties—Kulakov recognized him as a junior minister whose photograph had recently appeared in *Pravda*—shook hands with half a dozen men. A woman thrust a bouquet of lilacs wrapped in cellophane into his arms as he turned to climb into the plane. Three aides followed. Everyone was very polite, very deferential. The minister himself found places for his aides before he permitted himself to be ushered to a seat across the aisle from Kulakov. *A new breed,* Kulakov thought, taking in the cut of the minister's suit, the new leather attaché case, the discreet hammer-and-sickle pin in his lapel. *This is how Gregori would have ended up if only he had . . . if only . . . if . . . if . . . if . . .*

Kulakov was still struggling with the *ifs* when he spotted the embassy heavies who had come to hold his hand between planes. They were waiting just beyond passport control in Athens airport. Their eyes, glazed with a kind of passive professionality, passed over the minister and his aides, the two colonels and the inspector general, and settled on Kulakov and the worn leather diplomatic pouch chained to his left wrist. "You are invited to come with us," said the one who appeared to be in charge. Then he smiled and thumped Kulakov on the back and added, "There is a hot lunch waiting for you at the embassy."

The two Mercedeses, moving slowly through heavy traffic, turn into Constitution Square and come to a stop at a red light. Crowds of lunchtime strollers surge across the intersection just ahead. *Now,* Kulakov tells himself, *now or never.* His fingers tug gently at the handle; the door opens a crack. Up front the heavy is concentrating on the red light, waiting for it to change. The pale second secretary is fumbling for another American cigarette.

The light turns green. The heavy jars the Mercedes into gear. Kulakov pushes the door open and leaps into the crowd just as the car starts to roll. Behind him there is a screeching of brakes,

8

then the sharp sound of doors being flung open against their hinges. Several men jump from the cars after him. "Kulakov," the pale secretary screams in a hysterical voice. "Do you know what it is you do?"

Kulakov is in full flight now, careening off a kiosk, reeling wildly through the scattering crowd that senses danger but doesn't know what direction it is coming from, tripping over a baby's stroller filled with celery stalks, knocking down an old woman, stumbling over the outstretched metal legs of a beggar. Police whistles sound in the distance.

At an intersection, Kulakov casts a quick glance over his shoulder, sees two of the heavies bullying their way through the crowd behind him. One of the heavies catches sight of Kulakov, calls triumphantly to the others, snatches a large-caliber pistol from his jacket and levels it at him. Dozens of people dive for doorways. Kulakov, riveted, peers down the flight path of the bullet, sways on the balls of his feet, *leans toward the bore of the pistol to meet the bullet.* It is suddenly just another solution. Sound ceases, motion slows; Kulakov has the sensation of being under water. Floating on emotionless currents, he waits. It is with a sense of disappointment that he sees the pale second secretary reach out and knock the heavy's arm up.

"Kulakov," the pale second secretary pleads in a high-pitched voice. "For the love of God, come back."

For Kulakov, there is nothing to go back to. He turns almost reluctantly—the game hasn't been played out yet—and runs across the street, bounces blindly off the fenders of a taxi and just misses being run down by a bus. Gasping for air, fighting the nausea mounting in his throat, he rounds a corner, dashes diagonally across the street and ducks into an alleyway. The pavement pitches under his feet like the deck of a ship. Halfway down the alleyway, he finds the open back door of a hotel kitchen, lumbers through it and the restaurant, knocking over a serving table, scattering waiters, and emerges through a revolving door into another boulevard. The sidewalk is drenched with water gushing from an open hydrant; dirt floats on thin currents

9

into sewers. A line of taxis is parked in front of the hotel. Kulakov hikes his trousers, tiptoes through the water, climbs into the first taxi on the line.

"Take me," he says in heavily accented English—and stops because of the fierce pain deep in his chest. With the back of his sleeve he wipes foam from his lips, sweat from his eyes. "Take me," he begins again, the driver eying him with curiosity, "to the American Embassy."

Some forty kilometers outside Moscow, near the village of Nikolina Gora, a single-lane macadam road leads off into a forest of snow-covered white birches. An international road sign indicating "No Entrance" is planted at the turnoff, and another marked "50" half a kilometer into the road; it indicates the speed limit for those who decide to ignore the first sign.

The road, which is cleared of snow and sanded daily, leads to a small military compound surrounded by an electrified fence. There are several wooden buildings in the compound. Smoke rises from chimneys. At the center of the compound is a two-story cement structure with a forest of antennas on the roof.

Inside the building, a lieutenant colonel with a thin scar over his left eye is patiently decoding, from a one-time pad, a message from a Soviet military attaché in Athens. The decoded message, which will be read by the officer who is decoding it and one other person and then destroyed, says:

"The diplomatic courier Kulakov has defected. Implementing Contingency Plan Bravo."

CHAPTER

2

Stone is trapped on the surface of things: moisture fogging a plate-glass window, paint peeling from a storefront, fleeting thoughts clinging like a scab to an idea. "Yes . . . sure . . . uh huh . . . no kidding. . . ." Speaking English with a vague trace of some foreign accent, he inserts comments in Thro's pauses as if he is slipping coins into a slot to pay for a recorded announcement. His voice is all undertone, his gestures edgy: he hooks a finger over his shirt collar, constructs a tower with blocks of sugar, demolishes it by adding one too many, fidgets in his chair, glances at his watch again without seeing it, stares off into some middle distance, focusing on nothing; on everything.

"You spray fluorocarbons into the atmosphere," Thro explains patiently, "where they're bombarded by sunlight—right?—and what do they do when they're bombarded by sunlight? They break up, releasing atoms of chlorine, is what they do. Then the chlorine atoms react with the ozone, which is a kind of oxygen whose molecules contain three atoms instead of what's normal, which is two, converting it. . . . You're sure I never told you this one before?"

"No, no, this is all new to me." He thinks: *Everything will be riding on the first contact. That's the moment when it either goes right or it goes wrong. The first contact.*

". . . converting it to conventional oxygen, and there goes your

11

ozone shield and in pour the ultraviolet rays, and zingo, everyone comes down with skin cancer."

"My God!" He thinks: *I've got to handle him carefully. Any sudden motion, he'll take off like a panic-stricken pigeon.*

"That's one possibility," continues Thro. She laughs nervously. "Then there's the possibility we're moving into a new ice age. Indisputable scientific fact number one: The earth is colder than it was ten years ago. Indisputable scientific fact number two: The icecap over the poles is growing thicker each year. Are you listening, Stone? You sure you're interested to hear this? If that doesn't finish us off, there's always the possibility that we'll use ourselves up." Thro is becoming agitated by her own story. "We dig out of the earth 2.7 billion tons of minerals a year. Okay. If you figure on the basis of a three percent annual growth rate a year, which figure is modest to say the least, the consumption of minerals in a single year one thousand years from now will be greater than the weight of the earth! Can you imagine that, Stone? *Greater than the weight of the entire earth.*"

"Holy cow!" Stone tries to imagine it, but draws a blank. He thinks: *If I went according to the manual, I wouldn't be doing this myself. I'd send in Kiick or Mozart. But I'm curious to see him—I'm curious to see the face of the man whose life I plan to ruin.*

Thro bites viciously into a croissant, sucks noisily at her cup of American coffee, takes another bite of croissant. "Then there's the distinct possibility that the Antarctic ice sheet will slip into the ocean, which would raise the sea level twenty feet and flood every coastal city in the world. And you have to confront the fact that someday the sun is going to burn out. And if all that doesn't get us"—she breaks into a slightly hysterical laugh—"we've got to live with the very real likelihood that there is less than one atom for every eighty-eight gallons of space, which means the universe is going to expand forever, with the result that the stars will all fizzle out like candles and we'll be adrift in an endless empty black graveyard of space."

"That would be a pity." Stone thinks: *I hope I don't like him.*

I hope to God he rubs me the wrong way. I'm ready to go through with it even if I do like him, but it'll be easier if I don't.

"What worries me sick," Thro sighs, "is that something will happen that we don't have enough imagination to imagine." She bangs down her coffee cup. "You haven't heard a word I said, Stone. The fact is you don't give a damn how the world will end."

"You want to do me a favor," Stone says in an undertone, irritated at the heads starting to turn their way, "stop flashing that goddamn ring of yours when you talk. It makes me nervous." He thinks: *What if the heavies refuse to let him out of their sight? What if he tumbles to the microphone? Or the camera? What if?*

Thro's eyes—they look brand-new—suddenly lift and focus on Stone's face; she looks deathly pale in the cold lilac light sifting through the leafless branches on Boulevard Saint-Germain. "Sometimes," she says softly—when she is really hurt, she always talks softly—"I can't believe how aggressive you are."

"Everyone's aggressive," he says sullenly, "except the dead."

"My aggressions are less violent than yours, Stone," she retorts. "They're physical."

Stone, embarrassed by her stare, shakes his head, waves a hand—vague gestures of apology for his natural acidity, which is the way he responds to pressure. There is a long silence. *Why is it,* he thinks, *that my relationships with women start off in poetry, slip into prose and wind up in strained silences?* "I'm sorry, sweetheart." He is conciliatory now. "It's just that every time the ring turns black, you have a way of waving it around like a flag."

An elegant woman at the next table turns quickly away, whispering to her companion in French, and Stone, annoyed at being overheard, switches to what Thro calls his "BBC Russian"; it always manages to get a laugh out of her. "I've got an idea for you, Thro. Why don't you put an ad in the *Tribune*. Or hire yourself a skywriter." He reaches up and traces a phrase in Cyrillic in the air with the tip of a spoon. "N-y-e-t s-e-x."

13

The accent has the desired effect; Thro cannot help but smile. "Love, it's my way of signaling you," she answers in a Russian only slightly less fluent than his. "All lovers have signals. I happen to have a gold ring that turns black when I get my period." She tugs playfully at the hairs on the back of his wrist, leans closer until her mouth is next to his ear, switches into what Stone calls her "BBC sexy." "Remember," she says playfully, "our first trip to Paris together?"

As if Stone could ever forget it. He had been scouting the Soviet frontier near Hamina, Finland, for crossing points. Thro, five pounds overweight and wandering around with a degree in psychology she wasn't sure what to do with, was on her way back from the Hermitage in Leningrad. Their paths crossed in Helsinki, in a hotel sauna, to be exact. Stone was flat on his back, being scrubbed down by an old woman he nicknamed "Mama Wash" when Thro turned up, round and pink and bare and unconcerned by five extra pounds or the bareness, carrying it off as if it were the most natural thing in the world to walk into a sauna stark naked and find yourself alone (Mama Wash soon disappeared) with a strange man trying to will away an erection. Unsuccessfully, as things turned out. They made love in the sauna, showered together, made love again in his hotel room, then took their first long look at each other: Stone with his natural acidity and his brooding way of peering out at the world and his permanent fixture of a frown, as if he were pondering the absence of a great scheme of things; Thro with her run-on sentences describing all the ways the world would end— the list was never-ending. Both of them liked what they saw, and said it, so they teamed up and went on to Paris for what turned out to be a glorious week, with Thro falling in love with an outdoor café in Palais Royal while Stone fell in love with Thro. "Get that company of yours to post you here," she commanded—it was before she knew what Stone's company did; before she herself went to work for it—"or at least invent some assignments that will bring us back once in a while."

Which is why, when Stone got the bright idea to set up a Russian diplomat, he picked one who was based in Paris.

Stone glances at his watch, sees it this time, calls for the check, argues (in BBC French; another smile from Thro) with the waiter attempting to hold them accountable for four croissants instead of three, counts out change. "I've got to get going," he says in English. "I'll be back at Kiick's shop around two-thirty, three maybe, to tie up the loose ends. Which should put me back at the hotel around six at the latest. Did you see what Kiick painted on the window of the showroom? 'Père et Fils depuis 1977'!"

Thro smiles, but there is a tightness to her lips, and lines at the corners of her eyes. "Traditions have to start someplace." She hesitates. "This isn't . . . dangerous, is it, Stone?" she asks quietly.

Stone shakes his head and smiles, and she smiles back, though the tightness is still there. "I'll never get used to you with a three-day beard," she says. "You look like a Polish Jew from the shtetl."

Stone answers in singsong Yiddish. "A Polish Jew from the shtetl is what I am. Gold rings turned black by your endocrine balance are what I detest. *Sholom aleichem.*"

Thro waves her black ring in his face. "Are you a Hasid," she taunts him in English—the elegant lady at the next table visibly cringes—"that you're afraid to have sex during menstruation?"

Stone picks up a *Tribune* at a kiosk, scans the headlines, is mildly surprised to see it is already February. He is all business now, and the first order of business is to tuck the *Tribune* under his arm so that the crossword puzzle is clearly visible.

Stone was trained as a street man, but he has had very little opportunity to put to use what he knows. Now he operates on memories of old textbooks with a very limited distribution, and an instinct for the street that caught the eye of his instructors when he started out twenty years before.

Halfway across the Pont des Arts, he stops to watch an unshaven young man at work on all fours. (He is trying to pass

15

himself off as a poverty-stricken art student, but the Gucci loafers give him away.) He has printed, in large Gothic letters, on the walkway:

LES QUOIQUE SONT DES PARCEQUE MÉCONNUS

M. PROUST

and is illuminating, with bits of colored chalk, the first letter of each word.

Where, Stone wonders, *does Kiick find them?* Shrugging, he drops a franc onto the chalk drawing of a hat already filled with coins.

"Kiick said you'd be stingy," the young artist mutters without looking up. His voice is neutral, without tone, without shadings. "In case you're curious, you're clean as a whistle."

"You do that well," Stone comments, nodding toward the illuminated letters, trying to sound mildly sarcastic.

"I'm a medievalist at heart," the young man replies seriously.

"Aren't we all," moans Stone.

He continues across the bridge, feeling more secure now that he has confirmed he is not being followed. To be on the safe side, he mingles for a while with a large group of German tourists gaping at the Louvre, then doubles back on his tracks, wandering (not so aimlessly) through the park. A church bell is chiming the hour as he enters Palais Royal from the Louvre side.

He spots the two heavies almost immediately; the one he is supposed to notice is sitting on a bench scattering seeds to pigeons that peck around his trousers, which are baggy and have wide frayed cuffs. The other, dressed in clothing he bought in Paris, sits on the edge of a fountain, which has been turned off for the winter, buried in a right-wing French newspaper called *Minute*. The third heavy he learns about from the Gypsy woman (another one of Kiick's free-lancers) with a baby under her arm (Stone doubts the baby has been thrown in free of charge). "There's another one in the café," simpers the Gypsy woman, holding out her hand for a coin. "Crew cut. Blue tie. Also a team photographing from the apartments."

16

Stone comes up with a franc for the Gypsy, then strolls across the park toward La Gaudriole, Thro's hangout when they first came to Paris together. They were drawn to the small café with the white metal tables outside because of the name; Thro was forever telling off-color jokes, which is what *gaudriole* means. Stone, his face tense beneath the mask of beard, approaches the Russian diplomat who is sitting at a table, his feet planted flat, knees apart, a copy of Céline placed conspicuously in front of him. He looks exactly like his passport photograph, Stone thinks: tired, with a grainy complexion; one-dimensional. He is fiftyish, with thick hair brushed straight back without a part, and very ill at ease; he wears black silk stockings that have long since lost their elasticity and sag around his thick ankles. Two tables away, the heavy with the crew cut and the blue tie sizes up Stone; his look is so open, so frank, that Stone has the impression he is soliciting.

"Good day to you," Stone addresses the diplomat. He speaks French with a slight German accent now. "I invite you to come with me."

The Russian diplomat, whose name is Boris Gurenko, looks around uncertainly. "I understood the meeting would be here. You specified La Gaudriole. You said nothing about following you elsewhere."

"The meeting is here," Stone explains patiently. "The exchange of my documents for your money, if it takes place at all, will take place in an excellent restaurant not very far away." Stone glances casually at the line of apartment windows overlooking the park. "Here it is too ... observable for my tastes."

The diplomat hesitates, turns questioningly toward the heavy two tables away, who takes another long slow insolent look at Stone before he makes up his mind. He nods once. "All right," the diplomat says, collecting his copy of Céline. "But I don't see what you'll gain. They'll follow wherever we go."

Without a word, Stone starts off with the diplomat in tow. The three heavies fan out behind them; two in their wake, the third (the one Stone isn't supposed to notice) angled off to one side. With Stone leading, this odd procession makes its way to

17

the entrance of Le Grand Vefour, a three-star restaurant on the far side of Palais Royal, backing onto Rue de Beaujolais.

Inside, Stone—vaguely ill at ease; dining at a three-star restaurant was Mozart's bright idea of how to ditch the heavies—mumbles a name to the maître d'hôtel, who scans his notebook, confirms the reservation, offers them the last two vacant seats. Behind them at the door, there is a frantic conference as the three heavies (the one in French clothes has dropped all pretense of being there by accident) study the menu posted in a glass case; it is impossible to get out of Le Grand Vefour, a restaurant where the *vin ordinaire* is a reasonably *grand cru*, for less than two hundred francs a head. After an animated discussion, the Russians pool their resources, dispatch the one with the French suit inside—where he is turned away by the maître d'hôtel; one dines at Le Grand Vefour by reservation only.

"That was neatly done," the Russian diplomat comments, warming to the ambiance, licking his lips at the thought of the *haute cuisine* that he will soon feast on. Outside, two very worried heavies have taken up positions on either side of the entrance to the restaurant; the third has raced off to find a telephone.

"The Americans have a saying," remarks Stone. "Two's company, three's a crowd."

The Russian watches intently as the waiter serves lobster in a milky sauce to someone at the next table. "They are only here to protect me," he explains, "in case you aren't what you say you are."

"You have no need of them," Stone says flatly. "I am what I say I am: Someone who has four single-spaced typed sheets of military information to sell if the price is right."

The maître d'hôtel approaches. "Would you care for a cocktail?"

"We'll order immediately," announces the Russian diplomat. "My friend here has a lean and hungry look." Gurenko studies the menu as Stone squirms uncomfortably; Le Grand Vefour is not his cup of tea. "We'll begin with some *gravettes*," the Russian instructs the maître d'hôtel. To Stone, he explains: "*Gra-vettes* are very small sweet oysters from the Arcachon Basin. I always make it a habit to begin a meal eating something with my fingers. It's very important to touch food, I think." To the maître d'hôtel, who is visibly impressed: "Then we'll attack a plate of your young leeks with truffles in olive oil. After that"— Gurenko purses his lips, as he tries to decide—"ah, after that we'll try your Rouelle de Langouste Bretonne à la Vapeur de Verveine aux Girolles et Chicorée." To Stone: "You'll like that. The transparency of the green chicory leaf complements the translucence of the *langouste*. Now, let me give this some thought. Yes, yes, after that we'll have a salad of white endives and mushrooms—*canaris, lactaires, girolles, charbonniers* and *trompettes de la mort* would make a superb bouquet. Don't bother with the cheese platter; only bring us a perfect Reblochon. For wine, you'll have to put up with my unusual tastes. Bring us a bottle of your Mouton Lafitte, 1964. Ha! I can see the choice astonishes you." The Russian explains to Stone. "I'm one of the very few people who appreciate the '64. Most people consider it too tart. But it suits me."

The maître d'hôtel backs off, still scribbling on his pad. The Russian says conversationally, "I've always thought the world was divided into two groups—those who prefer a good year of a bad wine, and those who prefer a bad year of a good wine."

Stone, out of curiosity, asks, "What made you choose Céline as your recognition signal?"

This is the last thing that the diplomat expects to be asked. "I happened to be reading Céline," he answers carefully—he's not sure where the question is leading and feels his way. "Many people consider him a great writer."

"There are many who consider him a great anti-Semite," retorts Stone.

The sommelier lets Gurenko inspect the label on the wine bottle before he opens it, lays the cork alongside the bottle, tilts Gurenko's glass and measures out a small amount, swirls it around with a practiced gesture before he offers it to him. The

19

Russian sips, nods his acceptance. The glasses are half filled. The sommelier withdraws.

"About Céline," Gurenko says. He thinks he understands why the subject was raised now; the man in front of him with several days' growth of beard must be a Jew. "There were many great artists who were anti-Semites. That shouldn't stop us from appreciating the genius beneath—"

"Céline was an anti-Semite at a time when millions were murdered for the crime of being Jewish," Stone bursts out. There is a passion, a sudden intensity, a sudden bitterness, to the rush of words. The conversation is like a squall; Gurenko is rubbing him the wrong way. "You look past his anti-Semitism to the genius beneath, assuming there is a genius beneath, because you don't give a goddamn about the killing of the Jews. Oh, intellectually you recognize it as a crime. But you don't *care.*" Stone catches himself, suppresses the intensity, forces himself to look casually around; he spots Kiick and Mozart and a lady friend across the room, notes that the lady's oversized handbag is planted on the table and pointing their way. "Céline," Stone continues more quietly, "isn't a favorite of mine."

Gurenko notices the waiter heading their way with a tray full of food, tucks the tip of his napkin into his shirt collar. "I was told you would show me some papers with information about NATO bases in Germany. If the information was ... suitable, I was instructed to pay you twenty-five thousand United States dollars."

"I expected more," Stone says. "I expected twenty-five thousand."

Gurenko is confused. "That's what you'll get, if the information is worth it."

The first course—the oysters—is placed before them. Gurenko rubs his palms together in anticipation. Stone studies the assortment of utensils available to him, settles on a small fork.

"No, no, with the fingers," Gurenko insists.

"I prefer a fork," says Stone.

They eat in silence, Stone with his head angled down, lifting his eyes quickly every now and then to study the Russian. Gurenko chews noisily, helps himself to more wine, says with his mouth full, "Why me? Why not someone else at the embassy? This is not my line of work. There are others—"

"I wanted you," Stone tells him, "precisely because it isn't your line of work. This is a one-shot affair for me. I don't want to deal with professionals who will try to find out who I am and come back for more. Which is why I prefer your bodyguards outside."

"Yes, I see the logic of that," Gurenko says. "Still, you might change your mind; you might decide to do it again. After all, this"—he gestures to the room full of well-dressed people talking in undertones, to the bouquets of flowers strewn with impeccable attention around the old restaurant, to the waiters hovering discreetly and silently—"this could become a habit. You might change your mind. You might decide to do it again."

Stone smiles faintly. "I'm not fool enough to risk this twice."

The table is cleared and the second course—leeks and truffles in olive oil—is laid before them.

"This time you are permitted to use your fork," the Russian informs Stone with a straight face.

At the next table, a heavily made up American lady raises her voice in mock horror. "Look what we've been reduced to," she complains dramatically to her companion. "Happiness is an empty parking space."

Gurenko snorts. "She is speaking American," he whispers to Stone, showing off his linguistic abilities. "She tells that happiness is when you find a vacant parking space. The Americans are a special race, I think."

They are finishing the endives and mushrooms—the Reblochon has been judged by Gurenko overripe and sent back—when Stone casually pulls a long envelope from his breast pocket and slides it across the table to the Russian diplomat. Across the room Kiick and Mozart stop talking, and their lady friend opens her handbag to look for something.

"At last," Gurenko says. He pushes away his plate, wipes his mouth on his napkin, begins to examine the documents. The American lady at the next table explodes in laughter. "Nothing's sacred," she tells her table companion.

"If you'll excuse the intrusion," Stone addresses the lady directly in slow, accented English, "there are still things that are sacred."

"Name one," the American lady challenges.

"The speed of light squared."

Stone signals for the bill, which is quickly placed before him on a small silver dish. The Russian nods as he reads, then reaches into his breast pocket and extracts a thick brown envelope, which he passes to Stone, who glances at the contents. "Is this all?" he asks, disappointed.

"What did you expect?" the Russian inquires.

"At least twenty-five thousand dollars," says Stone. "The material I gave you is worth more than ten thousand dollars."

Gurenko's eyes narrow. "What ten thousand dollars? There is twenty-five thousand dollars in the envelope. What game are you playing?"

Stone looks again at the contents of the envelope. "I'm a bit confused," he says vaguely. He pockets the envelope, starts to get up. "Let us hope," he says, "that we don't meet again."

A waiter dashes over to pull back the chair. Stone smiles and gestures with his thumb toward the Russian. "My friend here will take care of the check."

"You should have seen his face"—Kiick laughs—"when he realized he would have to pay."

"You should have seen it when he saw the size of the bill," says Mozart.

Stone comes out of the bathroom, wiping his face with a towel. The three-day growth of beard is gone; clean-shaven, Stone looks younger than his forty-four years, but tired—an accumulation of restless nights full of dreams he remembers only too well; he has the face of someone driven by things he deeply believes in but doesn't stop to question for fear of

22

wearing away the edges of his commitment. Now he says, "No trouble cleaning up afterwards?"

"No, no," Kiick replies. He is an overweight, balding, shabby man in his fifties, given to making gestures that are delicate, effeminate almost. "We recovered the bug without anyone knowing it was even there. Carted it off with the flowers. The film looks to be first-class. I don't think he suspected a thing."

"Other than the fact that the handbag was pointed our way," says Stone, "I wouldn't have either."

Kiick takes this as a compliment and beams like a schoolboy. "We'll doctor the tapes before the end of the week. I found a pro who works for the Israelis and free-lances on the side."

"Make sure he doesn't get to know more than he has to," cautions Stone.

"He doesn't even know my nationality," boasts Kiick.

"What about the bank account?" asks Mozart, Stone's lazily efficient second-in-command; he makes everything, including brilliance, seem effortless, something one does with one's left hand. He is lounging on a couch, his vest and jacket unbuttoned, his Ivy League Phi Beta Kappa key dangling on a gold chain stretched across his generous stomach.

"The bank business will be taken care of when Gurenko makes his next run to Geneva," Kiick explains, a noticeable tightness to his voice; it makes him uneasy to deal with ambitious people. "The fifteen thousand dollars will be deposited in a numbered account under a phony name. The signature will be in Gurenko's handwriting, no mistake about it. Christ, the signature alone is costing me two grand, but it's worth every penny."

"Everything will depend on how you play him," Stone says. He throws the towel back into the bathroom and settles into Kiick's swivel chair. "There's a tendency in these affairs to rush things, but the secret is to go slow. The slower, the better."

Kiick nods in eager agreement. "We let him know we've arrested a German for selling him NATO documents for ten thousand dollars, and we say we found out he pocketed the other fifteen thousand dollars and stashed it in a numbered account. We play him the doctored tapes to prove you only got ten thousand dollars."

"He'll deny it," Mozart offers, competing with Stone. "He'll be angry as hell. Remember it's an anger that comes from innocence."

Stone ignores Mozart. "That'll be the crucial moment," he tells Kiick. "He could go either way. It's your business to make him go our way. He'll be angry, but he'll be frightened too— frightened to death. You've got to play to the fright. The important thing is to ask him for a favor so inconsequential that it'll seem easier for him to do it than go to his security people and open up the can of worms. In the back of his mind he'll know that even if they believe he paid over the whole twenty-five thousand dollars, there'll be that minuscule grain of doubt, and that doubt will ruin his career."

"Once he does you a small favor," Mozart chimes in, "you reward him, but the reward has to be small enough so that he'll accept it. Send him a Sony portable, or better still a kitchen appliance that his wife won't want to give back."

"If he keeps the reward," Stone says, "you'll have him. The next time you go back at him, you'll have the original business to hold over his head, plus the fact that he's already done you a favor—"

"—and accepted a gift," says Kiick.

"—and accepted a gift; exactly," agrees Stone. "So then you escalate. You wait a few weeks and ask him for a second favor, hardly more important than the first—the makeup of an economic delegation due to turn up here, or the guest list at one of their receptions. Then you come across with another reward. Not cash; never give cash. A fur coat for his wife. A color TV. Something like that. Something a friend would give to another friend who does him a favor. If you take each phase slow and easy, if you play him like you would a fish, you'll have the combination to the office safe in six months and copies of the embassy's coded correspondence in a year."

"We could use a coup like that," Mozart says pointedly. "It would put an end to all those rumors about us going out of business."

"You can get a lot of mileage out of a good coup," agrees Stone.

Kiick smiles and nods. He knows the story only too well. There are very few professionals who don't. Back in the early sixties, Stone had put the company on the intelligence map with a coup that was a classic in its time. In those days, the Russians were ahead of the Americans in nuclear missile development, and Washington was worried sick about it. To offset the Soviet advantage and buy time, Stone came up with an idea whose beauty was in its utter simplicity. American agents were ordered to monitor Soviet submarine ports, military units, code traffic, deliveries of spare parts to air bases, call-up of specialists, for any indication that the Russians were mobilizing for war. When the Russians discovered, as they were meant to, that the Americans were monitoring them for signs of mobilization for war, they asked themselves the question they were supposed to ask: "What are the Americans doing which, if we found out about it, would cause us to mobilize?" The Americans, of course, weren't doing anything except play catch-up ball, but the ploy kept the Russians off balance and guessing for two full years before they tumbled to this.

"You pulled off some beauties in your day," Kiick says admiringly.

"Let's hope my day isn't over," Stone says, looking directly at Mozart, who makes no bones about being unhappy acting (in company argot) as Stone's "deputy dawg."

"You guys at the top have to make a mistake sometime," Mozart says quietly. There is a glint in his eye, a hint of mischief. "Then us youngsters will get our turn at the helm. It's a law of nature in our business. Survival of the youngest."

The intercom buzzes. Mozart is summoned to the top floor of the town house, which serves as a communications center. As soon as he leaves, Kiick leans toward Stone. "These young guys

25

get on my nerves," he says. "Listen, Stone, before I forget, I want to thank you again," he adds earnestly. "If it hadn't been for you, well . . ."

Stone waves away Kiick's thanks. "The CIA's loss is my gain. They were dumb to dump you, is how I look at it."

"I want you to know I'm grateful, is all. And I won't let you down. If there is ever something I can do for you, well, you get the idea."

Mozart comes back into the room on the run; he is amazingly light on his feet despite his size, a characteristic that Stone attributes, with no substantiating logic, to the fact that Mozart is a very wealthy young man; work, for him, is indoor sport. "Looks like we have a Soviet defector on our hands in Athens," he says excitedly. "A diplomatic courier with a pouch full of goodies. The admiral wants us to pick him up at the starting gate. I've already checked. I figure I can be there in six hours if I get a move on—"

"If anybody's going to Athens, it'll be me," says Stone. "Rank has its privileges. You head back to Washington and mind the store. I'll collect the pouch full of goodies and the warm body attached to it."

"What a very nice guy you are," sulks Mozart.

Stone, already scribbling a note to Thro, smiles sweetly. "It's a law of nature in our business: Nobody is nicer than he has to be."

The antennas on the roof are being whipped about by an icy wind that cuts in from the Moscow River, bending even the birch trees in its path. Inside the cement structure, at a desk behind the double winter windows with the seams stuffed with cotton, the officer in charge puts tiny tick marks next to items on a yellow pad.

✔ *Recall three embassy security men assigned as escorts (dereliction of duty, 15 years)*

✔ Recall second secretary (go through motions)
✔ Fire general in charge of courier service, order revision of procedures for clearing couriers for foreign assignments
✔ Issue general alert to military intelligence agents in Middle East, Europe, United States (use code Americans known to have broken)
✔ Get copies of all documents in pouch, advise senders that documents may have fallen into American hands, invite reports on consequences and suggestions for cutting losses
✔ Put our team in Geneva on 24-hour alert status
✔ Invite minister of defense to order us, and not KGB, to backtrack on defector (family, friends, etc.) to uncover motive

"You've left off the duty officer," points out the lieutenant colonel, looking over his shoulder. "You've forgotten about Gamov."

The officer in charge writes in longhand:

"Duty Officer Gamov to disappear. No trial."

He studies the item for a moment, then puts a small check mark before it.

CHAPTER

The image that leaps to Stone's mind is that of a lap dog in heat—a combat between instinct and decorum. With decorum coming out second best. He spots it first in the taut faces of the Marine guards at the entrance, in their hands making edgy passes over the undone flaps of their Navy-issue holsters. He sees it in the maniacal gleam in the eyes of the ambassador's woman Friday, a near-sighted career officer who speaks seven languages, none of them really well. Muttering under her breath in ancient Greek, she plucks Stone out of a gaggle of journalists being held at bay by the Marines, plows through corridors full of milling staffers as if she is the prow of an icebreaker, barges past the civilian security contingent into the oak-paneled inner sanctum, with the limp American flag at one end, hissing hysterically, "He's come, he's here, I have him in tow."

Stone sees it—shoots of panic breaking through what appears to be an ordered surface—in the person of his holiness the ambassador, a tall, heavy-handed, very rich political appointee whose name appears regularly on someone or other's ten-worst-dressed list. "Welcome aboard—yes, indeed—welcome aboard," gushes the ambassador, wringing Stone's hand as if he is trying to pump up water from a reluctant well, smiling all the while with his facial muscles but not his eyes. "Mighty glad," he mutters, and he repeats it several times without specifying precisely what he is mightily glad about. He takes Stone by the elbow and steers him toward an enormous suede couch, out of earshot of the half dozen or so first and second and third secretaries, clipboards at the ready, parked around the vast room. Stone, worn out from the trip, sinks gratefully into the soft cushions, catches a glimpse of several framed photographs over the couch. One shows the ambassador chatting amiably with a woman Stone takes to be his government-issue wife; others show him chatting amiably with various Presidents or Heads of State or Film Stars. In every photograph his expression is precisely the same: his shoulders are hunched, his head is thoughtfully inclined, frozen in a nod of agreement, his lips are pursed, his eyes are squinting as if he is hard of hearing.

"Let me put you in the picture," the ambassador begins. In keeping with the atmosphere, which has more in common with a library reading room than an ambassador's inner sanctum, his voice is a hoarse whisper. "What I've got is trouble with a capital *T*." He impatiently waves off one of the young second secretaries, who tiptoes over with an outstretched clipboard marked "Incoming—Eyes Only." "I've got this Russki courier, name of Kulakov, holed in upstairs with a diplomatic pouch chained to his wrist which he says will blow up if anybody tries to take it away from him by force. I've got State breathing down my neck to open the pouch and take a look-see what's in it, never mind the guy it's chained to. That's for starters. I've got the Russian ambassador lodging diplomatic protests with anybody dumb enough to return his calls. I've got security people at the airport telling me the Russkies are flying so many warm bodies into town you'd think they booked the Parthenon for a convention of Old Bolsheviks. I've got—"

One of several phones on the large mahogany desk purrs. The woman Friday lifts the receiver, listens, says something in modern Greek, smothers the mouthpiece in her ample bosom. "Mr. Ambassador," she stage-whispers, "I'm afraid it's the undersecretary of foreign affairs, Mr. Tsistopoulos, on the line again. He is very insistent. They have him on hold."

"Hold him on hold," whines the ambassador. To Stone, he offers this as a potential last straw. "I've got the Greek undersecretary of foreign affairs, Mr. Whoosis—"

The woman Friday coughs discreetly to catch the ambassador's attention. "Mr. Tsis-to-poulos," she prompts him.

The ambassador's eyes strain for a moment at the top of their sockets. "I've got the Greek government climbing the wall for us to get this guy out of here, with or without his pouch, before the whole diplomatic shebang comes down around our heads. I've got the English and French and Germans—our Germans, of course, not theirs—clamoring for a piece of the action. I've got a passel of congressmen of Greek ancestry flying in day after tomorrow. I've got a reception on some Sixth Fleet aircraft carrier scheduled for five P.M. I've got an operation that's ground to a dead standstill. Did you see them standing around the halls downstairs? You couldn't get a passport processed here in anything under two months, for love or money. What else I got? I've got journalists from countries I never heard of shooting questions I'm not sure I'm supposed to answer even if I knew the answer, which most of the time I don't. Sweet Jesus! For all I know, the only thing in the damn pouch is Brezhnev's unpaid laundry bills!"

The catalogue of trials and tribulations has worn the ambassador down; feeling very sorry for himself, he sinks back onto the couch and presses a large palm to his large forehead to calm a migraine he senses is lurking just behind his eyes. "What I need," he says weakly—for a fleeting instant Stone is actually afraid the ambassador will burst into tears—"is *official guidance.*"

Drained, the ambassador stares hopefully at Stone. The woman Friday and the army of first and second and third secretaries actually take a step or two in his direction.

Stone studies his shoes longer than he has to; he can't resist. He wonders at what point silences become silly, at what point someone will suddenly see the ridiculousness of it all and burst into laughter. But everyone holds out. When Stone finally looks up, the faces peering at him are still intense. "Mr. Ambassador,"

30

Stone says slowly. The sound of a human voice speaking out loud echoes through the vast office and appears to shock several of the secretaries. "I'm going to do better than give you guidance. In two hours, two and a half on the outside, anybody asks you about the Russian upstairs, you'll laugh and say, 'What Russian are you talking about?'"

There are two Marine sergeants posted in the stairwell, and two embassy security men outside the door of the room within a room, constructed by the Seabees so embassy people could talk shop without worrying whether their conversations were being picked up by hidden microphones or delicate sensors that can lift voice vibrations off windowpanes. Inside, the décor is State Department Conference Room, beige, with the only touch of color coming from a bouquet of plastic daffodils in a vase filled with the stale water that nobody has changed for years. Two more civilian security types are playing gin across a corner of the conference table and casting an occasional bored look at their charge, the diplomatic courier Kulakov, who is stretched out on the cot that has been set up for him. His face at first glance seems like a death mask: leaden features that will never change expression, eyes that appear to have closed from the weight of the lids. The diplomatic pouch, still chained to Kulakov's left wrist, is in full view on his chest.

As Stone enters, Kulakov swings his legs off the bed, sits up, gazes dully at the feet of the new arrival.

Stone addresses the security men. "Could I trouble you gentlemen to step outside for a few moments?"

They look at one another, then back at Stone. "We got instructions to maintain ourselves here," one starts to protest.

"It's all right," the ambassador's woman Friday stage-whispers from the doorway. "He's from Washington."

Obediently, the two collect their playing cards and cigarettes and leave. Stone scrapes one of their chairs over to the cot, sits down, without a word offers Kulakov a cigarette. The Russian studies the pack as if he is drawing lots and there is a prize to be had for a good guess. Eventually he settles on a cigarette and plucks it from the box. He accepts the book of matches, looks without curiosity at the advertisement on the cover, strikes one. His fingers tremble on the match. Stone looks away so as not to embarrass him.

"What ... are ... you?" Kulakov asks in his slow, accented English.

Stone answers in Russian. "I'm a representative of the American government. I'm here to help you."

There is a spark of interest in Kulakov's eyes—the first Stone has seen. "You speak Russian"—Kulakov reverts to his own language—"so you are from the famous CIA."

Stone isn't from the CIA, but he doesn't correct him, not now, not ever. "I'm here to protect you," he says. "To protect you and to help you. This is the beginning of a new life for you. The first step."

Stone is careful to use short sentences, to deal with Kulakov as he would deal with a child, but Kulakov's attention wanders anyhow. "My stockings got wet," he complains. He takes a deep drag on his cigarette, chokes on the smoke. "I don't know how they got wet. I must have walked somewhere in water. I must have ..." The thought trails off; Kulakov makes an effort to hang on to the thread, but it slips through his fingers. Suddenly he leaps to his feet and starts pacing agitatedly. "Why is there no window in this room? Where is the window? What month are we, January or February?" He returns to the cot, grips Stone's wrist. "I must telephone Moscow," he argues vehemently. "I must explain to them why I ran away. I must convince them I'm not a traitor...." This thought slips away too, and Stone is reminded of other defectors he has handled: men going through the motions with an energy that comes mainly from force of habit. Experience kills, Thro told him when all the trouble over his daughter began. It kills whatever you were before you had the experience.

Stone's eyes drift to the diplomatic pouch. Kulakov follows his gaze, clutches it to him. A cloud passes across his face. Dark

32

suspicions hang there like suits in a closet, cleaned, pressed, ready to wear.

"Would you be willing," Stone asks quietly, "to let me have the pouch?"

"When I arrive in America, I'll give it to you," Kulakov says. "I warn you, don't try to take it from me. If there is a struggle and I pull on the chain, the contents will be destroyed."

"Do you have any idea what's in it?"

Kulakov can't restrain a sneer. "Papers that are too important to send through the mail."

The woman Friday suddenly pokes her head in the doorway. "Do you have the pouch?" she stage-whispers in English. Kulakov, startled, clutches the chain in his right hand and prepares to pull on it.

"Get out," Stone coldly orders her. "Don't open that door again until I tell you to." The woman Friday shrinks back in confusion. The door clicks closed.

"Have you eaten?" Stone turns back to Kulakov. "Have you had something to drink?"

The Russian nods. "They gave me a sandwich, a beer."

"Listen to me carefully," Stone tells him. "If all we wanted was the goddamn pouch, we could have slipped you a drug and taken it. All we had to do then was find the key. It will be hidden in a coat lining, or tucked behind a collar. We could have taken the pouch. We could have dumped you back into the hands of the local KGB. But that's not how we operate. We're not like them. You'll see that for yourself, Kulakov. *You'll see we're not like them.* You keep the pouch. I'll take you to America. You can give it to me when we get there. Okay?"

"Okay," Kulakov agrees.

"Okay." Stone stands up. "I know this is very difficult for you—not knowing what's going to happen to you, wondering if you did the right thing after all. You have to hang on to two things. You can't undo what you've done. If you go back, they'll kill you. The second thing to hang on to is the belief that it will all work out." He puts a kindly hand on Kulakov's shoulder—

33

the first of many gestures Stone will make to win his confidence. "It will work out, I promise you. It always works out."

The arrangements take longer than Stone thought they would. He has difficulty getting authorization from the Navy to commandeer one of their mail planes parked on the Athens tarmac, and once he gets the authorization he has trouble tracking down the pilot and crew. They are finally run to ground in a Piraeus nest called the Black Cat Inn and brought back to life with pots of black coffee mixed with dire threats about what will happen to them if they don't turn to. Four hours after his conversation with the ambassador, Stone is ready to put the show on the road. All the embassy's Cadillacs, including the ambassador's pride and joy, which is bulletproof, along with several civilian cars belonging to the security people, are pressed into service. The convoy, when it finally pulls down the curved driveway, is very impressive. In the lead are two Greek police cars with flashing blue lights on their roofs. (The Greek government will later deny any of its vehicles participated, and will confiscate photographs that prove the contrary.) Then come nine embassy cars, with the bulletproof Cadillac sandwiched in the middle. Halfway down the first narrow street, the last of the nine cars swerves to a stop across the road, blocking the dozen or so cars full of journalists chasing after the convoy.

Fifteen minutes after the convoy departs, a small Greek van with the faded markings of a laundry company on the panel sides pulls unobtrusively to a side door. Two workmen in white overalls carry in several large straw hampers, and return moments later with the hampers full of dirty linen, which they stow in the back. The van starts off down the side streets in the general direction of the coast. In one of the narrow back alleys in the rat's maze of roads between Athens and Pireaus, a Mercedes suddenly veers in front of it, forcing it to the curb. A second Mercedes jams up behind. While two heavies hold the two frightened workmen at gunpoint, four others pull open the rear doors and rip the straw lids off the hampers. Much to their astonishment, all they come up with are armloads of dirty napkins and tablecloths from official embassy dinners.

At that moment, the ambassador's bulletproof Cadillac, with Kulakov in the back seat and Stone riding shotgun, is pulling through an unmarked gate of the Athens airport straight onto the tarmac. On the far side of the runway, its engines warmed, its takeoff clearance already granted, sits the Navy mail plane that will carry them to Malta, where an Air Force Globemaster will take them, with only a fuel stop in the Azores, to a SAC base in Virginia.

The throbbing of the Globemaster engines makes Stone drowsy, and he has to struggle to keep his eyes open and the conversation, however intermittent, going. Kulakov, in a window seat, seems to be mesmerized by the thin wisp of smoke that spirals up from his cigarette in the ashtray. "I can't remember," he says slowly, troubled by the lack of memory, the failure to come up with names or details that he is sure he knows.

Stone does his best to reassure him. "The peasants say you have to forget something seven times before you can commit it to memory."

"Yes, that's so," Kulakov says thoughtfully. "The peasants know many things we don't know."

After a while Stone asks, "Considering all the things that happened to you in the last—what was it?—six or eight months, how is it they let you leave the country?" His tone is casual, the delivery offhand, but the question is the first direct one Stone has put. It is the start of a very precise debriefing process that will go on and on until Kulakov has been drained of every last drop of information.

"I don't know how to answer," says Kulakov. He stares out the window into the darkness. "I saw a memorandum—the colonel conducting the investigation showed it to me—ordering my name eliminated from the courier list. I was told I was not permitted to leave Moscow. I was told there was every chance I would be formally charged, and that it would be in my interest

35

to hire a lawyer. I was told that if I didn't hire a lawyer, the court would appoint one. And then . . . then . . . out of nowhere, that phone call . . ."

Kulakov is losing the thread again, but Stone gently nurses him along. "What phone call?" When this gets no response, he says, "You were talking about a phone call."

"Yes, out of nowhere. Summoning me to the duty officer. In civilian clothes, they specified. As if nothing had ever happened. As if . . . and he . . . said I was to take this"—Kulakov taps the pouch—"to Cairo. He said I was elected by one vote. His." Kulakov's lips twist into a vicious smile. "You can bet that's the last time that poor son of a bitch will vote for anything. He's probably on his way to Siberia right now."

The copilot, a young man with a blond mustache and a broad open smile, makes his way down the aisle to them. "Everything all right?" he asks conversationally. Without waiting for an answer, he hands Stone a metal message board that opens like a book. "I reckon this here's for you. You're Mr. Simon, aren't you?"

Stone reads the message, which has been decoded and printed out in capital letters. "Reception preparations laid on as per your instructions. Judging from the fuss the Russians putting up on all fronts there is nothing less than solid gold in the pouch, so handle with tender loving care. FYI White House plus State Department plus CIA plus various foreign governments expressing curiosity bordering on interest. Treat affair like proverbial hot potato. Report only to me." The cable is signed "Elbow Room," which is the operational code signature of the crusty admiral who is the chairman of the Joint Chiefs of Staff—and the man Stone happens to work for.

"Our estimated time of arrival is 2230," the copilot informs Stone. "Weather conditions will be clear but cold, somewhere in the low twenties."

"We're not listed on the manifest, are we?" Stone checks. He doesn't want to leave any trace of how he came into the country.

"Just like you specified, there's nothing on the manifest. As for us monkeys, we haven't heard nothin', we haven't seen

36

nothin', we don't know nothin'." The copilot flashes a conspiratorial grin as he leaves.

Kulakov drifts into a fitful doze, his cheek pressed to the windowpane. Stone looks at his wrist watch, calculates the time left to the flight, settles more deeply into his seat, his mind going over for the thousandth time the details of the court case that his lady lawyer with a good line to the judge says he stands every chance of winning. "When you explain how it happened," she reassured him—he reproduces her exact tone of voice, her precise words; she seemed so sure, he remembers, so confident— "you'll get your rights back. Look, it could have happened to anyone, so stop worrying."

With a stifled scream, Kulakov straightens in his seat. Stone sees that his body is rigid, his forehead laced with perspiration. "I always wake myself up like that," Kulakov explains sheepishly, "but I never seem to be able to remember what I'm screaming about." Almost apologetically, he adds, "I have a lot to scream about." He takes out a handkerchief and mops his brow. "It's strange: we call a man who has lost his wife a widower, and we call a child who has lost his parents an orphan, but there's no word to describe a father who has lost his children."

"It's the same in English," Stone observes grimly. "We have no word for it either."

Kulakov obviously wants to change the subject. "Tell me," he asks, "if you are permitted to tell me, what will happen to me in America?"

And so, in very general terms, Stone explains the drill: a farm tucked away in some remote part of the countryside; a staff that will take him under its collective wing, teach him English, American history, American money, American sports; will teach him how to blend into mainstream America on the assumption that the powers that be will one day be finished with him and throw him back in. "Eventually we'll set you up with a brand-new name and a brand-new identity. You can have a business if you want one, or you can retire on a pension. While all this is going on, we'll debrief you, of course."

"Debrief? That means you will ask me questions. But I have

37

no answers. I don't know secrets. I am just a messenger. Whatever you find in the pouch is all I have to give you."

"There are things you can tell us, just the same," Stone insists. "Look, Kulakov, you're an intelligent man; figure it out for yourself. We must make absolutely certain, to begin with, that you are a genuine defector."

All this seems to astonish Kulakov. "And how long will this debriefing take?"

"It's already started," Stone says in his disarmingly frank way. "It will end when we know more about you than God."

The touchdown is as smooth as any Stone has ever experienced; one moment they are airborne, then the eight giant wheels kiss the earth, the engines reverse, the plane vibrates slightly, and they are in out of the night, taxiing toward a distant hangar with military police posted at every entrance and two cars, their motors idling, waiting in the semidarkness.

"This is where we part company," Stone tells Kulakov as they walk toward the second car. Half a dozen men in civilian clothes are standing around, but their faces are masked in shadows. Kulakov peers anxiously inside the car, then looks over his shoulder at the airplane as if he is weighing the possibility of going back—to the plane, to Russia. He shrugs imperceptibly, takes a deep breath, and starts to duck into the back seat.

"Kulakov," Stone says gently. The Russian turns to face him. "You agreed to give me the pouch when we got to America. We're in America now."

The men in the shadows move forward into the light; their faces are anxious. Stone tenses. Since he is the closest one to Kulakov, it will be up to him to punch him in the stomach with all his force at the first sign of hesitation. But Kulakov doesn't hesitate; he only nods tiredly, retrieves the key from his shoe, unlocks the chain from his wrist, and hands the key and the diplomatic pouch to Stone. "There are two small locks," he explains. "You must first turn the left one left, half a rotation, then the right one an entire rotation to the right, then the left one another half rotation to the left. If you don't follow the sequence, the contents will be destroyed." As if guessing what Stone is thinking, he shakes his head. "Don't try it. There is no other way into the pouch. If you try to cut into it, you will trip a circuit and it will all go up in smoke. You must use the key." He smiles almost sadly. "And you must take my word for the sequence. It goes without saying, I understand the consequences if I should . . . disappoint you."

Kulakov takes his place in the back seat; he seems to have shrunk in size and looks lost against the cushion. One of the men in civilian clothes climbs in alongside him, two others take their places in front. Just before they move off, Kulakov rolls down his window. "Tell me," he asks Stone, "if you are permitted to tell me, how is it you can know more about someone than God?"

"All right, Stone, in ten words or less, what's he got?"

The admiral, in dress blues and gleaming black shoes (he spit-shines them himself every morning, claims it is his only completely serene moment of the day), leads the way into the private dining room just off his suite of offices in the Pentagon. The metal Venetian blinds are drawn; the admiral feels ill at ease in bright sunlight. Philippine stewards in starched whites hold the backs of two chairs at the only table in the room. The admiral settles his bulk into place, sets his leather cigar case and a pocket calculator on the table, switches on a small black box with a circular antenna (which emits "noise" designed to jam any microphone in the room), turns his full attention on Stone for his ten words or less.

Stone and the admiral are ill at ease with each other the way people who complement each other often are—the admiral with a cerebral squint to his eyes, totally at home with computer printouts, ballistic trajectories, tables of probabilities; and Stone, all fingertips, nerve ends, intuition.

"Of course, I've only had time for a quick look," Stone tells him evenly, "but from what I can see, it could be one of the biggest hauls we've ever had."

The admiral, who has often boasted that he is prepared to be

39

bored by the start of World War III, takes Stone's assessment in his stride, nods impatiently, adjusts his reading glasses and starts to leaf through the dossier. "Looks like the sight on a tank turret," he comments, holding up one sheet to the light. Stone cranes his neck, skims the Russian text, tells the admiral, "That's what it is, all right—a night sight which they plan to install in their T-62s already in Egyptian hands. The sheet gives the specifications for the sight—the ranges at which it's effective, that sort of thing."

"Hmm," the admiral says. He is, as usual, professionally noncommittal.

One of the waiters offers the admiral a typed menu. He gives it the same attention he gave to the night sight. "Jellied madrilène, T-bone steak well done, carrots, jello. No bread. No butter." He looks at Stone. "That suit you?" Without waiting for an answer, he tells the waiter, "Same for him. And we'll take a bottle of that New York State red wine I had the other day." To Stone: "The gnomes over at General Accounting won't let us have French wines in the mess anymore. Some crap about balance of payments. Hmm. What's this one say?"

The admiral offers another sheet of paper to Stone, who reads it quickly. "It looks like a report on our fleet movements in the Mediterranean for the next six weeks"—Stone shakes his head in amazement—"including the patrol routes of the two Polaris submarines on station." Stone is whispering now. "They must have access to our movement reports, which means they've broken one of our naval codes. This one"—he hands the admiral another sheet—"is a letter to the Soviet ambassador in Cairo from his brother-in-law, who's the general in charge of Soviet logistical support facilities in Kazakstan, on the border with China. He says the Chinese are thinning out their forces along the frontier, that the troops are being pulled back to garrison cities, which leads him to believe that Mao's death has caused more internal trouble than most people are aware of." Stone picks up the next page. "This one looks like a report on a defect in the low-level parallax input on the radar tracking system for the SAM missiles."

The admiral attacks his jellied madrilène as if nothing unusual is happening. He finishes leafing through the dossier, listens with only an occasional "Hmm" to Stone's running translation, hands the dossier across the table when he is through with it. "Obviously we're going to have to go over these papers with a fine-tooth comb. Now tell me what you know about the defector Krolokov, isn't it? What's he like?"

"His name is Kulakov," Stone corrects him. "He's in his mid fifties, short, tired, frightened. It's hard to characterize what he's like. I was raised on coasts, Admiral—in China, in Brazil, later in New England. After a good storm, we always used to scour the beaches for driftwood. Friend Kulakov reminds me of a piece of driftwood washed up on the sand. He's high and dry, beached, abandoned by the waves; he's been rubbed smooth, if you see what I mean. He's without edges, without a center. He feels cut off, isolated, though the isolation is psychological rather than physical. He's cut himself off from everything behind him, and he has no idea of what's ahead of him."

"What prompted him to up and run for it?"

"Reading between the lines, I gather a lot has gone wrong with his life in the last six or eight months. I'm not sure of the details yet. Then they were going to bring him up on some kind of charges. So when he got the chance, he flew the coop."

"Hmm."

Stone, who has dealt directly with the admiral since he became chairman of the Joint Chiefs nineteen months before, thinks again how wrong first impressions can be. At their initial meeting—the admiral didn't even know that such a group as Stone's existed, never mind that it was directly answerable to him—Stone came away thinking he was dealing with someone who was slow on the uptake, a time-server who doled out ideas as if there was a limited supply. Now he sees him as one of the cleverest minds in Washington, a man naturally suspicious of conventional wisdom, an expert on so many subjects, not the least of which is Congress, that Stone has long since lost track of them.

"What's next on the agenda?" Stone asks now.

41

The admiral ignores the question, slices into his steak, cuts it in small pieces of equal size, chews each morsel methodically, almost for a fixed time, before swallowing. When there is nothing left on his plate but the bone, he wipes his lips on his napkin, looks up to contemplate his guest. "I've been meaning to ask you for some time, Stone: Do you have a first name?"

Stone is caught off guard by the question. "I had one once," he quips, "but it's been lost somewhere in the bureaucratic shuffle."

The answer, for some reason, seems to please the admiral, who nods and twists his facial muscles into what could pass for a smile. "Tell me something else, Stone: If you had your choice, which would you take—the warm body of Kulakov or the papers?"

Stone doesn't hesitate. "The warm body, any day of the week."

"Why?" The admiral levels his gaze on Stone.

Stone's intuition is at work now. "Because," he explains, "if there's a fly in the ointment, something tells me we'll find it in the warm body. The papers, if they've been set up, will be perfect."

Again Stone's response pleases the admiral. "Thought you'd say that," he mutters. He leans back, reaches for his cigar case, clips the tip off one, puts it in his mouth. One of the Philippine stewards appears from nowhere with a light. "Here's where we're at," says the admiral, exhaling a cloud of cigar smoke. "Charlie Evans over at CIA was furious when I put you onto the defector instead of one of his boys. Their station chief was out of town at the time, and one of our military attachés—a Navy captain, I might add—had the good sense to latch on to the Russian when he walked in the embassy door. Anyhow, the modus operandi I've worked out is this: Charlie Evans gets the cold paper, and you get the warm body. I had to promise Evans that his boys could have the courier, if they still want him, when you get through with him. You speak a bunch of languages, don't you, Stone?"

"Five fluently, not counting English."

"You don't happen to speak Eskimo, do you?" the admiral asks seriously.

Stone has to smile. "Eskimo? Not a word."

"Hmm. Well, in the Eskimo language there are four future tenses: the immediate future, the middle future, the far-in-the-future future, and a future that will never arrive. I was conjugating in this tense when I spoke to Evans."

"I think I read you, Admiral," Stone says. What he understands is what all the insiders in Washington understand: that there is a long-standing bitter feud between the admiral and Charlie Evans that dates back to the days when Evans, then a middle-echelon regional chief at the CIA, tried to pressure the admiral, then the captain of an aircraft carrier, into launching an air strike attacking the Bay of Pigs against Castro's troops. The admiral refused (so, eventually, did the President when he was approached directly by the CIA) and Evans did his level best to ruin the admiral's career, filing a scathing report accusing him of being personally responsible for the fiasco by failing to provide air cover at the crucial moment. In later years, the mere mention of Evans's name would bring an instantaneous glint to the eyes of the admiral, who neither forgot nor forgave.

The admiral puts his cigar case back into his breast pocket. "How much time will you need with the warm body?" he wants to know.

"Hard to say, Admiral, until I've made a pass or two at him."

"Hmm." The admiral appears lost in thought for a moment. "All right. Start the debriefing and set up a coordinating link with Evans's people who will be working over the papers. But don't tell them anything you haven't told me first. What I mean, Stone, is don't give away the family jewels"—he winks slyly—"if you find any family jewels."

Again Stone says, "I read you, Admiral."

"Hmm." The admiral glances over his shoulder, checks to make sure that the stewards can't observe him, removes a dead fly from his jacket pocket and, holding it by a wing, drops it

43

onto the uneaten jello. "That'll keep them on their toes," he whispers, and he laughs wickedly.

Thro is working herself up again; her slightly hysterical laughter rings through the room like crystal being tapped with a spoon. "Then there's the dreadful possibility that we'll be sucked into the black hole at the center of our galaxy which is pulling in stars the way a vacuum cleaner pulls in dust. Do you understand, Stone, what will happen? The gravitational force of the black hole will shrink the earth to the size of a green pea. All the Picassos and Brandenburgs and Beatle records and Porches of Maidens and Pentagons and Top Secret Eyes Only documents will be crushed, Stone, crushed and pulverized and disintegrated, their molecules and atoms intermingling."

"I'm more interested in the gynecologist," Stone tells her, "the one you said danced so close he gave you a Pap smear on the dance floor, while I was off on the frontier of freedom, which this time out happened to be Athens."

"My God, Stone, don't you know a joke when you hear one anymore?" She adds coyly, "He did dance a bit closer than I'm used to."

Mozart buzzes on an interoffice line. "Anytime you're ready," he says. "Everyone's primed."

"Be right in," says Stone. He rocks back in his swivel chair, his head against the photostat of the front page of the *New York Times* dated November 9, 1917. "Revolutionists Seize Petrograd; Kerensky Flees," reads the main headline. A small one, circled in red crayon, says: "Washington Reserves Judgment, Hoping Revolt Is Only Local."

Thro says, "Ah, Stone, don't be sulky. I was only trying to bug you. You made such a fuss about my ring turning black in Paris. . . . I was just getting back, is all I was doing."

"The chemistry of couples"—Stone shakes his head in annoyance—"is a fascinating thing."

"And what, pray tell, is the chemistry of couples?"

"I have a theory," Stone explains—he starts to gather the

44

notes he wants to take with him—"that couples have a fixed amount of time together, and the chemistry of their relationship at any given moment depends on their perception of how much of this time is behind them, and how much ahead."

"Working the equation backward," Thro says, "you ought to be able to figure out how much time they have ahead by observing the chemistry."

"You ought to," agrees Stone.

Thro's voice is barely audible. "Oh, Stone, it used to be so good, our chemistry. There used to be an endless amount of time ahead of us."

"I don't know what you want anymore," mutters Stone. He puts his notes in a blue folder with the words "Topology—Current" stenciled on the cover.

"I want what I've always wanted," pleads Thro. "I want to be imagined."

Stone's unit is carried on the Pentagon books under the innocuous nomenclature "Task Force 753—Topology." Its budget, which has been hovering around the $2.5 million mark for the past several years, is buried in the Defense Intelligence Agency appropriations. The money is funneled from the DIA director's current contingency fund to the Joint Chiefs current contingency fund to Topology Project Chief current contingency fund, where it pays for the twenty-eight staff members on the books, the two European bureaus (in Paris and Vienna), half a dozen safe houses scattered around the world, and the top two floors of the Georgetown town house which serves as the headquarters of Task Force 753—Topology. Actually, only the top floor is used for Topology work. The floor underneath was originally bought and left vacant to "insulate" the top floor; one of Stone's innovations has been to install a working business to go along with the unit's cover. Thus was born John Pierce Associates Inc., an international mail order house that netted $245,488 in the last calendar year, enough to pay for the upkeep (without dipping into contingency funds) of the small Virginia debriefing operation which is the only other physical entity under Topology control. The particular advantage of raising funds this way is that it permits Stone to run an operation that is totally untraceable through funding links, even to the handful of people in Washington who know what Task Force 753—Topology really is.

And what it really is is this: the elite private intelligence arm of the chairman of the Joint Chiefs. The unit was originally created in 1946, as the cold war was getting under way, under the title "Penetration Feasibility Studies." Its mandate then—and it has never been altered—was to train penetration agents, and organize support facilities, against the day when they would be sent into the Soviet Union, under the direct control of the Joint Chiefs, on one-time missions.

In all the years of its existence, Task Force 753—Topology has never sent a single agent into the Soviet Union. But it religiously maintains the capability. It has its own Clothing and Accessories Section (with a sign on the door of the storeroom that reads "Buy Russian"), which can outfit an agent with everything from a Soviet-manufactured valise to toothpaste to underwear. There is an Identity Section, which deals in internal passports, work books and various ministry or military identification cards. (The section chief's pride and joy is a secondhand Soviet-made lamination machine, bought some years before from a source in Yugoslavia.) There is one middle-aged woman who does nothing in life but keep up to date on train and plane schedules, and someone else who compiles lists of places where a potential agent might stay in various cities without coming to the attention of the local militia. Still someone else keeps track of Soviet soccer scores, which are posted on a bulletin board; Stone's staffers are the only Americans in Washington who run an office pool on Russian teams. Even the dentistry (for the few, Stone among them, who are carried on the books as potential penetration agents) is performed by a Russian exile who drills and fills exactly as he did when he practiced in Minsk. (One of the running arguments between Stone and Mozart has been on just this sore point, with Mozart representing the staffers who prefer high-speed drills and more modern dentistry techniques, and Stone insisting on verisimilitude down to the poorly done lead fillings in his molars.)

What makes all this accumulated expertise possible is the fact that Task Force 753—Topology is staffed by second- and third-generation anti-Communists, all of them the offspring of people who at one time or another fled the motherland—or died trying. The first requisite for membership in Topology is fluency in Russian. Russian is the office language. Copies of *Pravda, Izvestiya, Literaturnaya Gazeta* (preferred by most, though not at all for its articles on literature), *Yonost, Oktyabr* and *Novy Mir* are scattered around desks. All told, Stone's unit subscribes—via a cover library facility in the Pentagon—to one hundred and twelve Soviet publications.

With all this Russian expertise at its fingertips, the unit—under Stone's prodding—took to performing odd jobs in its spare time. (The admiral describes this as "honing the blade.") Stone's attempt to turn a Soviet diplomat in Paris was a typical extracurricular activity. Before that, the unit had concentrated its resources on examining the private life and loves of a first-term congressman who was rallying his colleagues on the Hill against military appropriations. Topology got into the debriefing business when it was charged by the Joint Chiefs with questioning the American scientist Lewinter, a rare bird who defected to the Soviet Union several years ago and was then unaccountably handed back to the Americans. Stone concluded that the Russians had released him to convince the U.S. that they didn't believe Lewinter really possessed the signature trajectories for America's ballistic missile force. Ergo, they did have their hands on the crucial trajectories, a breakthrough which would permit them to distinguish, during a missile attack, the decoys from the real McCoys by their flight paths. Stone's conclusion was instrumental in obliging the Joint Chiefs to change the missile trajectories, a project that cost the American taxpayers four billion dollars over a three-year period.

47

After the success with Lewinter, the odd job that Topology undertook more often than not involved debriefing Soviet defectors who, for one reason or another, had aroused the interest of the Joint Chiefs.

Kulakov is just such a defector.

The woman who follows the soccer scores is making book on an upcoming match between the Moscow Dynamos, known for playing unflappable position soccer, and a squad from Bratsk, which has a reputation for improvisation, a rare trait among Soviet teams. The smart money (led by Mozart, who has put himself down for five dollars) is on the Dynamos. Stone, characteristically, risks two dollars on the boys from Bratsk as he makes his way through the small, crowded room to the desk.

The atmosphere, as always, is casual. The woman who has as her bailiwick Planes and Trains is describing how a Washington hostess organizes the dinner parties for which she is universally famous. "Picture it," she says, her voice pitched high, her penciled eyebrows dancing. "She starts off by choosing the dessert. Then she figures out what cheese goes with that dessert, then decides what main course goes with that cheese, and *then* selects what guests go with that main course!"

"She must be Jewish," quips the man in charge of Clothing and Accessories. "I mean, organizing her dinners from right to left, sort of thing. . . ." His voice trails off. The moment is awkward. Everyone is aware that Stone is Jewish. Not to laugh would be more noticeable than to laugh, so everyone laughs.

Stone, shuffling through his notes, finally looks up. His voice is low, modulated; his manner is slightly nervous. He is uncomfortable with groups, and feels more at home when dealing with people on a one-to-one basis. "I thought," he begins—he speaks, as he always does in meetings of this kind, in Russian—"we'd keep this session down to section chiefs—"

"Better fewer but better," interjects Mozart. All the section chiefs recognize the phrase; it is the title of the last article Lenin ever wrote. More laughter. Even Stone is obliged to smile.

"Here's the drill," says Stone. "First and foremost, penetration readiness must not be allowed to suffer. One of the advantages of access to a hot defector is that it gives us a way of updating our penetration files. Everyone can benefit from a defector—Clothing and Accessories, Identity, Entries and Exits, Internal Contacts. That having been said, let me add that in this case, there's more to it—a good deal more. Your normal defector is debriefed for information, and then the information is checked and double-checked. Our defector won't be debriefed for information; he has none. He's a run of the mill military courier who has been carting around secrets for years without ever getting to see them himself."

"Aside from updating our penetration readiness, why debrief?" asks the woman who follows the soccer scores.

"The admiral feels, and I agree, that if anything's fishy about this affair—to dot the *i*'s, if it's a Soviet operation—we're not going to find out about it by looking at the paper. That would have been prepared meticulously. No, the place to look is the defector himself. Now, the few times we've done this kind of thing in the past, we've taped the whole debriefing, transcribed and distributed the end product for in-house use. This time around I propose we work somewhat differently. I'll handle the actual debriefing myself. I'll tape every morning for three or four hours, depending on how much he can take. We'll transcribe in the afternoon and you'll start in on the material the next day. Mozart here will run this end of it." Stone is looking directly at Mozart now. "What you'll do is make lists of every fact that is checkable: addresses, phone numbers, ages, descriptions of people and places, dates that certain things happened. Everything. Then you'll distribute the list in-house to the section chiefs, who will start to run down the confirmations."

"Sounds simple enough," says Planes and Trains. "If everything checks out, he gets the Topology stamp of approval on the inside of his left thigh."

"Wrong," snaps Stone. "Bear in mind that nobody can accurately remember every detail of his life—except someone who

49

has memorized an identity that's not his. Which is why I've always told you, in working up identities for penetrations, to build in, without the agent's knowledge, some minor errors."

"The trouble is," the man in charge of Identity says thoughtfully, "they may have done the same thing."

"They may have," agrees Stone. "But they won't program any *inconsistencies* into an identity they've created. And it will be up to us to see if we can come up with inconsistencies. Which is what all the checking will be about."

"What about the pouch?" asks Mozart. "Do we get to see what's inside?"

"I was just coming to that," says Stone. "CIA will be doing with the paper what we're going to do with the warm body. I'd appreciate it if you would personally establish a liaison link on this, Mozart. You'll deal with Charlie Evans directly. I would hope it will be on a daily briefing basis, but you may not find him that forthcoming, so take what you can get."

"Will I be filling him in on our product too?" Mozart wants to know.

"In principle, yes."

"That'll give me all the leverage I'll need," says Mozart. "Tit for tat. If they want information, they'll have to trade."

"I knew I picked the right man for the job," says Stone. "You wouldn't give away the time of day unless you got something in return." Stone says it lightly, and smiles, but Mozart doesn't smile back.

An elderly man in charge of Entries and Exits raises his hand at the back of the room. Stone nods in his direction. "I beg your pardon, Stone. As I understand it, you've already spent some time with the subject of this debriefing. I think it would be helpful for us to know whether you actually entertain the idea that he may be a plant."

Stone chooses his words carefully. "It seems to me," he says, "that we've got to accept this as a very real possibility in order to attack the debriefing material with any kind of enthusiasm."

There is some discussion of Topology business. One of the

section chiefs has come up with a newly arrived Russian émigré in Israel who, through a bureaucratic oversight, still owns his own cooperative apartment in Moscow, just off Gorky Street. The section chief is interested in exploring the idea of setting it up as Topology's first and only safe house in Moscow. Stone vetoes the project. "There are too many unknowns," he says. "Who is the Russian in Israel? What do we know about him other than the fact that he claims to own an apartment in Moscow? Also, a safe house in a Communist country, according to our operating charter, would have to be registered as a 'potentially dangerous asset' with the Senate Select Committee on Intelligence. And that just might prompt this same Select Committee on Intelligence to inquire what the hell a group called Topology is doing with a safe house in Moscow."

"We could probably get the DIA to front for us," suggests the section chief lamely.

"And they'd scream their heads off to the admiral about us poaching," warns Stone. "No, it's just not worth the candle. I think our penetration readiness will survive nicely with the methods already worked out—living with people who take roomers without residence permits, whorehouses, that sort of thing."

Mozart asks if Stone has decided about budgeting three thousand dollars to finance the Russian-speaking Cornell student on a summer camping trip through European Russia. "The boy is an excellent prospect," argues Mozart. "His grandfather fought with Wrangel, his father fought with Vlasov in the Ukraine during the war, and escaped through Czechoslovakia afterwards. His Russian is fluent. He'll make a good recruit for us someday."

"I'm okay on the three thousand dollars," agrees Stone, "on the condition that the money isn't linked to Topology."

"The money will be funneled through a DIA front in New York that hands out summer scholarships," Mozart explains. "The guy who runs it is a Harvard classmate of mine."

"If there's nothing else?" inquires Stone.

The elderly man who specializes in Entries and Exits has his hand up again. "I'm sorry to bring this up, Stone, but there have been too many rumors making the rounds in recent weeks for comfort. They all point to the same thing—that penetrations, which is our basic brief, are no longer considered to be even remotely possible; that Topology is going out of business."

"I have every reason to believe," Stone answers, looking around the room, "that these rumors are completely false. To my way of thinking, we may have the most difficult brief in the intelligence establishment—preparing for something that may never happen, sharpening a knife that may never cut. But the option is everything. Penetration is an option that the Joint Chiefs want to keep open."

The old man with white hair nods slowly in agreement. Stone has told him what he wants to hear.

"Admit it, Stone," Thro whispers. She presses the buzzer to the apartment just under Topology's in the Georgetown town house. "Admit I changed your life."

"I admit it," Stone whispers back sarcastically. "I give credit where credit is due. You changed my life. I'll give you an affidavit if you want one. 'Thro changed Stone's life. Signed, Stone.' I'm not the man I was. At the ripe age of forty-four, I've given up pajamas completely and wake up every morning with a serviceable erection."

"That's not what I mean," hisses Thro furiously. "You distort every word I say."

Stone can see Cross bouncing across the room, his latchkey thrust forward, to open the glass door with "John Pierce Associates Inc." stenciled in gold letters on it. "Words awaken other words"—Stone reverts to Russian—"like ants touching antennas."

Cross, who is the business manager of John Pierce Associates, flings open the door. Once again Stone is struck by his appearance; seen in three-quarters profile, Cross is the spitting image of Harry Truman, so much so that Cross was once called upon to portray Truman in a television semidocumentary about the Korean War. "Ah, Stone, if you knew how delighted I am to see you." Cross's voice even has something of Truman's nasal twang to it. "Good of you to squeeze in time . . . absolutely essential . . . taken on items . . . anxious for you . . ." Disjointed phrases spill from his chapped lips as he leads Stone through a maze of rooms. Cross is one of those people who fall just short, not for any lack of trying, of being eccentric. At any given moment he generally has more solutions than there are problems. But he produces a profit, and doesn't interest himself in where the money goes when it is siphoned off. "Yes, indeed, now look at this . . . going to star them in our next catalogue . . . yes, indeed." He produces for Stone a glossy soft-cover booklet entitled "Everything You Want to Know About Mushrooms," then a second volume, thinner than the first, with the words "Body Hair" printed boldly on the cover, and finally a boxed three-volume soft-cover series with the title "E-Z Guides to Theosophy, Anthroposophy and Pyramidology." "I've already had half a dozen phone calls on body hair," boasts Cross. "Word of mouth will make a volume like this . . . surprised if it became a best seller . . . yes, indeed, ah."

Later, at the apartment they share, Thro teases Stone about Cross. "From Topology to body hair in one easy leap. The eclectic mind takes it all in its stride."

"Don't knock Cross or John Pierce Associates," Stone says. "It pays for the farm. And speaking of the farm, that's where we're going to be for the next few weeks."

"You got the warm body?" Thro is surprised. "Will the CIA sit still for that?"

"They'll sit still for the admiral," says Stone. "You'll be in charge of resettlement. I'll give him to you for an hour every afternoon. Use any Topology facilities you need when it comes time to work up a new identity for him."

"What about settlement money?" Thro asks.

"A lot will depend on how valuable the paper he brought with him turns out to be. We'll decide that later."

"He's going to want to know right off," Thro says. "They always ask about money first."

"You can say there'll be a pension, plus a lump sum in a bank somewhere. But stay vague on the numbers until we come up with some."

After dinner, which they both eat in silence, Thro reaches across the table and makes small circles on the back of Stone's wrist with a fingertip. "I'm desperately sorry about what happened," she says softly. She avoids looking him in the eyes. "You know it was an accident, Stone. If I could undo it, I'd give anything. It would mean a great deal to me if you didn't hold it against me."

"If it turns out all right in court," Stone replies coldly, "I won't hold it against you."

Her voice instantly changes tone; the circles stop. "That's not what I wanted to hear," she snaps.

"What you want to hear," says Stone, "is not my voice, but an echo of your own."

"We all of us want to hear echoes," says Thro sadly. "We *need* to hear our voices come back at us. Echoes give us the illusion we're not alone."

Outside, the guards trudge through the new snow with the body of a dog that lunged into the electrified fence during the night when he spotted a fox on the other side. "That's the second one we've lost this year," notes the oldest of the three men in the room.

One of the aides, wearing the insignias of a lieutenant colonel on his uniform, scans the batch of morning cables. "Nothing from Geneva," he notes worriedly.

"Too early for Geneva," says the older man. "This kind of thing has to ripen like a peach."

A second lieutenant colonel knocks once on the door, which is made of metal and not wood.

"Come," the older man calls.

54

The second lieutenant colonel, a squat man with a thin scar over his left eye, hands the older man a folder with the words "Incoming—One-Time Pad" and "Warning: Burn both pad and message after delivery" typed on it. The older man scans the message, written in a precise, slanted longhand, then looks up. "The peach is ripening, but it's not ready for the table yet," he comments, and he passes the message, which originated with the Soviet military attaché in Washington, to his aides. It reads:

"Americans appear very excited with catch. Contents of pouch in CIA hands. Courier accompanied by American male in civilian clothes landed at SAC base but disappeared and untraceable to any known intelligence organization. Assume he being debriefed. But by whom?"

CHAPTER 4

Swallowing, digesting, defecating and remembering all come more easily now. His mind still wanders, but never very far afield; Stone is usually able to pick up where they left off the day before with a simple, "You were saying that..." And for the first night since he's been at the farm, which is three weeks and two days, Kulakov didn't wake up screaming.

"I've never seen anything like it," he is telling Stone and Thro over the breakfast table. He looks excitedly from one to the other as he describes a television quiz program he saw the previous afternoon. "They opened a curtain and there was a dishwashing machine, a color television and a sewing machine. They said all three were brand-new, but I wasn't born yesterday. Ah! New, old—what do such things matter? They gave the girl three price tags. She had thirty seconds to race across the stage and put them on the items. If she put the right tag on the right item, she got to keep it. When she discovered she had all three right, she started to cry and leaped into the arms of the announcer." Kulakov stirs a spoonful of jam into his tea, noisily blows on the cup to cool it, sips while it is still, by Stone's standards, scalding. "What I don't understand," says Kulakov, "is the advertising."

"What don't you understand about it?" Thro asks.

"In the Soviet Union," Kulakov explains, "they only advertise products nobody buys. And nobody is buying because they aren't well made. The products that are good don't need public-

56

ity. Word spreads quickly. You could have a queue a kilometer long ten minutes after it goes on sale. In your country, I can't make out whether the government is advertising the products because they're good, or because they're bad and aren't selling."

"It isn't the government that advertises," says Stone. "It's the company that makes the product. Most of the time a number of companies make the same thing. So they advertise to convince people that their model looks prettier or works better or lasts longer or costs less." Stone smiles at Kulakov warmly. "It's a different world, Oleg, but it will all fall into place. Give it time. Don't become impatient."

But Kulakov is impatient: with the daily routine, with the English lessons, with the scenery, with the food, and most of all with the questions that Stone fires at him from nine to twelve every morning, seven mornings a week.

"Can't we break off now?" Kulakov had a habit of complaining, his eyes glued to the Japanese wrist watch Stone had given him the second week they were there.

"It's only eleven-thirty," Stone answered. "Let's give it another half hour."

"But we've been over this before," Kulakov groaned.

The debriefing, in fact, had reached the point where there was almost nothing they talked about that they hadn't talked about before. But Stone, poring over the transcripts of previous sessions late into the night, was purposefully leading Kulakov over the same ground again and again, and then once again, looking for a word, a phrase, a hesitation, an inconsistency, a flaw, a discrepancy; looking even for a failure to change wording, which could indicate that a response had been memorized.

"Tell me about your daughter again," Stone urged him.

"Don't you get tired of listening to the same thing over and over?" Kulakov whined. He plucked a cigarette from a box and inserted it in the ivory holder that Thro had given him when he had admired hers. "Nadia," he began—he leaned toward the match that Stone held for him—"was an open book from the day she was born. If she was ever sad, or lonely, or anxious about something, if she was falling in love or out of love, it was written on her face." Kulakov sucked on the ivory holder and stared out the window.

"You met some of the boys she fell in love with, didn't you?" Stone prompted.

"She brought them to the house if she really liked them," Kulakov said. "She respected her parents. She wanted us to like the people she liked. It was normal." And more forcefully: *"She was normal."* Again Kulakov's gaze was fixed on the rolling hills that surround the farm.

"She also brought girl friends home," Stone said carefully. "You told me she brought girl friends home."

"Yes, she brought girl friends to the house," Kulakov replied quietly. He had himself under tight rein. "But she never thought of them in that way. I tell you, I knew her like a book. I would have known." Kulakov was talking more for himself than for Stone by then; if he had been rehearsed, Stone thought, it was a brilliant job of acting. "When my wife showed me the photographs—"

Stone cut him off. "Describe the photographs."

"They were taken with a telephoto lens. They came in the mail. No letter. No return address. Just photographs. One showed her holding hands . . . one with her arm around the other's waist, laughing, kissing a shoulder. The black-and-white one was taken head on and said 'With love, from Lina' on it. I used to carry it around in my wallet. I had a vague idea about trying to find this . . . this Lina. I noticed it was gone when you returned my wallet the other day."

"I didn't think you'd want it any longer," explained Stone. "What was Nadia's attitude toward the photographs? Did she admit the liaison?"

"She admitted everything, yes," Kulakov recalled. His eyes were moist by then, and red-rimmed. "She said she was in love with this . . . this girl . . . this Lina. She asked where was it written she had to fall in love with a boy. . . . She was only nineteen—
. . . only nineteen."

"Was it difficult getting her committed?"

"What do you mean, committed?"

"You told me"—Stone checked a detail in the folder on his lap—"yes, you said you committed her to an asylum outside Moscow that more or less specialized in people with sexual problems."

"Ah, yes, committed. My wife's brother-in-law had a brother who worked at the hospital. Normally you wait two years to get someone treated, but we pulled strings." Suddenly Kulakov stood up. "It's almost noon," he said dully. "Enough for today."

The next day Stone began the session with: "You were saying you pulled strings to get Nadia committed. Did she object to going? Did she object to being separated from her . . . friend?"

"At first she wouldn't consider it." Kulakov started off briskly. "We had some terrible scenes. The woman we shared the flat with—she was the widow of a wartime comrade of mine, actually—called the militia one night, and I had to take them outside and give them a couple of bottles of vodka before I could convince them it was a family argument. I worked on Nadia for weeks about the asylum. She resisted, but then she became unsure of herself. She knew I loved her more than anyone in the world. In the end she was very nervous. She had bitten her fingernails down to the quicks. She had an ugly rash that wouldn't go away. She had trouble breathing—a pain deep in her chest. One day she shrugged and said she would go. And so I took her . . . I took my own daughter—" Kulakov's voice broke. When he regained his composure, he said, "You know, the only difference for me between one day and the next is that some days are less sad than others."

After that session, over lunch, Kulakov turned suddenly to Stone and asked him if he had any children. Stone and Thro avoided each other's eyes. "A daughter, yes," he answered softly. Thro quickly changed the subject; she was trying, for the dozenth time, to explain to Kulakov how a checking account worked. Stone, watching them talk, let his mind wander; for no reason at all, he remembered how his daughter used to confuse kissing with making love. When he would come in to say good night, she would giggle and say, "Let's make love," and start planting kisses on his mouth. The next morning she would proudly announce in her high-pitched voice that she and her daddy had made love fifteen times the night before.

That happened when she was six. Now she was eight going on nine. Stone wondered if she still confused kissing and making love. He didn't know. He hadn't set eyes on her in two years.

Thro's end of it got off to a slow start; for the first few days, all Kulakov wanted to talk about was money. Thro was as reassuring as she could be, but necessarily vague. Kulakov grew suspicious, and then bitter. "What does it depend on?" he wanted to know. "How many secrets I give to your Mr. Simon? How many times must I tell you, I don't know any secrets?"

Thro was patient. She explained that he would get a lump sum settlement, and a military pension roughly equivalent to what a retired major, which was Kulakov's rank, would receive from the United States Army after twenty-eight years of service. He would also receive private medical insurance, and be eligible for Social Security payments when he reached the age of sixty-five. Kulakov remained anxious. "What," he asked, "is Social Security?"

Thro questioned Kulakov closely on what he had done in the courier service ("I carried sealed diplomatic pouches from point A to point B for twenty-eight years"); what he had studied in the military academy ("Artillery; I was a specialist on how rifling affected the spin and accuracy of a projectile"); his hobbies ("What," he asked, "are hobbies?"). She finally wormed out of him that during one of his vacations at a Ministry of Defense rest home on the Black Sea, he had borrowed a secondhand easel and started to dabble in oils. The next afternoon, Thro turned up with a professional easel, oils, brushes and an assortment of canvases. Kulakov smiled weakly and thanked her profusely, but he didn't go near the easel for two weeks. Then one day, Thro arrived in his room to find him painting furiously near the window. His canvases, which he began turning out at the rate of one every two or three days, were colorful primitives with tiny figures clawing their way up hills or struggling through fields of grass in which ferocious beasts and oversized snakes lurked.

"It would be my dream to run an art gallery," Kulakov agreed the first time Thro suggested it. "Is such a thing possible?"

"We could arrange for you to work at a big gallery for six months to learn the ropes," Thro told him. "After that, we'll find a good-sized city that doesn't have a decent gallery and set you up in business."

"It could also be a cultural center," blurted Kulakov, bubbling with ideas. "I could show art films one night a week and serve tea from a samovar and hold discussions."

"You could invite artists to lecture," offered Thro.

"I could organize a lending library of art books," said Kulakov. "I could start an art newsletter."

In the sessions that followed, while Thro slowly developed an identity for him to slip into when he left the farm, Kulakov kept coming back to the art gallery. "You make it sound possible," he commented. "Please don't build up my hopes if such a thing is not possible."

Even Stone noticed the change in Kulakov; the morning sessions, for the Russian defector, became a means to an end: The sooner he gave Stone what he wanted, the sooner he, Kulakov, would be able to realize his new-found dream of opening an art gallery.

"You were saying that your wife left you for another man," Stone prompts. "Did you see any signs of what was in the air before the event?"

"Absolutely nothing," Kulakov responds almost eagerly. He tilts his head and studies an unfinished canvas on the easel in front of the window: it shows a cat about to spring on a tiny man in a dark forest. "It came like a bolt of lightning."

"But you said she had been moody—"

Kulakov interrupts him with an impatient wave of his hand. "Who wouldn't have been moody?" he says. "A daughter in an asylum being treated for . . . problems. A son expelled from the university for using drugs. Her mood had nothing to do with it."

"How was your sex life?"

This gets a snort out of Kulakov. "My sex life was normal, which is to say we made love once every week or two when she rolled over and began to touch me."

"She only attempted to stimulate you once every week or so?"

"My God, do you have to know everything?" Kulakov shakes his head quickly, as if he is clearing it. "She tried to stimulate me more often, of course, but I usually acted as if I was asleep. I also drank a lot, which meant I often *was* asleep."

"How long were you married?"

Kulakov purses his lips, calculates. "Twenty-two years."

"Whom did she run off with?"

"I don't know his name," Kulakov mumbles in exasperation. "She never said. She just told me she couldn't take any more and was leaving."

"Did you try to stop her?"

"Yes," Kulakov says, and then corrects himself. "No. Not very hard."

Stone lets a moment go by. "What made you think another man was involved?"

"I asked her. I asked her if there was someone else. She laughed hysterically and started screaming at me that she was going off with some tank commander."

"Did you ever hear from her after that?"

"Indirectly." Kulakov jams a cigarette into his holder and lights it. "A friend of hers I'd seen occasionally, a typist in one of the ministries named Natalia—"

"What was her family name? Her patronymic?"

Kulakov thinks a moment. "Natalia Viktorovna Mikhailova. Her husband was a captain in the Army transport section. Yes. Mikhailova."

"And she came to you—"

"She turned up one day at the door—"

"Before or after you were living with the actress?" Stone asks.

"After," Kulakov says. "The actress had moved in, but she wasn't there when Natalia came by."

Stone nods encouragingly. "We'll come back to the actress. Tell me about Natalia."

"There's not much to tell. She said my wife was well. She said she was living in Alma-Ata with this tank commander." Kulakov closes his eyes, concentrates, and gives Stone the address. "She asked if she could collect my wife's effects—her clothing, her cosmetics. My wife was very proud of her collection of Western cosmetics. I left Natalia alone in the apartment. When I came back, she was gone, along with my wife's things."

"And you never heard from your wife again?"

Kulakov is lost in thought, staring out the window. Stone repeats the question. "I got a picture postcard in the mail once," Kulakov recalls. "On one side was a photograph of the sports stadium outside Alma-Ata. On the other was a note, in my wife's handwriting but unsigned, that said, 'You are weighted down, like a diver, by the sense of your own specialness. Come to the surface.'" Kulakov is suddenly very intense. "I tell it to you frankly—if she rots in hell, it's all the same to me."

Kulakov, agitated, stares from the strange man, whom he has never seen before, to the array of electrodes and meters in the open suitcase. "I categorically refuse," he announces. He looks at Stone with a pleading expression. "Why are you humiliating me like this? I've told you the truth. I swear it to you."

"I believe you," says Stone. "But the people I work for must have this before they'll believe you."

"Isn't there another way?" begs Kulakov.

"There are certain drugs," Stone says vaguely, "but they are generally used on uncooperative subjects. There is a voice print analysis procedure, and eyelid observation; people tend to blink more often, and more rapidly, when they are lying. We've already used both techniques on you, with negative results. But voice printouts and eyelid observation are experimental methods. They will want the lie detector results to confirm the feeling we all have that you are telling the truth."

Obviously unhappy at the turn of events, Kulakov allows himself to be led to the chair set up in the middle of the room. The curtain is drawn, the electrodes are attached, a floor lamp is pulled over and placed just next to Kulakov's elbow. All the other lights are turned off.

Kulakov squirms uncomfortably. "The peasants say," he jokes bitterly, "that the darkest place in a room is under a lamp."

"The peasants know many things we don't know," Stone agrees. Kulakov half smiles at the line, which he used to Stone on the Globemaster.

The civilian adjusts several dials in the suitcase, starts the printout, nods to Stone, whose voice comes out of the darkness. "All right, let's begin. Will you state your full name, your age, your rank, your last assignment and your military serial number."

"Kulakov, Oleg Anatolyevich. I'm fifty-three years old. I hold . . . I held the rank of major. I was assigned as a courier attached to the Ministry of Defense. My military serial number is 607092."

Again the civilian monitoring the dials nods toward Stone. "That's fine," he says. "You can start in now."

Stone walks over and hands Kulakov a lighted cigarette. "You all right?"

"I'm all right," he says tensely. "Your friend is a painless dentist."

"Oleg," Stone says, "I'd like you to describe the events surrounding Gregori's dismissal from Lomonosov University. Talk slowly, take it chronologically."

Kulakov pulls several times on his cigarette. "The first I knew about my son being in hot water was when the rector of the university sent for me. I thought Gregori had gotten into trouble

64

with the Komsomol again. He had been in difficulty several times before—once for not turning up for a Komsomol work party, another time it was for telling a joke about the Soviet intervention in Czechoslovakia. Each time I had been able to smooth things over—I was, after all, a very trusted member of the Party—so I didn't expect this one to be any more serious."

The civilian says, "So far, so good."

Stone says, "And that's when you found out about the drugs?"

"Yes," says Kulakov. "The rector was actually very understanding. He said he had no choice except to expel him. He gave me the name of a doctor I could go to—"

"Gregori had treatment?" Stone sounds surprised. "You didn't mention that before."

"It didn't last very long," Kulakov admits. "In the end, I found out that all the time I thought he was going to the clinic, he was wandering around Moscow with some hooligans."

"Is that when the militia picked him up?"

"It was during that period, yes. The militia thought he was drunk and held him overnight. Then they found the needle marks. And that was the end of his Moscow residence permit. He was sent to work on a Hero Project in Irkutsk—building a railroad spur, I think. About a month before I left, I got a note from him in the mail. He said he couldn't remember my birthday, but he wanted to wish me happy birthday anyhow. He said he was on his way to live with his mother in Alma-Ata. That was the last I heard from him."

The civilian lets the printout run through his fingers onto the floor. He looks up at Stone and nods.

"Children never remember their parents' birthdays," Stone comments.

"I always remembered my father's," Kulakov offers. The civilian behind him leans closer to the printout "He was born September twenty-fourth."

The civilian signals with a finger to Stone.

65

"You told me your father was dead," Stone says carefully. His voice is exactly as it was before. "Do you remember the date of his death too?"

Kulakov answers quickly. "He died in the summer," he says. "Early August. The fourth, I think it was."

The civilian looks across at Stone and shakes his head. Stone says, "I'm sorry, Oleg, but you're lying!"

"Why would he lie about his father?" Thro asks. "Why would he say he's dead when he's alive?"

"Because his father is Jewish," Stone explains. "Kulakov was very ambitious when he was young. When he applied for entrance into the military academy, in 1942 I think it was, he was smart enough to realize he wouldn't get very far in Stalin's bureaucracy with a Jewish father on his record. So he bribed someone to change the name of the father on his birth certificate and substitute the name of a family friend who had died in the war. This kind of thing was done all the time. Instead of a Jew for a father, he had a party member and a war hero. In the confusion of the war, with records being lost all the time, nobody caught up with him."

"And what happened to the real father?"

"That's the odd part," explains Stone. "He's still very much alive. His name is Davidov. Leon Davidov. He works as a janitor-handyman in the Ministry of Defense. Kulakov used to see him every now and then in the corridors. Sometimes they met in the men's room for a few minutes. They would pee at adjoining urinals and exchange a few words. The last time Kulakov saw his father was when he came out of the duty office with the diplomatic pouch chained to his wrist and written orders to take it to Cairo. Davidov was on a ladder changing light bulbs in the hall. It must have been quite a moment. Kulakov passed right next to him, knowing he would never see him again. He gripped the old man's ankle by way of goodbye. He broke down when he told us about this." Stone shakes his head sadly. "What a world we live in."

Thro asks, "What was the real father like?"

"Apparently the old man was frightened out of his skin during the Stalin years. He was arrested twice, once because he shared an apartment with someone accused of being a Trotsky-ist, another time because he listened, along with several others, to an anti-Stalin joke and didn't denounce the storyteller. Somebody else did, and the law of the land specified you could be sent to prison for failing to denounce an enemy of the people. Davidov wound up doing what many people did: he was so frightened he'd be accused of being anti-Stalin that he became an ardent Stalinist. In a manner of speaking, he became more Catholic than the Pope. He read Stalin's speeches in *Pravda*, memorized them and quoted them back word for word to everyone. Anybody who spoke to him came away convinced he was a great Stalinist. He was just crazy with fear, is all it was."

"My God, what a secret for Kulakov to carry around with him all these years," says Thro.

"The irony," recounts Stone, "is that the charge they eventually brought against him was for lying about his family background in official documents—*but they had him on the wrong lie.* The man who was listed as his father turned out not to have been a war hero at all, at least that's what the military prosecutor claimed. He showed Kulakov an old divisional war diary proving that the real Kulakov had been executed for desertion under fire. Kulakov denied knowing this so convincingly that the prosecutor gave him a lie dectector test—which he promptly flunked, since he was lying. Kulakov was caught. He couldn't explain he wasn't the son of an executed deserter and trot out as proof the Jewish father he'd hidden all those years. It would have only made matters worse."

"It's an incredible story," says Thro. "Stone, this must prove that he's a genuine defector. They could never have set all this up."

"Oh, Kulakov's telling the truth, all right," agrees Stone. "That's not what's worrying me."

"What is worrying you?"

"What I'm worrying about," Stone answers evasively, "is how the world will end. And when."

"Aside from the fact that you part your hair on different sides, you're really very much alike," Thro says out of the blue. She has slipped into his room to see if Stone wants to make love and has found him poring over the reports that came back from Topology.

"How alike?" Stone asks, watching her strip off her bathrobe and climb into his bed. "Alike how?"

"God, these sheets are cold," she says. "You're both victims, is how you're alike. Kulakov once told me he went around for twenty-eight years carrying a sealed pouch from point A to point B. It strikes me as a pretty fair description of what you do, Stone."

Stone climbs into bed alongside her, presses his knee into her crotch, runs a hand over her breasts. "There's a difference," he says. "I know what's in the pouch."

"Do you, Stone? Do you really?"

Stone makes it a point to arrive at the motel room early, and routinely goes over it for bugs. As an added precaution, he has rented three rooms in a row, and uses the middle one for the meeting. Mozart arrives, as usual, precisely at the appointed time, lugging a briefcase with a new batch of Topology reports.

"Morning, Stone." Mozart greets his boss with no visible sign of deference. "How's our courier holding out?"

"Better than I am," replies Stone. "What've you got for me today?"

"Lots of dirt," says Mozart, tossing a thick folder onto the bed, "but no nuggets." And in his maddeningly efficient monotone, he gives Stone a rundown on what the Topology people have come up with. Kulakov, it seems, has gotten several addresses wrong. At one point he mentioned a film he had seen in Moscow, but according to Topology records, it didn't open until a month after he said he saw it. He made an error in describing

68

Natalia's husband as a captain; at last listing, he was still a lieutenant. There is no railroad spur Hero Project in Irkutsk; there
were avalanches in the area at the time, and some teams were
sent out to reopen lines that had been cut.

"That doesn't add up to much either way," muses Stone.
"What else have you come up with?"

"On the positive side, we've got the Russians trying to close
the barn door after the horse has skedaddled," says Mozart.
"There are confirmed reports of military intelligence cleanup
teams in Cairo and Athens, and cleanup is what they've been
the embassy heavies in Athens who let Kulakov slip through
their fingers have been flown home and charged with dereliction
of duty. The second secretary who was in the car with them has
been relieved and brought up on charges. The general in charge
of the diplomatic courier service has been relieved. The deputy
director of military intelligence has been transferred to the
boondocks. Just about everyone who touched Kulakov has been
in hot water. The driver who drove him to the airport, a civilian
attached to the ministry car pool, was sent packing to a kolkhoz
in the Ukraine. The admiral thinks—"

Stone looks up sharply. "You've been in to see the admiral?"

Mozart is very cool. "He summoned me," he says, a pleasant
smile spreading across his jowly features. "I didn't initiate. He's
following this on a day-to-day basis."

"I'll bet," says Stone. "Have you come up with anything on
Gamov?"

For once Mozart looks blank. "Gamov?"

"The duty officer who sent Kulakov on a courier run even
though his name had been stricken from the active courier list,"
Stone explains, not without some satisfaction.

"That Gamov." Mozart recovers quickly.

"That Gamov," says Stone, "should be in very hot water indeed."

Mozart chuckles gleefully. "He may be in the hottest water of
all," he tells Stone. "He's disappeared without a trace. For all
purposes, there simply is no Gamov."

Mozart also fills Stone in on what Charlie Evans over at the CIA has come up with on the cold paper. "The pouch was a gold mine," he says. "There's a series of letters from people at the Ministry of Defense to their Egyptian counterparts listing which spare parts for MIG 17s, 19s and 21s are available, and which aren't. Working from these lists, the CIA expects to be able to make a very educated guess on how many of the MIGs in Egyptian hands are operational. The Israelis are already talking about some very attractive trade-offs for access to this information; they have an agent in place in Iran that they are offering to make available for starters. Then there is a personal letter to the ambassador's daughter from a boyfriend of hers, describing bread riots in the city of Nordvik on the Laptev Sea. There's another note to the military intelligence resident in Cairo, instructing him to tell a certain Ahmid—it's obviously a code name—that ten thousand Swiss francs have been deposited in his account in the Swiss Bank Corporation in Zurich. There are also several personal letters, two typewritten, two handwritten. One's a love letter, actually. And there's a curious item that nobody's figured out yet. It's a note from a Russian in Geneva to his brother-in-law, who is a third secretary in the Soviet Embassy in Cairo. The letter, written in longhand, has five words: *'Ti minyeh dolzhen sto rublei.'* 'You owe me one hundred rubles.' It's signed, Khrustalev-Nosar."

"Did you check out the name at Topology?" Stone wants to know.

Mozart nods. "Khrustalev-Nosar is a diplomat at the SALT disarmament talks. Thirtyish. Brilliant. Technocrat. He's got scientific credentials and specializes in air-to-ground missile systems. There is apparently some suspicion that he's connected with military intelligence."

Stone takes all this in. "What are your relations with Charlie Evans's people?" he asks.

"Cold. Correct." And he adds sarcastically, "None of us is nicer than he has to be."

"You were talking about the actress," Stone reminds Kulakov. "You were saying that it was her idea to move in with you, not yours."

They are strolling along an unpaved road that winds through the rolling hills near the farm. A civilian with a shotgun cradled in his arms follows discreetly behind. The air is cold, but clear. Kulakov has the collar of his sheepskin coat turned up and his head tucked turtlelike into it. The pace is brisk—too brisk for Kulakov, who has trouble walking and talking at the same time.

"She didn't have a Moscow residence permit," Kulakov explains. "It was either move in with me or go back to Leningrad. Naturally, I preferred her in Moscow. So when she asked, I said yes."

"It didn't strike you as unusual—her asking, I mean? Normally it's the man who suggests this kind of arrangement."

Kulakov actually laughs. "You speak Russian like a native," he says, "but you don't really know Russia. There are thousands—maybe even tens of thousands—of people living like Gypsies in Moscow. They have no residence card, and without a residence card they have no right to a job or an apartment. It's a vicious circle. They can't get the residence card without the job and apartment; they can't get the job and apartment without the residence permit. So they move in with friends or lovers and live *na levo,* as we say—on the left. She worked at a theater company in Leningrad, but she wanted to live in Moscow, so she was hunting for a film studio or a theater that would take her on. Meanwhile she had to live somewhere. It's as simple as that."

Stone walks on for a while in silence. "How did you meet her?"

"Meet whom? Oh, the actress. I met her at the Actors Union. I was dining there one night with a cousin who is the widow of an actor who looked exactly like Lenin from the back and always played him in films. Galya was at another table—we had exchanged looks two or three times, the way people will. At midnight they turned off the overhead lights to signal everyone to leave. We were lingering over cognacs. Galya walked straight up to me, leaned down and planted a kiss on my lips." Kulakov smiles bitterly at the memory. "Just like that. She was very—how to put it?—unconventional. When I ran into her again, purely by accident, in the record store on Gorky Street—I was buying some new records to take to Nadia at the hospital—well, you know how it is. One thing led to another. And she asked if she could move in. I was alone, so I thought, where's the harm?"

"But things didn't work out the way you thought they would?"

Kulakov's head emerges from his collar; his features are drawn, his eyes half closed and moist. "For which of us," he says quietly, "do things work out the way we thought they would?" He shakes his head sadly. "Galya was a very beautiful woman on the outside, but very warped inside."

"How warped?" Stone asks.

"Sexually, for one thing," replies Kulakov. "She made demands that no man could satisfy. And she didn't hide her lack of satisfaction. She seemed to take pleasure in humiliating me. She boasted about other loves she had known; about what she had done to them, and what they had done to her. She loved to describe things in great detail. No matter how much I tried to please her, it was never enough. She always wanted more."

They walk on for a hundred yards without saying anything; ahead, the farm comes into view on a rise: a main house, whitewashed clapboard, two stories, and two smaller outbuildings, one in brick, one in wood. The entire complex is surrounded by a whitewashed picket fence. Four cars are parked in various places around the complex, and two men with shotguns can be seen lounging in the shadows of the buildings. Stone knows that two more, also with shotguns, are playing cards inside the brick building, which serves as a storehouse for the farm's arsenal—an assortment of Uzi submachine guns, grenades and one light mortar.

"Did your actress friend leave before or after the charges were brought against you?" Stone asks.

Kulakov thinks a moment. "I can't remember," he says. "It was a bad time for me, you understand. I lost track of the sequence. I remember a vicious argument when she turned up one night with another man and kissed him on the lips in front of me. But I don't remember if it was before or after the charges."

"About the charges," Stone says, "what was the first you heard of them?"

"I had just come back from a run to Paris, and was due for a few days off. I got a phone call from someone at the ministry ordering me not to leave Moscow, and to be available at my phone between nine and six every day. I thought maybe there was another diplomatic run in the works. Two days later, I think it was, though now that I think of it, it might have been three or four, the call came through."

"But it wasn't a diplomatic run?"

Kulakov nods. One of the men with the shotguns waves from the farm, and Kulakov and Stone wave back. "I was ordered to report to room 666—I remember the three sixes—at ten the next morning, in uniform. The uniform part made me nervous; I seldom wore a uniform."

"And that's when you met Colonel Koptin."

"Yes." They are up to the picket fence now, and Stone stops so they can finish before they go in. "He was a decent enough fellow," Kulakov says. "He seemed sorry to be doing what he was doing. He said that a routine background investigation, which is ordered up periodically for people who have access to very secret material, turned up the fact that I had lied about my father. I must have turned very pale when he said that; you see, I thought they had discovered the truth about my father being Jewish. Koptin came around the desk and brought a seat over for me, and then gave me a glass of water. And he explained that it had come out that my father had not been a war hero after all, but rather a deserter who had been executed for collaboration with the Nazi invaders. He even showed me the handwritten entry in the war diary noting the execution of someone named Kulakov. I denied everything—all this was news to me—and he

73

noted my denials in the dossier. He even appeared to believe my denials were sincere—he asked me if I would submit to a lie detector test and became openly sympathetic to me when I instantly agreed. Then he showed me a memorandum, signed by his superior, ordering my name stricken from the active courier list. And he advised me to hire a lawyer, as there was a good chance that the case would come to trial. I asked him what the consequence of a guilty verdict would be. He said that for someone in my position, which is to say someone with access to very secret material, a conviction would go very hard. He said I could expect a jail sentence of not less than ten years, along with a dishonorable discharge and loss of all pension rights."

Thro comes out of the front door of the main house. "Anybody for lunch?" she calls.

"Let's eat," says Stone.

Thro's skin is tingling from the Chinese tea disease. "I read it in *Newsweek,*" she says, pressing her fingers to her cheekbones. "By burning fossil fuels, we're increasing the amount of carbon dioxide in the atmosphere. This curtain of carbon dioxide produces a greenhouse effect. So far, so good. Now, if we keep burning fossil fuels at the present rate, the atmosphere will be 5.4 degrees warmer than it is today by the year 2050. And that will turn the corn belt into desert." Thro giggles hysterically. "The fact that there are enough nuclear weapons around to annihilate the world population 690 times over will be the least of our problems!"

Mozart serves some Cantonese rice to the gorgeous blonde who claims her name is Clyde. She flashes a smile that has been perfected in front of a mirror and bats her false eyelashes at Kulakov as she passes the plate of rice to him.

"Where'd you find her?" Mozart asks in English. (Kulakov doesn't know she is a high-priced hooker, and Stone doesn't want him to find out.)

"It's Thro who organized it," Stone says.

"You'll have to fix me up sometime," Mozart tells Thro.

74

"Not on company money or time," remarks Stone.

They have been drinking whiskey and water, and are all slightly drunk.

"Don't you ever stop playing the boss?" taunts Mozart. "Don't you ever let go?"

Thro belches delicately into her hand and says, "Fair question."

The hooker leans closer to Kulakov so that her breast presses into his arm and whispers something in his ear. Stone holds his breath to get rid of hiccups, gazes at Mozart through half-closed eyes. Suddenly his breath spills out, along with a flow of words he can't stop. "You know something, friend," he blurts out, his face very close to Mozart's. "I detest your generation. I really do."

Mozart takes the assault in his stride. He leans back in his chair and toys with his Phi Beta Kappa key. "What did you do to us that makes you hate us so much?" he asks arrogantly.

"You see," cries Stone. "That's exactly the kind of smart-assed response you get from an Ivy Leaguer." He appeals to Thro. "They're always turning everything inside out." Stone sways a bit, turns his gaze directly on Mozart. "My generation has the saving grace that it is honestly and deeply anti-Communist; we did what we did to avert a greater evil. But your generation is without beliefs. You have no center. You do what you do because you enjoy doing it. Espionage is an indoor sport to you. Jesus, you don't really care about Communism one way or the other. If there were no Communists, you'd invent them to have someone to play with."

There is an embarrassed silence; Kulakov looks from one to the other, unable to follow the English.

"Stone?" Thro tries to break it up.

"You'll never get my job, you know," Stone tells Mozart evenly. He turns to Thro, who is tugging at his arm. "Over my dead body he'll get my job."

Kulakov says in Russian, "What means, 'The victor belongs to the spoils'?"

75

The hooker hangs on Kulakov's every word. "What's he saying?" she asks out of the corner of her mouth.

"I read it in my English lesson yesterday," Kulakov explains. And he repeats the F. Scott Fitzgerald phrase in halting English: " 'The victor belongs to the spoils.' "

The hooker laughs at Kulakov's accent. "He's cute," she says.

Mozart says belligerently, "What makes you think I want your stinking job? Topology is a fossil fuel."

Thro explains the Fitzgerald phrase to Kulakov. "It's a play on words, Oleg. The original is, 'To the victor belong the spoils.' "

Mozart repeats the phrase in Latin. Stone sneers.

Kulakov says, "To this victor, no spoils. By the time I got to Germany, there was nothing left." He raises an empty whiskey glass and clinks it against Stone's bowl of rice. "To tell the truth, I had a great war. I was never bored."

Stone nods more than he should. "Me too," he says. "I had a great war. I was sorry when it was over." And he turns fiercely on Mozart. "How was your war, friend?"

"It's just started," says Mozart. "It's going, thank you for inquiring, very nicely."

The hooker tiptoes out of Kulakov's motel room, finds a guard cradling a shotgun on duty outside his door. "Who pays me?" she whispers.

The guard motions with his head to the next door. The hooker raps softly. Stone opens a crack, sees who it is, tells her to wait a moment. He returns and hands her an envelope through the partially open door. "How'd it go?" he asks.

"He performed normally," she answers. "They almost always do with me. Funny thing," she adds, not a little touched, "is he cried like a baby afterwards."

Stone takes the shuttle from Washington, and a taxi from La Guardia Airport to the courthouse, all the time rehearsing pretty speeches—how a daughter needs a father figure in her life, how he will devote himself to her, how he is not competing with the mother but only complementing her. The lady lawyer, whose first name is Margaret and who signs her letters with an "Ms." before her name, buttonholes him on the courthouse steps and leads him around the corner for a quick coffee. "Whatever you do," she instructs him, "no pretty speeches. You keep quiet unless you're asked a direct question. Remember that the judge has had every pretty speech in the book thrown at him. What he will be impressed with is a quiet, contained man who has his wits about him. Relax. Look confident. Leave everything to me."

Stone's ex-wife is there, looking leaner and meaner than he remembered her. "Alice." He calls her name and moves toward her, but she turns her back and says something to her lawyer, a heavy-set man who looks like a monseigneur in civilian clothes.

The judge, a frail, near-sighted man in his sixties who appears to peck like a bird at the papers in front of him, barely glances on the attorneys. The talk, for the first twenty minutes, is a good-natured exchange of legal mumbo-jumbo—affidavits, jurisdiction, statutes, precedents. Eventually the judge comes to what Stone considers the point.

"If I understand you correctly, Mr. Stone, you are contesting a ruling handed down in this court, by a judge now deceased, prohibiting you from having any contact whatsoever with your daughter, Jessica."

"Yes, Your Honor. I believe—"

"And you, Mrs. Stone, contend that the original reasons for denying access are still valid." The judge shuffles through some papers, finds the one he wants, pecks at it for a moment, then looks up again. "Yes, I think I have it now. The original case concerned Mrs. Stone's allegations that on such and such a day"—the judge is scanning now—"in such and such a place, the father, then exercising weekend custody of the child, was negligent in that he permitted a woman who was his mistress to punish the child by scratching her fingernails across the child's arm and shoulder, thereby inflicting wounds that required

77

emergency medical treatment, and subsequent psychiatric therapy sessions for the child, who was badly frightened by the incident." The judge looks up at the lawyers. "That's quite a mouthful. Well, where do we start?"

"Your Honor." Stone is on his feet—they are seated around the judge's desk in his chamber. "I swear to you it was an accident. We were roughhousing, and—"

"Mr. Stone." The judge waves him back into his chair. "What's in question in this new hearing you've requested is not the original incident, which led to a ruling denying you access. What's in question, now as then, is the best interests of the child. Your attorney has represented you as claiming that loss of access for two years has had a profound effect on you *and* the child; that any negligence on your part was unlikely to be repeated, given what was at stake; that the best interests of the child would be served by reinstating reasonable visitation rights. And she has attached various affidavits from child psychiatrists and pediatricians and prominent people who are acquainted with you. Am I correct in assuming that the admiral who put his name to one letter of recommendation is in fact the admiral who is currently serving as the chairman of the Joint Chiefs of Staff?"

"One and the same," says Stone's lady lawyer, obviously content that they have scored a point.

"Well, there's no getting around it, is there?" The judge appeals good-naturedly to Mrs. Stone's civilian monseigneur. "That's a very impressive testimonial." The judge clears his throat, pecks again at various papers. "Now, your attorney, Mrs. Stone, has represented you as saying you still fear for the physical and emotional well-being of your daughter, inasmuch as the lady who inflicted the original fingernail wound, for which Mr. Stone has been held accountable, is still very much associated with Mr. Stone. Another mouthful! And he has attached various affidavits from child psychiatrists and pediatrians"—Stone thinks he detects a hint of mockery in the judge's tone—"and the like to support your claim."

"My client," the monseigneur says smoothly, "maintains that her daughter has grown accustomed to living without a father, that to reintroduce visitation rights would reopen what in effect has become a closed chapter in the child's life. In essence, Your Honor, reinstating visiting rights would create a problem for the child where none presently exists."

The judge fixes his attention on the two attorneys again. "What I would like to do, if it meets with no objections from you, is invite each of the parties to respond to the legal presentation of the other side, in writing, with counterarguments. Secondly, would either side object to my ordering a social inquiry into the private lives of the two parties?"

Stone's lawyer leaps at the offer. "We'd be delighted to cooperate, Your Honor. My client is a well-respected man making a valuable contribution to his country."

"Naturally," chimes in the monseigneur, "we would not object. Mrs. Stone has nothing to hide."

"Ask the child," Stone's ex-wife blurts out. "Ask her if she wants to see him again."

"She'll say what she's been told to say." Stone is on his feet again. "How can you ask an eight-year-old—"

"We were doing so nicely," the judge says mildly. Stone sinks back into his chair. "Naturally, we will interview the child," the judge tells Mrs. Stone. He turns to Stone and adds, "And naturally, we will bear in mind we are talking to an eight-year-old who may or may not have been influenced to say what she says by her mother. Our social people aren't idiots. They know how to deal with situations such as this one. So we'll follow the procedure I've suggested. And then we'll see what we'll see."

"It went very nicely," the lady lawyer with the "Ms." before her name assures Stone.

"How could you tell?" he asks. He isn't sure how it went.

"The business about the letter from the admiral. The fact that he bothered to order the social inquiry; if he was going to rule against you, he would have done it on the spot. In my opin-

79

ion, he's looking for the factual basis to rule in your favor. It made a very bad impression on him when she blurted out, 'Ask the child,' at the end. Remember what I told you about speaking out of turn? The trick, in all court cases, is to keep your mouth shut. The one who talks the least gives away the least."

"What about my still being with the woman who accidentally hurt Jessica?" Stone asks. "How will that stand up under scrutiny?"

The lady lawyer shrugs. "I told you when you began this it would be better to be able to say that she no longer figured in your life." She sees Stone's gaze drift dejectedly to the empty coffee cup. "Cheer up," she says brightly. "With or without her in your life, it's in the bag. I wouldn't have taken on the case if I didn't think I was going to win it."

"You were saying that the duty officer phoned—"

"It wasn't the duty officer who phoned," Kulakov corrects Stone. "Someone else phoned and told me to report to the duty officer in civilian clothes."

"Oleg, I want you to concentrate on this. I want you to try and remember every detail, no matter how trivial," Stone tells him. "Didn't you consider it odd that one day you could be called before an examining officer, informed that charges were being lodged against you, shown a memorandum ordering your name stricken from the active courier list, and the very next day you could be summoned to the duty officer as if nothing had happened and sent abroad?"

"I've thought about it a great deal," admits Kulakov. "It was a bureaucratic mistake. Every bureaucracy makes mistakes. Memorandums have to circulate. That takes time. They can get lost, or misplaced. Or lie around unopened and unread on desks. I've seen it happen dozens of times. So have you."

"In all your years as a courier," asks Stone, "have you ever heard of someone being sent out of the country by accident?"

Kulakov is silent.

"If it was an accident," says Stone, "it was one hell of an accident."

"It has to be an accident," insists Kulakov. "Why would they want a diplomatic pouch to fall into your hands?"

This time it is Stone who falls silent. He stares out the window for a long while. Finally he says, "Coming back here on the plane, you described your conversation with the duty officer. Do you still remember it?"

Kulakov nods. "He said someone had to deliver the pouch to Cairo by that night."

Stone finishes it for him. "He said, 'You're elected. By one vote. Mine.'"

"Yes," agrees Kulakov. "That's what he said. What of it?"

"What was his rank?"

"He was a major," answers Kulakov, "same as me."

"'Someone has to deliver this pouch to Cairo by tonight. You're elected. By one vote. Mine.' That's not the way one major talks to another. It sounds more like a superior talking to a junior."

Kulakov shrugs.

"How old was this Gamov?" Stone asks.

"Sixty. Sixty-two maybe."

"Old for a major," Stone muses. "Describe him again."

Kulakov closes his eyes. "He was missing an arm—his left arm. The sleeve was pinned up. He had dandruff on his shoulders, which he brushed off with his right hand. His fingers were not the fingers of a man, but more like a woman's—long and thin. He wore his wrist watch on the inside of his wrist. He had a tendency to sneer. He had quite a few medals on his chest."

"Can you remember which medals?" Stone asks intently.

Kulakov shakes his head.

"Try," insists Stone.

Kulakov closes his eyes again, concentrates.

"Try, damn it!"

Kulakov says slowly, "One was all red with a hammer and sickle in the middle."

"The Order of the Red Banner," murmurs Stone.

"Another was . . . red with black stripes."

"Vertical or horizontal?"

Kulakov opens his eyes. "Horizontal," he says. "The stripes were horizontal!"

"The Order of Stalin!" Stone walks over to the window and stares out at the white picket fence. "The rows of ribbons. The Order of Stalin. The missing arm. He was a war hero. But only a major. Why was someone with an Order of Stalin to his credit still a major? And what was he doing as a duty officer in the Ministry of Defense?"

Kulakov laughs nervously. "He was giving me a chance to save my neck."

Stone looks at Kulakov without seeing him. "That's one possibility," he says. "There are others."

And then it is over. Spring has come; the air is suddenly soft and warm and moist, the ground spongy underfoot. The civilian guards, carting valises and locked metal boxes to the station wagons, squint because of the brightness of the sunlight.

"I feel as if I'm graduating," Kulakov tells Thro happily. "Sometimes I thought it would never end."

One of the guards knocks twice on the door, and comes in without being invited. Thro points to two brand-new leather valises. "Those are his. They go in the Plymouth."

When the guard has left, Thro opens a very thick attaché case. "Here is the new you," she says. "Your name is Martin Kemp. It was shortened from Kempny when you became an American citizen in 1970. Your father was Czech, your mother Russian. Your parents divorced when you were a baby. You lived in Moscow with your mother, who died in 1964. You were visiting your father in Prague when the Russians occupied it in 1968. You left Czechoslovakia in the chaos that followed. Crossing to Austria was no problem. The frontier was open for weeks.

Thousands left. You were one of the thousands. You spent two months in a Red Cross camp in Vienna before you received permission to emigrate to the United States. Here." Thro hands him an account, in Russian, of a Czech who fled after the Soviet occupation in 1968. "You'll find this full of useful details. Your date of birth and age have been changed on all your documents. You must memorize the new ones, along with all the other material—parents' names, their dates of birth and death, et cetera. Now, in Moscow you worked in an art gallery across the street from the Hotel Ukraine. There was a man who was half Czech named Martin Kempny, incidentally, who actually worked at that gallery."

"Where is he now?"

Thro looks up brightly. "He's dead, of course." She hands Kulakov a packet of documents. "Here is your original birth certificate—"

"It looks very old," Kulakov says admiringly. "How do you manufacture such things?"

"It's not manufactured," Thro explains. "It's the genuine article. Here are your citizenship papers, your American passport, a New York driver's license, a Social Security card, an American Express credit card, a bankbook from the First National City Bank—"

Kulakov opens the bankbook. "Is this money mine?"

"The twenty-five thousand dollars in the account is all yours," says Thro. "So is the Plymouth parked outside. Here's the registration for the car, made out in the name of Martin Kemp. There's an apartment in Los Angeles waiting for you. The rent has been paid for one year. The furnishings in the apartment are yours. Here is one thousand dollars cash to get you started. Also, you're being carried, for pension purposes, on the Army books as a retired major, which means you'll receive nine hundred and sixty dollars a month for the rest of your life."

Kulakov is overwhelmed. "You have been very generous. . . . I have never had a car of my own."

Thro has saved the best for the last. "Oleg, we've organized a

83

job for you in Los Angeles. It's in a very fine art gallery. . . ."

"Ah, it is all coming out as you said it would," Kulakov says softly. "I thank you from the bottom of my heart."

"Be careful," Stone tells Kulakov. They are shaking hands in front of the Plymouth. The civilian guards, Kulakov's English teacher, the cook and Thro all look on from a distance. "Grow a beard, memorize your new identity. If anyone looks as if they're too curious about your background, all you have to do is call the number I gave you and we'll find out who they are."

"This is like a dream," says Kulakov. "To get in a car and drive across America like this . . ." There is a nervous edge to his voice. "You make it sound so easy, so possible."

"Here people do it all the time," says Stone. "Here getting in a car and going where you want is an everyday occurrence." He opens the driver's door for Kulakov. "I told you we weren't like them, Oleg."

"I didn't dare believe it," says Kulakov. "I still don't dare believe it."

Two men wearing electrician's overalls, sneakers, long gray smocks and surgeon's gloves crouch before the door of an apartment on the eleventh floor of an apartment building in downtown Geneva. One has a walkie-talkie pressed to his ear. The other fiddles with a ring of passkeys, finally opens the door. Soundlessly, the two men let themselves in, wait inside the threshold in the dark until they hear two soft clicks on the walkie-talkie, then make their way to a wall safe hidden behind a mirror in the bedroom.

The taller of the two men hands the walkie-talkie to the other one, adjusts a stethoscope and places the business end on the tumblers. In less than a minute, the tumblers fall into place and the safe snaps open. Inside is a cardboard shoe box. The shorter man photographs the open safe with a Polaroid before removing the box. He lifts the cover and photographs the letters scattered loosely inside, then starts to hand them one by one to his companion, who flattens each letter on the floor and photographs it with a Minox. When they finish, they put the letters back in the box, last letter first. One of the two carefully checks the Polaroid photo of the shoe box and meticulously adjusts the letters until they match the photograph. Then the shoe box is returned to the safe, and the Polaroid photograph is again consulted to make certain the box is exactly where they found it. The safe is closed, the dial returned to the number it had been on. A last look around. Two soft clicks on the walkie-talkie, and the two men are out the door and down the fire stairs to a waiting car.

From start to finish, the operation has taken eighteen minutes, involved six men, two inside, four outside, and cost (including bonuses and bribes) $18,745.

The cleanup team waits in an apartment two floors below until the telephone rings once. They mount quickly to the target apartment and begin work. One probes the front door lock with a long, thin strip of metal, extracting barely visible magnetized filings, which he examines under a powerful magnifying glass. Two others, on their hands and knees, search the living room carpet to recover the bits of straw they planted. One of them motions with his head toward the bedroom. The mirror is scrutinized, removed, the safe dial is photographed, then the door is opened. Measurements are made with draftsman's instruments, more photographs are taken with a camera fixed to a tripod, angled straight down, the tripod feet and the shoe box on predrawn marks on a sheet of paper.

From start to finish, the operation has taken forty-eight minutes, involved eight men, six inside and two outside, and cost (including bonuses and bribes) 3,137 rubles.

CHAPTER

5

If Washington, D.C., is, psychologically speaking, a mixture of Wall Street and Disneyland, then the Forty Committee, that discreet interdepartmental big brother that watches over the shoulder of the American intelligence community, is its spiritual halfway house. It represents a judicious mix of reality and fantasy essential for the successful pursuit of its goals (which unfortunately—or perhaps fortunately—are only vaguely defined). It is, for instance, keenly aware of precedents without being tied to them; by the same token, it has nothing against an occasional flight of imagination—as long as everyone concerned takes along a parachute.

The director of the Central Intelligence Agency, Charlie Evans, a tall, handsome, impeccably pin-striped man whose wife obliges him to wear garters so his pale skin will not be visible when he crosses his legs, is entertaining Senator Howard, the chairman of the Senate Select Committee on Intelligence, with tales of cloaks and daggers; Evans, a career CIA officer who came up through the ranks, has found over the years that it is easier to deal with senators as if they were children—make them feel you are letting them in on trade secrets.

"What he do then?" demands the senator eagerly. "How'd he get his self out of that pickle?"

"He didn't," Evans says dramatically. He leans back in his chair and crosses his legs; the only thing that shows is stocking.

"The moment he saw the hair he'd planted was gone, he knew he was blown, so he went around putting notes in dead-letter drops that implicated *the wrong general*. When he thought they were about ready to pick him up, he killed the man who was staked out at his apartment—broke his spine with his knee sort of thing—and disappeared into a safe house. He had to stay out of sight fourteen weeks before our people could spirit him out of the country. By then the general he implicated had been shot by a firing squad, and *our* general had moved up a notch in the junta." Evans taps the senator on the knee. "See what I mean about planning? In this business, you've got to anticipate. There's no substitute for doing your homework. When the roof fell in, he had an alternative plan ready at hand that took advantage of adversity."

"You boys have sure come a long way from the days when you tattooed secret messages on stiff upper lips and then hid them with mustaches." The senator chuckles. "Ah, here's the admiral. And Nicholas. Morning to you, Nicholas. I guess we can put our little show on the road now."

Nicholas Toland, the short, secretive assistant to the President for national security affairs, waves everyone to places around the large circular table, activates the black box that jams any eavesdropping microphones. Toland appears uncommonly moody today; a *New York Times* review of his most recent speech, delivered to a Harvard audience, called him a "literary Sisyphus rolling clichés up a hill." The conferees take their seats; Stone sticks close to the admiral. The décor is State Department Conference Room, off green, with the only touch of color coming from the red rose in Senator Howard's lapel. Unlike most interdepartmental groups, there is no pecking order here; Toland, as the President's representative at the table, is the unofficial chairman, but each man defends his department's territory. When interests conflict, which is more often than not the case, the problem is generally avoided, if possible, or sent up to the Oval Office for a judgment.

Toland unstraps his wrist watch, a gold Patek Philippe, and

places it on the felt-covered table. "Incidentally, Charlie"—he turns to Charlie Evans—"the President is curious to know whether your people have come up with an identity for Volkov. It's almost two years now since he took over as chief of Soviet military intelligence. It's almost a year since he pulled off that coup in West Germany, of which the less said the better. It's seven months since he managed to buy the blueprints for our new Day-Track System before we could even put it into production. The man has given us a lot of trouble in the past; he's obviously going to give us a lot of trouble in the future. And we don't even know what he looks like!"

Evans doesn't appreciate the question. "There have been some leads," he reports, "but nothing we can pin down. There's a possibility that Volkov may actually be two people, one in charge of domestic activities, the other foreign. But it's unconfirmed. Volkov is still a name without a face."

"In other words, you still don't have the vaguest idea who Volkov is," Toland says. He is a stickler for restating things precisely.

"That's correct," Evans says tightly.

Toland makes a note on a yellow pad. "All right. We've got two items on the formal agenda," he announces. "First is the delicate matter of one war versus one and a half wars. Second is the Russian defector. Andrew, why don't you start the ball rolling."

Andrew is Andrew Horrick, the deputy secretary of defense, a cool, brainy West Coaster who began life in Washington as one of McNamara's whiz kids. "The Defense Department," says Horrick, "takes the view that worst-case contingency planning is still the basis of scenario construction. Now, it's all well and good to pinpoint Soviet weaknesses in production, in procurement, in translating existing forces into field potentials, but the fact of the matter is that the Russians are capable of launching a major land conflict in the European theater, and a brush-fire affair in, say, the Gulf area. In other words, they can get up steam for one and a half wars—"

"Nicholas, this is something we're going to have to iron out at a higher level," sighs Al Prentice, a scholarly undersecretary of state for political affairs. "Aside from the obvious drawback of us spending billions for weapons we don't need, worst-case contingency planning has had the effect of frightening the Russians about our intentions—"

"Of making them spend enormous sums to catch up to *their* worst-case estimates on us," agrees Charlie Evans.

"That's it exactly." Prentice leaps on the point. "We construct a military response to a supposed worst case—the one-and-a-half-war bogey this year; a missile gap ten years ago; an ability to sweep across Europe to the English Channel ten years before that—and then they construct a response to our response. And then your boys, armed with computer printouts, come in trying to scare the pants off us with how much the Russians spend in dollar equivalents—"

"The dollar equivalent calculations are extremely valuable in estimating Soviet capabilities," insists Horrick.

"Capabilities don't tell you anything about *intentions*," Prentice argues earnestly. "Look at the difference between our capabilities and our intentions. My God, we have the capability of wiping out the Soviet Union a hundred times over, but we don't intend doing that. Or do I have that wrong too?"

Nicholas Toland asks quietly, "We're not against dollar equivalent calculations, are we?"

"They're extremely useful tools," says Ohm Berenson, the director of the Defense Intelligence Agency.

"They sure are useful when it comes to prying money out of Congress for military hardware," quips Senator Howard.

"Which is pretty much what they're for," mutters Prentice. "Listen, the State Department is just against getting locked into worst-case contingency planning as methodology. We're dead set against accepting as fact that the Soviets *will* wage a war and a half simply because they may, in the worst case, be *capable* of waging a war and a half."

"In general, I concur," says Charlie Evans. "I think we should structure our assessments to take into consideration the likelihood that the worst case won't be the case we have to deal with."

The admiral, who carries a good deal of weight in his role of chairman of the Joint Chiefs, catches Toland's eye. Toland, preoccupied with trying to remember which clichés he threw at the Harvard audience, nods toward the admiral. "What do our professional soldiers think about all this?" he inquires.

"I think Charlie here, and Mr. Prentice, are missing the boat," he begins. He speaks slowly, as if he is picking his way through a thicket. "All of our intelligence assessments point to the inescapable conclusion that the worst case is a plausible case. The hard truth is that the Soviets are capable of launching and supporting, for a prolonged period of time, one and a half wars. It seems to me that once you grant this capability, it would be criminal insanity to fail to accept the capability as a possibility. If it is not a possibility, why is it a capability?"

"Just because they have a capability for waging one and a half wars doesn't mean they can wage them efficiently," Al Prentice says sullenly.

"The possibility that one and a half wars might be waged inefficiently," the admiral says sternly, "doesn't relieve us of the responsibility of having to prepare a response to them."

"If they're going to wage one and a half wars inefficiently," comments Charlie Evans, "they'd have to be crazy to wage them."

"They'll go to war," the admiral says quietly, "when they conclude they have no more to gain by not going to war. It's no secret where I stand on this." He appeals directly to Nicholas Toland. "I told the President, when he offered me the chairmanship, that I believed in my heart that we would one day find ourselves at war with the Soviet Union. And I want the United States to win that war, gentlemen."

"You mean war and a half," mocks Prentice.

"Win what?" asks Charlie Evans. "What's the prize?"

"Victory is the prize," says the admiral angrily, focusing directly on Evans.

Evans uncrosses and recrosses his long pin-striped legs. "Would the admiral care to define victory?" he asks, staring straight back at him.

"The admiral would be delighted to define victory," the admiral says with cold contempt. "Victory is being around to write the history of what happened."

"Even if nobody is around to read it?" sneers Prentice.

"Gentlemen, gentlemen," Nicholas Toland intervenes. "I'll take memos on the efficacy of worst-case contingency planning from anyone who cares to put his two cents in. Keep them reasonably short; you know the President's attention tends to wander at anything that spills over an eight-by-ten file card. We'll put it to him and see what reaction we get. Now, what about this defector? We're all of us curious to know what we have."

Charlie Evans nods to Stone. "Why don't you start," he says politely. To the others he explains, "The defector was a military courier on a run to Cairo. Stone here has debriefed the warm body. We got to debrief the diplomatic pouch."

"Mr. Stone," Nicholas Toland says, "has the floor."

Speaking in a low, deliberately unemotional voice, Stone fills in the members of the Forty Committee on the Russian defector Kulakov. He carefully explains the personal tragedies that made Kulakov wake up screaming every night, though he was never sure which of the tragedies he was screaming about. "We caught a number of small errors in his story," says Stone, "but they were inconsequential things that anyone could slip up on, such as someone's rank or address. We only caught him out in one outright lie." And he explains about Kulakov's father being Jewish, and the fact that Kulakov hid this, apparently successfully, from the Russians too.

"Then as far as you can determine," inquires Charlie Evans, "Kulakov is a genuine defector?"

"He thinks he is, yes," answers Stone.

"I detect a nuance there," says Senator Howard, peering across the table at Stone through his bifocals. "He thinks he's a genuine defector, but you seem to have reservations. You'll have to explain that, I'm afraid."

"Senator," Stone says, "intelligence activity, as you have good reason to know, is the process of great numbers of people laboring over a period of months, and sometimes even years, to put enough pieces of a puzzle together to come out with a morsel that can prove useful to those like yourself who make political decisions. When a diplomatic pouch full of morsels lands in your lap, through no effort of your own, you must begin by being extremely cautious—"

"Caution is a laudable quality," says the senator, "but we'd be damn fools to not use something that falls into our lap just because you don't believe, as a matter of faith, that things fall into laps."

Charlie Evans asks Stone, "Do you have any specific reason to think that Kulakov is not a genuine defector? Has he tried to contact anyone since he left the farm?"

Stone shakes his head. "He's clean in that respect," he says. "We bugged his car, we bugged his apartment in Los Angeles, we've watched him twenty-four on twenty-four. If he's contacted anyone, he's been pretty clever about it."

Nicholas Toland has forgotten about rolling clichés uphill for the moment. "Have the Soviets reacted in a way that indicates the defection isn't genuine?" he asks.

"On the contrary," says Stone, "every motion they've made since the defection, starting with some of their heavies waylaying a laundry truck that left the Athens embassy just after Kulakov, looks like the desperate reactions of people trying to close the barn door after the horse has fled. They've called home, and we have reason to believe they've punished, anyone remotely connected to the defection. The duty officer who made the fatal mistake of sending Kulakov abroad has disappeared from the face of the earth."

"Probably shot," offers Senator Howard.

"Dozens of their people have been called back to Moscow as a result of the Kulakov defection," continues Stone. "The Glavnoe Razdevyvatelnoe Upravlenie, which is the chief intelligence directorate of the Soviet General Staff—run by our faceless Comrade Volkov, as a matter of fact—has opened an inquiry into the causes of the defection. More heads will roll, you can count on it."

The senator peers at Stone quizzically. "You still haven't explained, then, why you don't think he's a genuine defector."

"I didn't say I don't think he's genuine," insists Stone. "I said *he* thinks he's genuine. And I'm suggesting that before we leap for joy over the contents of the pouch, we consider—I'm only suggesting we consider, you understand—other variations on the theme."

"For instance?" Senator Howard leans forward.

Stone glances at the faces around the table. "For instance," he says quietly, "the possibility that the Soviets organized the defection."

"To what purpose?" asks the senator, obviously skeptical. "Why would they go to all that trouble?"

"To make us swallow the pouch," says Stone.

"Which takes us to the pouch," says Nicholas Toland. He turns toward Charlie Evans.

"Which takes us to the pouch," agrees Evans. He places a single typewritten sheet of paper on the green felt. The page has been initialed by the woman who typed it, the six aides who subsequently read it, and Evans. In the upper-left-hand corner is stamped: "No Copies Exist."

"Gentlemen," Evans begins, letting his eyeglasses slip down along his nose and peering out, like a professor, over them. "I've been in the business of harvesting morsels, as Mr. Stone so accurately puts it, for twenty-four years. This is the first time I've ever been confronted by a feast." Evans plays to Nicholas Toland and the senator. "I identify nine items in the diplomatic pouch. Item: A diagram and operational specs on the night sight that our Russian friends plan to install in their T-62s in Egyptian hands. No positive confirmation here, but our tank ordnance people were able to identify several components that the Russians used in previous-generation night sights. They say the design and the characteristics are entirely plausible. Item: A memorandum on American Mediterranean fleet unit movements, including those of two Polaris submarines on station, for the six-week period starting 1 January. These movements were contained in a routine movement report summary sent by the Commander in Chief Atlantic, in Norfolk, to the British admiral in charge of NATO fleet units. The code used was NATO code Alpha Delta, December edition. The implication is that the code sheet somehow fell into Soviet hands. By backtracking on a basis of access, West German counterintelligence agents have arrested a female code clerk in Bonn and accused her of supplying Alpha Delta for December to her lover, who turns out to be a Soviet sleeper working for Comrade Volkov's military intelligence organization. So far nobody has admitted anything; there is some mystery as to how the clerk actually got the code sheet out, since surveillance is continuous. The best the Germans have come up with is that she memorized it line by line. Nevertheless, the Germans are positive that they've plugged a potentially disastrous leak."

"I assume," says Nicholas Toland, "that your people will be going over all traffic in the compromised code to see what the damage is."

"Berenson's people over at DIA are onto it," says Evans. "We both thought they would be in a better position to assess damage, given the fact that the compromised code dealt exclusively with military matters." Evans glances at the paper in front of him. "Item: Notification of a defect in the low-level parallax input on the radar tracking system for SAM missiles. Up to now, gentlemen"—Evans pauses for effect—"we've only had probable confirmations. Here we get into our first positive confirmation. The Israelis have owned up to being aware of the defect for some time. They ran a computer study on SAM firings in the '73 war and came up with the fact that supersonic passes at low altitudes led to an apparent displacement of the target and a subsequent lag in SAM tracking—"

"If I follow you right," says the senator, smiling broadly, "the SAMs missed the target."

"That's what happened," says Evans. "There is a defect that causes the SAMs to miss low-flying jets."

"Uh huh." The senator nods. "What else you got in that kit bag of yours?"

"Item," continues Evans. He has their attention now; the senator and Nicholas Toland are leaning forward, their elbows on the table, their chins resting on their hands. "Eighteen letters from various people at the Soviet Ministry of Defense procurement, to Egyptian procurement officers, listing which spare parts for MIG 17s, 19s and 21s are available, and in what quantity. Again, we have firm confirmation. The handwriting on one of the eighteen letters matches that of a Soviet Air Force procurement officer who served a tour as Air Force attaché in Tokyo a few years ago. Also, the first shipment of spare parts to arrive in Alexandria since Kulakov's defection—six crates of wheel-assembly housings for MIG 19s—matched exactly the notification of what was available." Evans regards the paper again. "Item: A letter to the Soviet ambassador in Cairo from his brother-in-law, who happens to be the general in charge of Soviet logistical support facilities in Kazakstan on the Chinese frontier. Once again, we can offer you positive confirmation. The handwriting is the general's; we have in our possession various letters he wrote to his wife while observing Warsaw Pact war games two years ago. In his letter to the ambassador, he mentions that the Chinese are thinning out their frontier forces and pulling units back to cities. This detail, too, has been confirmed by our satellite monitoring program."

"That's one program that's paid its way, and then some," says the senator. "Sorry, Charlie; go on."

"Item: A letter to the daughter of the Soviet ambassador in

95

Cairo from a young man who signed only his first name, Dmitri. He's apparently someone she knew from when she studied at Lomonosov University."

"No confirmation on this one, I take it?" asks Ohm Berenson.

"On the contrary, we have positive confirmation," says Evans. "The letter mentions, in passing, that there were bread shortages, and subsequent riots, in the city of Nordvik. One of the Russian dissidents in Moscow was visiting his sister in Nordvik at the time of the riots, and told Western reporters about it when he returned to Moscow. It was never published because they weren't able to obtain independent confirmation."

"We ought to play the riots back at them over Radio Free Europe," comments the senator. "Don't want to waste anything, do we?"

"It's already been played back," says Evans. "Went out a week ago."

"Might have known you wouldn't let a juicy one like that slip past you." The senator chuckles.

"Item: Four personal letters, two typewritten, two handwritten, to embassy staffers in Cairo. One confirmation here. One of the handwritten notes was a love letter from the niece of the minister of heavy armaments to a female translator—"

"You did say female?" asks Nicholas Toland.

Evans nods. "We were able to confirm both the handwriting and the homosexuality; both young ladies traveled with a student group to Paris several years ago. The niece of the armaments minister was tagged for possible blackmail on the homosexuality if she ever came out again; the female translator is being approached in Cairo now. Okay, we're getting down to the bottom of my list. Item: Instructions to the military intelligence resident in Cairo to notify a certain Ahmid that ten thousand Swiss francs has been paid into his numbered account in the Swiss Bank Corporation in Zurich. Here we were able to obtain one hundred percent confirmation. We traced the payment through our sources in Zurich—"

"Didn't know you people were into numbered Swiss accounts," the senator says uneasily. "I reckon nothin's what's sacred these days."

"The account was in the name of a Liechtenstein holding company, which in turn was controlled by a Panamanian company, and the Panamanian company was totally owned by one Khalid Tawfiq, who worked until the day before yesterday in the Egyptian cabinet secretariat."

Prentice whistles. "The Russians had a man in the cabinet secretariat! This material's got to be genuine—they'd never give that away."

"If I'm not mistaken," says the senator, "you've still got one item to go." He wags his finger playfully at Evans. "I've been down the road before with you, Charlie, and I know you save the best for the last."

"You've got my number, Senator," admits Evans. "Item: A short handwritten note from someone named Khrustalev-Nosar on the Soviet SALT negotiating team in Geneva to his brother-in-law, a junior diplomat in the Soviet Embassy in Cairo. The note has five Russian words. It translates, 'You owe me one hundred rubles.' "

The senator squints foxily. "What was the bet?"

"Well, we had some of our Swiss friends take a peek around one night when Khrustalev-Nosar was attending an embassy reception. We were looking for handwriting confirmation mainly, but I've got to admit, I was curious about the bet too. Our young Russian friend kept his letters in a shoe box—"

"That doesn't sound too difficult for people with qualifications." The senator laughs.

"The shoe box, Senator, was in a safe. The safe didn't give them much trouble. The problem in these affairs is to get in and out again without leaving a calling card. Which means the lock has to be picked without physically damaging the safe. But more important, the contents has to be put back precisely the way it was found."

"The bet," the senator prompts Evans. "What was it?"

"In the safe," Evans explains triumphantly, "was a letter to

Khrustalev-Nosar from his brother-in-law in Cairo offering to bet one hundred rubles there would be no SALT agreement before the negotiations adjourned."

"I'm not sure I follow all this," says Nicholas Toland.

"Me neither, I don't follow," says the senator. "There has been no SALT agreement, and there doesn't look as if there'll be one before adjournment—what's that, in six weeks from now?—unless one side or the other gives in on Cruise Missile force levels. . . ." The senator's voice trails off. His face lights up. "And your Russian would be in a position to know if they were going to give in to us?"

"He's an expert in air-to-ground missile systems," says Evans. "That's what he's in Geneva for."

"So his claiming the hundred rubles *before* there's an agreement means he knows there will an agreement. Which means he knows the Russians plan to give in to us on the Cruise. Which means"—the senator slaps the table in excitement—"all we have to do is sit tight, stick to our guns, and we get the new SALT treaty on our terms!" The senator turns to Prentice. "You realize, Al, what you boys over at State are being handed?"

"It's even better than it appears," notes Evans. "It's usual when you get a gem like this for the other side to know you have it, and that almost always undermines the usefulness of the gem. This time out, we have a gem that *they don't know we have.*"

Prentice is not convinced. "Khrustalev-Nosar will hear about the loss of the pouch."

"Sure he'll hear about the pouch," agrees Evans, "but he won't be sure that his letter was in it. Remember, he slipped a private note into the diplomatic bag going to Moscow. It could have gone on to Cairo in a dozen different ways. Even if he thinks we got our hands on his note, he'll check his safe, see nothing is missing, and figure we could never know what the bet was about. Also, if he tells his superiors what he's done, he'll be ruined, or even jailed. No, his instinct will be to sit tight and see what happens."

"His brother-in-law in Cairo can't blow the whistle on him either," the senator chimes in, "because he couldn't know the note was coming."

"And Khrustalev-Nosar will never tell the brother-in-law he sent the note if he finds out later that he never got it," says Evans.

Prentice shakes his head stubbornly. "What if this Khrustalev-Nosar is the patriotic type? What if, rather than see his country lose out in the negotiations, he owns up?"

"Careful," the admiral cautions coolly. "You're using the worst-case contingency."

General laughter around the table.

"Touché, Admiral," says Prentice, obviously annoyed but trying to hide it. "But where does it leave us?"

"Fair question, Al," says Evans. "If he owns up, if he tells his superiors what's in his five-word note, they will recall him and punish him immediately. First, because they'll be furious at him. And secondly, they'll do it to signal us that they are aware of the contents of the note, and hence we can no longer count on it being of value to us."

"I take it you're watching this Khrustalev-Nosar," comments Prentice.

"Twenty-four on twenty-four." Evans smiles. "Last night he had dinner with a woman clerk in the Czechoslovak Embassy. Then he slept with her. This morning he reported for work at nine. Yawning." Evans glances at his watch. "I don't know what he had for lunch yet, but I soon will."

Evans leans back in his chair, purses his lips thoughtfully. All eyes turn to Stone. "Given all these confirmations," says Nicholas Toland, "do you still hesitate to accept the defection as genuine?"

Stone refuses to let himself be intimidated. "It doesn't feel right," he says. "The pieces have fallen into place too easily."

He shakes his head briskly. "My instinct tells me to go slow."

Toland exchanges looks with Evans and shrugs. The senator snorts. "Looks to me, son, as if you've got a terminal case of euphobia." To the others he explains, "That there means fear of good news."

The admiral's back, straight as a ramrod, is turned toward Stone. He lights up one of his precious Havanas (smuggled in to him from Moscow by the naval attaché at the embassy), lets his head sink back on his shoulders as he enjoys the sensation. Then, slowly, like a main battery searching for a target of opportunity, he swivels one hundred and eighty degrees to face Stone. "Out with it," he orders, flicking on the microphone jammer. "In ten words or less, what makes you think he's a phony?"

Stone, sitting in one corner of the admiral's leather couch across the room, focuses on the framed clipping from the *New York Times*. It is dated March 18, 1970. Two sentences have been underlined in red. They represent the author John Barth as saying: "The fact that the situation is desperate doesn't make it any more interesting. I'm prepared to be bored by the man who murders me." Stone remembers a framed clipping from *Pravda* that his grandfather had hung over his desk. It had also been underlined in red. It quoted Stalin, in one of his six-hour marathon speeches, as saying: "Full conformity is possible only in the cemetery." At the time of the doctors' purge, in the early fifties, his grandfather shattered the glass with his fist. Stone remembers the old man, his white hair falling over his eyes, switching on the desk lamp and picking out, with a tweezers, splinters of glass from his bleeding hand.

The admiral sucks patiently on his cigar.

Stone strides across the room and sinks into a seat across the desk from the admiral. "It seems to me that we can observe the same set of facts," he says thoughtfully, "yet some of us see the tragedy of the human comedy, while others see the comedy of the human tragedy."

"Which do you see, Stone?"

"I've got a foot in both camps, Admiral," Stone says, smiling self-consciously. "Sometimes I go one way, sometimes the other, depending, I suppose, on what I had for breakfast, or whether the last time I made love, I made it well."

"Hmm." The admiral studies his cigar with admiration. "What you're saying, if I have it right, is the hell with consistency."

"Consistency is the last refuge of the unimaginative," says Stone. "That's Oscar Wilde."

"No one to my knowledge has ever accused you of being unimaginative," comments the admiral.

Stone closes his eyes for a moment, then opens them and plunges. "I've got a gut feeling, Admiral. Nothing more. No facts. No glaring inconsistency. No chapter and verse."

The admiral treats himself to another puff. "I'm listening."

Stone leans over the edge of the admiral's desk. "Everything that happened to Kulakov—to his daughter, his son, his wife running off with someone, the actress violating his sense of manhood, then the business of being accused of lying about how his father died—all this represents enough personal tragedy for two lifetimes. *But it all happened to Kulakov during an eight-month period.*"

"Hmm." The admiral is not overly impressed.

"Then there's the duty officer who made the fatal mistake of giving Kulakov an overseas run," continues Stone. "He was obviously a war hero—he was missing an arm, and wore a chestful of medals, including the Order of Stalin—yet he was still a major."

"Maybe he wasn't politically reliable," offers the admiral.

Stone shakes his head sharply. "He wouldn't have been in a politically sensitive job, dispatching couriers around the world, if he was unreliable. And since the defection, we can't find any trace of him. He's disappeared as surely as if he never existed."

"Maybe the senator hit the nail on the head," says the admiral. "Maybe the duty officer was shot."

"It's possible," Stone admits grudgingly.

101

"There's more, I hope?" asks the admiral.

"Not much more," concedes Stone. "The other detail that bothers me is that everybody associated with the Kulakov affair seems to be tied, in one way or another, to the military establishment."

"Spell that out for me," instructs the admiral.

"Kulakov's wife ran off with a tank officer. The wife's friend, Natalia, the one who came to collect her things, is married to an officer in the Army transport section. The rector who expelled Kulakov's son from the university is a retired Army general. The actress who seduced him is separated from an Air Force pilot. Kulakov was being charged with lying about his father by a military prosecutor. The evidence he was shown consisted of a notation in an Army divisional diary."

"Hmm. And the pouch?"

"It's the same with the pouch," says Stone. He is beginning to talk with more confidence, almost as if he is being convinced by the sound of his own voice. "Look what they gave away, Admiral. The night sight on their T-62. A defect in the SAM tracking system. Those are military secrets. The sleeper who supposedly passed our naval code to the Russians that his girl friend swiped worked for military intelligence, not the KGB, which is the party's intelligence arm. The eighteen letters about MIG spare parts came from Ministry of Defense procurement officers. The letter to the ambassador about Chinese troop movements came from a general. The love letter to the female translator came from the niece of the minister of heavy armaments, who happens to be a former tank general. The instructions to pay ten thousand Swiss francs into a numbered account were sent to the military intelligence resident, and led to exposure of an agent controlled by the military. Even Khrustalev-Nosar, who seems to be one hundred rubles ahead of the game, is suspected of being the military intelligence man on the Soviet negotiating team."

The admiral swivels back to face the window, and sits for a long while smoking and gazing out over the Capitol. At last his voice comes floating back over his shoulder. "You're not giving

102

me much to go on, are you?" Another long pause. "Still, if Charlie Evans is putting his head on the chopping block, I'd be an ass not to take a swing at it." He swivels briskly back to face Stone, all business. "What if you took another crack at Kulakov?"

"He's been wrung dry, Admiral," says Stone. "Even Evans didn't bother to ask for a turn. I'll go back at him if you like, but there's nothing more to be had."

"What about taking a look at the pouch, then?"

"Same thing," says Stone. "Evans's people are very good at what they do. He wouldn't have put himself on the line if he hadn't first examined every angle under a microscope."

The admiral studies Stone carefully. "What's left, then?"

"What's left," Stone says carefully, "is to take a closer look at some of the military threads running through Kulakov's life."

"Are you proposing we send someone in?" the admiral asks. The idea seems to amuse him.

"Not someone," replies Stone. "Me."

Stone sits cross-legged on the sheets, naked and surprisingly unaware of his nakedness. Thro, also naked, also cross-legged, her spine pressed to his, takes another drag on the hand-rolled cigarette, holds the smoke in as she passes what's left to Stone. The butt burns his fingers as he takes a last puff and drops it into the ashtray. His head angled back, his eyes closed, he grips his ankles to keep from rising like a balloon; it feels as if the top half of his head is about to lift off. "We drift through life," he says dreamily, slurring some of the words, "with one eye absently on a rear-view mirror. Somewhere 'long about the age of forty—yes, forty is about right—we become aware someone is tailing us."

"Who is it?" asks Thro, exhaling. "The angel of death?"

"It's us as we might have been," replies Stone.

"You see," cries Thro, turning in slow motion and twining her limbs around his body as if she is a vine. "You talk differently when you smoke. You'd never say something like that if you weren't high."

"I'd never even think it," admits Stone.

"I love to make you smoke," says Thro dreamily. "I love to smoke. The cold becomes colder. The hot is hotter. The luke-warm is lukerwarm—or is it lukewarmer?"

Stone laughs and folds her in his arms. "Fuck Mozart," he says. "Fuck Charlie Evans and Senator Howard. Fuck Nicholas Toland and Andrew Horrick and Ohm Berenson. Fuck Oleg Ku-lakov."

"What about me?" Thro asks coyly.

"Be patient," orders Stone. "I'll come to you. Fuck most of all the admiral—"

"He must have hit the ceiling when you told him your idea," whispers Thro, her head resting on his shoulder.

"He didn't hit the ceiling," says Stone. "The most dramatic he gets is a loud 'Hmm.'"

"What'd he say exactly?"

"He was quiet for a long while." Stone reconstructs the scene. "Then he swiveled back to me and thanked me for staying after class. Those were his exact words—thanks for staying after class!"

Thro sinks back on her haunches and stares at Stone. "You said you wanted to go into Russia, and he said thanks for stay-ing after class?"

Stone starts to lean toward her breast, but she fends him off excitedly. "Answer, Stone."

"That's what he said, yes," says Stone, puzzled.

"My God!" exclaims Thro. "Don't you see it?"

"See what, god damn it?"

"Stone, *he didn't say no!*"

It is a long moment before Thro's words penetrate. "He didn't say no," Stone repeats thoughtfully.

"The theory of plausible deniability," she reminds Stone. "You've always assumed the order to go in would never be a written one, or even a direct one, so that if things go wrong, ev-eryone could deny responsibility."

"It's true," Stone says, suddenly very sober. "He didn't say no."

104

Stone's informal note is hand-carried to the admiral. It says: "Due to pressing personal reasons, respectfully request four weeks leave."

The note comes back, by messenger, three days later. Below Stone's request someone has typed: "Accorded. Dictated but not signed, from the office of the Chairman of the Joint Chiefs of Staff."

Kulakov looks as if he expects Stone. "I knew it was too good to be true," he says gloomily. "I knew it would never end."

Stone installs Kulakov in a hotel room that he has already checked for bugs and patiently leads him over certain ground again. He tries to get closer to the identity of his daughter's lesbian friend. "I had the impression she was Polish," says Kulakov. "Nadia once spoke vaguely about going to live in Warsaw with her." Stone is also interested in the identity of his wife's lover, but Kulakov is unable to add anything other than that he is a tank commander. But most of all, Stone is interested in the duty officer Gamov. "You worked as a courier for twenty-eight years," he tells the Russian. "How is it possible you never saw him around the ministry before?"

"He must have been posted in the field," says Kulakov. "He must have been new to Moscow."

"Did the name Gamov ring a bell at least?"

Kulakov shakes his head. "No; I knew a Gabov during the war, but he was killed."

"Did the duty officer speak with any trace of an accent? Did his uniform look old or new?"

Kulakov turns away from Stone without answering. Finally he says, "If I were a plant, I would have to know about it. And I don't."

Stone nods. "You think you're genuine; we all agree on that."

"If I weren't genuine, that would mean that everything that happened to me—Nadia, my son, my wife—everything was *made* to happen to me."

Again Stone nods.

105

Kulakov runs his fingers through his thick hair. "I've got to go back," he says. "I've got to find out for myself."

"You can't go back," Stone tells him. "If you are a genuine defector, they'll kill you for defecting. If you are a plant, they'll execute you to convince us you were genuine."

Kulakov raises the window shade and stares out over Los Angeles. "My English is beginning to improve," he says absently. "This is a pleasant city." Suddenly he turns on Stone. "Things like this don't happen in real life," he moans. "I must know which way it is."

Stone assures him, "I'll find out for you."

The excitement is too much for the woman who follows the soccer scores; she bursts out of Stone's office and stares with moist eyes at the section chiefs waiting their turns. "It's really on," she whispers distractedly, clutching thick dossiers to her bosom. "After all these years, it's really going to *happen*." The emotion overwhelms her; tears stream down her cheeks as she hurries from the room, heading (for the sixth or eighth time this morning) for the ladies' toilet, which has a photograph of Akhmatova taped to the inside of the door.

Stone spends the day closeted with the various section chiefs, going over dossiers he knows by heart. Planes and Trains, nervously biting her fingernails, brings Stone up to date on transportation between Moscow and Leningrad, and Moscow and Alma-Ata. Entries and Exits, his ancient eyes red-rimmed from lack of sleep, traces with Stone how he will go in, and eventually come out, of Russia. Internal Contacts makes Stone repeat the precise location of the eight dead-letter drops, and the signals he will use ("To activate dead-letter drop number three, telephone 291-78-15, cough twice when someone answers and immediately hang up") to have one of the military attachés at the embassy fetch a message. Identity provides Stone with a French passport, a French driver's license, and several French credit cards which he'll use going into the Soviet Union, and four separate Russian identities, each complete with internal passport, work book, residence permit and various ministry ID cards, which will be smuggled into Russia (along with five thousand rubles in cash) in the false lining of his valise, which has already been supplied by Clothing and Accessories.

"What have we forgotten?" asks Mozart, who looks as if his Ivy League feathers have been ruffled for the first time in memory.

"As far as I can see," says Stone, supremely calm, supremely in control, "we're as ready as we'll ever be."

Mozart walks Stone to the stairwell. "Tell the truth, Stone, did you ever think the day would come?"

"I always thought it would come, yes," Stone answers. "It's what I've worked for for twenty years. If I didn't think it would come, I would have taken up knitting long ago."

Mozart accepts this. "I wish to Christ it was me going," he says passionately. "I'd give anything to be in your shoes."

It is a side of Mozart Stone has never seen before, and he almost feels sorry for him. Almost but not quite. "Your turn will come," he says. "Meanwhile, someone's got to mind the store. Remember, Mozart, when you deal with the admiral, don't mention me. If things go wrong, he wants to be able to deny under oath that he authorized a penetration."

"You really don't think it's risky?" Mozart asks.

"I've figured it from every angle," says Stone. "If Kulakov is a genuine defector, there's no way they can pick up on someone going over the ground again. They will have finished their own backgrounder, so there's almost no possibility of my running into their field teams. And if Kulakov's a phony, they'll keep their hands off me—as long as I don't come up with anything—so as not to tip their game. Either way, I should be all right."

"And if you do come up with something?"

"If I come up with something, I'll deposit it in one of our dead-letter drops, change identity and run for it. All I need is a reasonable head start."

"Fifty yards suit you?" Mozart tries a joke.

"Fifty yards will be just about right—if it's night."

"The SALT talks reconvene in Geneva in a little over three weeks," Mozart reminds Stone. "Does that give you enough time?"

"Three weeks should be about—" Stone opens the fire door and steps into the stairwell, to find himself before the Topology section chiefs and their assistants, sixteen people in all, lining both sides of the stairs down to the third-floor landing, quietly applauding as Stone makes his way between them. Planes and Trains and the lady who follows the soccer scores cry openly. So do several of the secretaries and assistants. The applause subsides. Entries and Exits offers his ancient hand to Stone. "The others have asked me . . . as I am more or less the senior man on board . . . we just want you to know, Stone, that our hearts go with you. . . ." The old man tries to summon up some graceful phrases, then bites his lower lip.

Thro keeps one eye on the big board with the flickering numbers for Stone's flight to Paris. "You picked a good time to skip town," she tells him huskily. She holds up her finger and flashes her ring in front of his face. It has turned black again.

Stone self-consciously kisses her cheek, and then her lips. "Don't you have any new ways the world will end?" he asks her.

Thro laughs nervously. "What a coincidence you should ask," she says. "I just read that the sun's surface temperature dropped eleven degrees—I'm talking Fahrenheit—last year. If it keeps up at this rate, Stone, the earth will become glacial in twenty years. Imagine, all the oceans of the world—" Suddenly Thro buries her head in Stone's neck. "Ah, Stone, my world will end," she tells him—he can feel the wetness of her lashes on his skin—"if you don't come back to me."

The melting snow is overflowing the tin gutters of the wooden buildings in the military compound near Nikolina Gora. Inside the smallest building, which serves as an informal canteen, three officers, their tunics open at the neck, are washing down spoonfuls of marinated red cabbage with vodka. A fourth man, older and (judging from the respect the others show him) senior to the rest, stares moodily out the double window, which is fogged with his breath.

"We must have the storm windows taken down soon," he says absently.

One of the vodka drinkers shakes his head in admiration. "You've got to give them credit," he says. "To the naked eye, it was a perfect job."

"They went in and out like cats," says another. "There wasn't a sound on our tape."

"To tell the truth," says the third, "I wasn't ready to concede they had been into it until I studied the enlargements. It was the measurements that convinced me."

The older man at the window turns back to the others and accepts a glass of vodka from one of them. It is yellower than the usual vodka because of the dried walnut shells that were added to the bottle by the supply officer who runs the canteen. The older man holds his glass up to the light to study the color, judges that the walnut shells have been left in long enough, and downs the vodka in one quick gulp. "I'd give five years of my life," he says lightly—but everyone understands that he is deadly serious— "to have had a seat at that Forty Committee meeting."

He holds his glass out for a refill. The others, who have never seen him drink two glasses of vodka in a row before, take this as a sign of the strain he has been under since the defection of the diplomatic courier Kulakov.

. . . Moscow, where the heart's fever burns.

—From Akhmatova's poem
"Boris Pasternak"

CHAPTER

One wing of the Air France 747 dips gracefully, like a gull's in free flight feeling for updrafts. The ground tilts into Stone's field of vision. Birch forests slip past. The ice-patched Moscow River bends around a cluster of wooden dachas. The tall brick chimneys of a factory complex intrude into the sky; their thin shadows probe like fingers into the folds of the countryside. The snow, everywhere melting, persists in the plowed fields, giving the impression of enormous white napkins spread out to dry in the sun.

It doesn't matter that Stone has never set foot in Russia before. Home is a question of recognizing the landscape of the heart. And Stone has the uneasy sensation of coming home. In his mind's eye, he sees himself hurtling forward into his past, rediscovering roots that his father and his father's father abandoned when they fled to China, one jump ahead of the Bolsheviks, so many years before.

Stone does his best to quell the curious mixture of fear and exhilaration that sets his head swirling; Russians out of Russia tend to be emotional cripples who have lost the habit of dealing with feelings and so usually suppress them. He concentrates on the plane's shadow racing along the ground, growing larger, rising to meet them. The wheels touch, scorching the tarmac with black skid marks; scorching the landscape of Stone's heart as well.

"I feel the same way," whispers the buxom Frenchwoman in the seat next to Stone's. She has been trying, with a noticeable lack of success, to strike up a conversation with him ever since he joined the group of French tourists at Le Bourget outside Paris. Now, seeing his expression, she leans toward him to take him into her confidence. "It's thrilling to think that everybody out there is a Communist, isn't it?"

Stone runs the back of his thumb along his mustache, adjusts his eyeglasses, smiles politely. "The museums are what attract me," he tells her, "not the Communists." He shrugs apologetically. "I teach art history in a lycée."

The airport is exactly as Planes and Trains described it: Uzbeks, with bulging cardboard suitcases sprawling across benches and using their coats as pillows; electric clocks that tell different times; candy wrappers overflowing the few ashtrays that haven't been stolen; whole families camping in corners waiting for planes that don't appear on any timetables; women with dirty fingernails playing with shrill cries of triumph a card game called Imbecile.

Intimidated, but doing their best not to show it, the French tourists file by passport control. The young frontier officer behind the desk signals for Stone to remove his eyeglasses, then scrutinizes the passport photograph and the face confronting him for a long moment. Apparently satisfied, he thumbs through a loose-leaf notebook, stamps the passport page with the visa on it, closes the passport with a snap and hands it back to Stone. There is a long wait for the baggage, and when it finally arrives, a rush to line up before the customs inspectors. Stone selects the youngest of the lot, a woman with a bouffant hairdo and a ridiculously short skirt which draws snickers from the Parisians, who have been wearing theirs midcalf length for several years already. The first member of the group, a loud insurance salesman from Lyons with a wig, runs into trouble when the customs inspector comes across a copy of *Playboy* in his valise. She calls over her chief, and he carefully studies the centerfold before nodding gravely and returning the magazine to its owner.

114

When Stone's turn comes, the woman makes a cursory inspection of his ancient suitcase and meticulously folded clothing. She is more interested in the two art history books she finds in his small shoulder bag, and the detective novel jutting from his jacket pocket. She strains to read every word of the blurbs on the back covers, then returns the books and fixes her expressionless gaze on the next tourist in line.

Stone, waiting for the others in the group to clear customs, watches absently as two young men, Muscovites from the sound of their accents, argue at another counter with a male customs inspector. He stands his ground and the two young men reluctantly begin to untie the ropes that bind their suitcases. The inspector's heavy-lidded eyes come alive as he begins to pull from the valises an assortment of blue jeans, Japanese transistor radios, phonograph records, cassettes, wrist watches, men's shoes with high heels, colorful scarves, and other bits and pieces of plastic junk that pass for treasure in Moscow. A crowd forms; two uniformed policemen impatiently wave people on. The chief inspector saunters over, fingers one of the silk scarves, tries to read the headlines in the newspaper used to wrap the cassettes, reaches into the leg of a pair of blue jeans and extracts a small red velvet sack with a Jewish Star of David embroidered on it. Then he finds a second, and a third. The mood changes. One of the boys begins to wipe his brow with a silk scarf.

Stone stares at the red velvet sack. A Jewish tallith! His heart aches with the memory of his grandfather formally presenting him, on the day of his bar mitzvah, with a tallith of his own.

Stone is shooed away with the others, and joins his group on the bus. A pert Intourist guide sitting on a swivel seat alongside the driver blows into a hand microphone to see if it is alive. "Welcome to Moscow," she says in careful French. "The airport you landed at is called Vnukovo. You'll be staying at the Hotel Rossiya, the largest hotel in the world, just off Red Square. The drive to the hotel will take three quarters of an hour."

The drive into Moscow proves to be an exhilarating experience for Stone. The Forty Committee and its babblings about one and a half wars are a world away; even Kulakov seems like a figment of his imagination. He is caught up in sights and sounds that stir faint memories; things he has never set eyes on before are painfully familiar. The first kvass wagons are on the streets, and the Muscovites are eagerly queuing up and counting out kopecks. The bus passes a parked truck piled high with cabbages from the nearest collective farms, factories with hammers and sickles and slogans plastered over their walls, prefabricated tenement clusters surrounded by potholes and mud paths with boards thrown across them to keep the residents high and dry. There is a huge statue of a thoughtful Lenin, and long lines of people at bus stops, and stores with their drab windows offering up a reflection of the road. Taxis and shiny black Zils with curtains over their passenger windows speed by. A policeman with white gloves and a baton holds up traffic so a kindergarten class, walking in double file with each child holding onto the coat of the child in front, can cross. A minor traffic accident between an Army truck and a taxi causes a jam at the Kaluga Gate, now known as Gagarin Square. Stone studies the crescent-shaped apartment houses on either side of the road. The Intourist guide doesn't say so, of course, but the houses were constructed by prisoners, one of whom later described the experience in a book called *The First Circle*.

And then they are in the thick swirl of downtown traffic that flows in enormously wide boulevards around the Kremlin, the sinister fortress where the Tartar invaders planted their horse-tall standards six hundred years before. The huge white elephant, the Hotel Rossiya, looms ahead beside the Moscow River.

The game plan, concocted by Entries and Exits, is simple enough. Stone, traveling under a French passport made out in the name of Bernard du Bucheron, age forty-two, celibate, instructor in art history at the Lycée Carnot in Cannes, goes through the motions of getting his room assignment from the Intourist guide. "Dinner in one-half hour in the dining room on the corner," she instructs her sheep, and they obediently trot off to unpack and criticize the plumbing and gawk at the colorful onion-shaped domes of Saint Basil's Cathedral. Stone carries his own valise to his room, locks the door and quickly goes to work. He empties the valise, cuts away the lining, stuffs some of the rubles in his jacket pockets and the rest in his shoulder bag, along with changes of socks, underwear and several clean shirts. He lays out the four sets of Russian identity papers on the bed. Three of them he sews into the lining of his suit jacket; the fourth set—the identity he will start with—goes into his breast pocket. The mustache is peeled off and flushed down the toilet, the eyeglasses pocketed (he will throw them away at the first opportunity). Stone checks to make sure that a copy of *Grani*, the anti-Soviet magazine published by émigrés in Paris, is still in the cut-away lining of his valise; when the Russians get around to searching his room, they will come across the copy of *Grani* and (hopefully) assume that the Frenchman who came in under the name of du Bucheron was merely a *Grani* delivery man with a suitcase full of subversive magazines. This sort of thing happens all the time; the police will look for the delivery man, Entries and Exits guessed, but not very hard.

Stone runs a comb through his hair, changing the part, and studies himself in the bathroom mirror; the overcoat is old, nondescript, the shoes Italian (available on the black market), the hat that of a typical Russian bureaucrat.

He is ready to disappear in the madding crowd of Muscovites hurrying home to the anesthetizing shot (of vodka, of poetry, of lovemaking) that will mark the passing of yet another day.

She is the kind of girl who stands out in any crowd, let alone a Russian crowd. Stone spots her just where Clandestine Residences said she would be: lounging against the side of a kiosk in the underground passage that runs between Gorky Street and Red Square. "She is in the neighborhood of twenty-five, with the features of a beautiful boy," Clandestine Residences (who had once been a beautiful boy himself) said. "My source, who was something of a poet *manqué* despite his military background, claimed she had all the innocence of a kitten looking into a mirror for the first time. Look for a thin face, thin lips, a long, thin nose—I believe it is usually described as aquiline—thick eyebrows, no hips to speak of, absolutely flat-chested. Wears her hair short, tied back with a scarf. Clean features. Profile of a bowsprit—nose, jaw thrust forward"—here Clandestine Residences did a reasonable imitation—"kind of face that looks perfectly natural with a wind blowing into it, if you see what I mean."

Several of the women shoppers, struggling with packages and dog tired from queuing, eye with obvious envy her pleated trousers tucked, paratrooper style, into her expensive Italian boots, the wide web army belt with the red star on the polished brass buckle, her waist-length fur jacket, salvaged from an elegant coat that had scraped the ground when it began its life forty years before.

"You'll have to get close to her to confirm the next item," Clandestine Residences warned. "Her pupils are so enormous, people think her eyes are black. Actually, one's green, one's khaki. Don't look at me like that, Stone! That's what the air attaché who slept with her swears."

Stone is close enough now to see for himself: enormous pupils, one eye green, the other khaki. And something else in her eyes, something he remembers seeing in the eyes of his grandfather as he peered, night after night, at old photographs of the civil war: a hunger that doesn't come from not eating enough.

"Who gives you a permit to stare?" the girl demands. The nose, the jaw, jut arrogantly. "If you're interested, make me an offer I can't refuse. If you're just licking windows, move on."

Stone manages a broad grin. "I'm interested," he says slowly. "What will ten rubles buy me?"

"She's extremely independent," Clandestine Residences warned. "If she doesn't like your looks, that will be the end of it."

The girl studies Stone from head to toe. "Me, for starters, with a glass of vodka thrown in if you're not rough."

"I need more," Stone says. He draws her back out of the flow of pedestrians. "I need a roof over my head."

118

"Try a hotel," the girl shoots back mockingly.

"Hotels don't suit me," says Stone. "They want to see all kinds of papers. I need something more discreet."

"At any given time," Clandestine Residences explained, "there are thousands of Russians in Moscow illegally—selling or buying on the black market, bribing officials, avoiding the draft, hunting for large shipments of raw materials for their factory, what have you. The ones who don't have relatives usually move in with prostitutes to keep out of the limelight. It's just a matter of paying them enough so that *they* won't tip off the militia."

The girl, all business now, asks, "How long do you plan to stay in Moscow?"

"Depends on how my work goes," says Stone. "What will twenty-five rubles buy me?"

The girl says, "Twenty-five a day, paid in advance, will buy you a warm bed, a warm breakfast, a warm me and no questions asked." Suddenly her face lights up in a smile. "I'm the curious type—I may make an educated guess or two."

Stone offers his hand. "There'll be another hundred in it when I leave if I haven't been bothered by the militia," he promises her. "My name is Pavel."

"I'll bet." The girl laughs, sealing the bargain with a handshake. "I'm Yekaterina. Friends, of whom I have more than I know what to do with, call me Katushka."

She links her arm through Stone's and sets off in long purposeful strides toward Gorky Street. "You're in luck," she tells Stone conversationally. "I just finished my period. When I have my period, I only sleep with women."

Katushka leads Stone to her small Zhiguli, the Russian-made Fiat. "Hungry?" she asks. Stone nods, and she says, "I can organize something at the Writers Union, if it suits you, or a private dinner at the apartment of a woman I know. Cost you twenty rubles for the two of us, which includes a bottle of Polish vodka and a Georgian red, though I prefer beer if it's all the same to you."

The meal, served in the ground-floor apartment of a building in one of the satellite communities twenty-five minutes out of

119

the city to the north, is home-cooked and the portions are generous. A small boy peeks in from time to time, and clears away the dirty dishes when Katushka signals to him. A phonograph record of Russian folk songs plays in the background, and the room is lighted by candles. Katushka stares into them—Stone again notices her enormous pupils—without talking for a long while.

"Why do you wear your rings with the stones on the palm side?" Stone asks.

She comes out of her reverie. "I wear them this way because my mother wears hers this way. And she wears them this way because palms don't age." She laughs gaily. "They say a woman's palm always looks fifteen." The candle flames, which are squat and steady, suddenly thin out and vibrate gently, as if they are being breathed upon. "The spirits are in the room with us," the girl whispers. "There"—she motions with her eyes—"above our heads, hovering, listening."

Stone has the impression that she is inventing herself as she goes along. "Do you believe in spirits?" he asks.

The small boy carries in a plate of *kurniki*, made of chicken and pastry and green peas, and places it before Stone. The boy's mother, who is doing the cooking, sets a second plate before the girl.

Katushka talks with her mouth full. "I am the seventh child of a seventh child. I am a spirit. I read palms, entrails, tea leaves. I can get news of someone by opening a book at random. When I dream, I dream someone else's dreams—I've been trying to find that person since I was a child. I always put sweaters on inside out for luck. You think I'm joking. Say it; you don't offend me. Here, give me your palm."

Stone hesitates, but Katushka insists. She studies it for a long while in the candlelight, tracing lines with the tips of her fingers, turning the palm over to observe his nails, then back again to stare some more at the lines. Finally she looks up. "You don't work with your hands," she says softly, "which means you work with your head."

"Anybody can see that," Stone scoffs.

Katushka smiles faintly. "You proceed slowly to avoid the arrival because it's the journey that intrigues you." She pauses. "You have the sense of being home again." Again she pauses. "You've had bad luck in your time, but good luck comes to you as a matter of course. You've had so much, you think it's your due. Me, I have to work at it day in and day out. I have to manufacture my good luck. It makes me sick." She touches with a finger a place where one line on his palm meets another and forks off. "In Moscow, you will find what you're looking for, but you will not use it."

Outside, in the Fiat, Katushka abruptly says, "I am pleased with you for leaving the boy a ruble." She uses the intimate *ti* almost as if it is a reward, but slips back immediately to the more formal *vui*. "Would you enjoy to hear dance music now, or do you prefer to make love and go to sleep?"

Stone indicates he would rather call it a day, and she heads for home, an apartment on the top floor of a building overlooking the Moscow zoo. "It has certain advantages," she explains, "for someone in my business. It is centrally located, the two people I share the flat with are discreet, and you can hear the braying of the animals below when they are in heat. It is a very arousing sound."

"Is that how you divert yourself," Stone asks, "listening to animals in heat?"

"I divert myself as best I can," she answers. "When I was young and cared a great deal about things that no longer interest me, I tried to sabotage the dance bands that played that awful Soviet music. I would walk up to the orchestra"—she leans on her horn, swerves around a slow-moving car and jumps a red light—"and suck on a lemon in front of them. It made the horn players salivate and ruined the song."

"And now?" Stone asks.

Katushka doesn't understand the question. "And now what?"

"What do you do for diversion now?"

Again she smiles, though it has a sadder quality this time.

"Now I hypnotize myself with maybes. For instance, maybe our universe with its billions of galaxies drifting through endless reaches of space is a molecule in a grain of sand in some gigantic world. What's so absurd about it? Every time our scientists look into a microscope, they see smaller and smaller worlds. Why shouldn't it be the same when they look into a telescope?"

They tiptoe through the lobby of the apartment building, past the night guardian, whose great head has sunk to the open page of *Pravda* on the desk. His goat cheese and bread and thermos of tea are in a basket next to his feet. "Some say he's so old he worked for the KGB when it was still the Cheka," whispers Katushka. She motions with a finger on her lips for him to be quiet. They walk up the five flights because the elevator would wake the old man. She inserts her key in the lock, leads him by the hand down a long dark corridor to the bedroom. "The toilet's there, the kitchen here," she whispers. "You'll meet my roommates in the morning."

Katushka snaps on the light and Stone takes in the bedroom. "Normally you can't tell what taste Russians have by the things in their apartments," Clandestine Residences warned Stone. "That's because they don't buy what they want, but what's available. She's the exception to the rule. She never buys; she barters. Services rendered for items that catch her eye. Would you believe she's even building a greenhouse on the roof?"

The room is soft, with apricot-colored cushions scattered in a heap at one corner next to the Japanese hi-fi set and the record collection. The rug, wall to wall, is off white. The mattress, which rests on a low wooden platform, is covered with a large patchwork quilt and another small mountain of pillows. There are double panes on the windows, and the space between is filled with moss spread over cotton, which keeps the windows from fogging over. On one wall is an exquisite eighteenth-century icon with a wafer-thin candle on either side of it. There is a low shelf full of books; Stone catches a glimpse of Pasternak poems and a rare volume of Mandelstam's called, simply, *Poems*. Hanging over the bed, illuminated by a spotlight from across the room, is a large oil canvas of the Virgin and Child that is at once realistic and romantic. Katushka catches Stone looking at it. "The painter who did that was not permitted to sell his canvases," she says. "The authorities who know about such things told him it was not art, and therefore to sell it would constitute a fraud. Several years later, when the painter emigrated to Israel, the same authorities told him he couldn't take his work out of the country with him because it came under the heading of art. So he left this with me for safekeeping. I am pleased with you for liking it."

A coal-black cat, its back arched, its hair bristling, appears from out of nowhere and rubs against Katushka's leg. She scoops it up and kisses it on the mouth. "This is my shadow," she tells Stone. "I call him Thermidor. He has the distinction of being the only left-pawed cat in existence."

Stone settles onto the low bed. "How can you tell?"

"Oh, I have an instinct for things like that," she says mysteriously. She gently places the cat in the middle of a large cushion and begins to undress. "I have a special feeling for cats. They have the same feeling for me. Thermidor, for instance, knows without my ever having said it that I am frightened of thunder. I always visualize two great clouds crashing together, something like ships drifting into each other. Boom!"

Katushka lights the candles on either side of the icon, turns out the other lights, puts on a cassette of Stan Kenton music she recorded off the Voice of America. Naked, thin as a rail in the flickering candlelight, her nipples casting long shadows across her flat chest, she sinks to her knees in front of Stone and starts to unlace his shoes. From somewhere below comes the distant sound of an animal braying.

"It's a zebra," she explains with a half smile. "She's in heat." She looks directly at Stone, her head cocked to one side. "How do you enjoy to make love?" she asks.

"Astonish me," Stone replies.

And she proceeds to do exactly that.

"Get up." Katushka pokes Stone in the ribs with her elbow. He rolls over on his side and buries his face in the pillow, but she insists. "Come on," she coaxes.

"What time is it?" Reluctantly, Stone turns toward her.

She ignores the question. "I have figured it out," she tells him.

"What have you figured out?" Stone asks, irritated that she woke him. He pulls the blanket up to his chin. "My God, it's freezing in here."

"Your Russian is what threw me off," she explains. "You speak it very well. Where did you learn it?"

Stone is instantly alert. "I thought our arrangement included no questions asked."

Katushka's mouth is very close to Stone's ear. "You're not Russian," she tells him excitedly. She puts a finger on his lips as he starts to deny it. "Don't bother lying. It's no use."

Stone finally manages to get a word in. He tries to keep the tone light, as if he is playing along with a good joke. "What makes you think I'm not Russian?"

She smiles in the darkness. "First there is the way you eat. You treat food as if it were fuel. A Russian who has a meal like the one you had tonight savors every mouthful. Then there is the way you drink vodka. You don't drink to forget, the way we do. You drink the way a mechanic puts grease on an axle—for lubrication. And then there is the way you make love. You don't make love like a Russian. I have made love with Frenchmen and Germans and Finns, and once with an American. He cut his hair in the military style and said he was a businessman, but I found out he worked at the American Embassy. My foreigners were like you in bed—they attempted to give pleasure as well as get it. Our men don't like so much oral sex, and they are very quick. Then there is this." Katushka reaches under the sheets and traces the outline of his penis with her fingertips. "I have never before seen a Russian with a circumcised penis. Even the Jews I have made love with don't have it, because they were born either during the period of Stalin, or during the German occupation, and it was dangerous to be circumcised. I have always wondered, do you feel less with a circumcised penis?"

Stone laughs uneasily. "I have nothing to compare it with."

"Where you come from, do girls take the sex of the man in their mouth as I do?" she wants to know.

"How would I know such a thing?" Stone answers. He feels on the edge of panic; all the years of painstaking preparation, and he finds himself bedded down with a prostitute who is sure he's not Russian because he is circumcised! Well, he has other identities, and other addresses.

Katushka reads his mind. "Not to worry," she tells him. "I am pleased with you for being a foreigner. I won't give you away." Oblivious to the cold, she leaps from the bed, snaps on the light, rummages in a straw trunk and comes out with a plastic folder, which she offers to Stone. "Here, you will read these," she instructs him. "And then I will tell you the story behind them."

There are two sheets of paper, both brittle with age, inside the plastic folder. Each sheet is stapled to a translation written out in longhand. Stone makes it a point to skip the originals, which are in English, and read the translations, which are in Russian. The first item is a British citation for bravery made out to one Aleksandr Yefimov. The citation specifies that Yefimov, while operating as a partisan behind German lines in Poland, saved the lives of four British airmen whose plane was shot down while trying to drop supplies to Warsaw during the uprising. The second item is a handwritten letter to Yefimov from Flight Lieutenant Frank Peterson. The letter, dated March 4, 1946, thanks Yefimov for saving his, Peterson's, life and organizing his escape to Soviet lines. Peterson ends his letter: "If you should ever come to London, you can be sure of a very warm welcome from my family. Our address is 4 Cambridge Gate, Regents Park, London. Yours faithfully, Frank Peterson."

"It's this way," Katushka says, curling up alongside Stone's tense body, placing her now cold hand on his penis. "Aleksandr Yefimov was my father. He was taken prisoner early in the war, and spent three years in a concentration camp in Poland. He and several others managed to escape and joined up with the Polish underground. That's when he saved Peterson's life. Because he'd been a partisan, my father didn't wind up in Siberia the way all the other returning prisoners of war did. But in 1946, he got a letter in the mail inviting him to come to the British Embassy to receive a medal for saving the lives of four British aviators. My mother warned it would bring trouble, but my father was a very proud man, so he borrowed a suit and went. He came home with the medal on his chest and this citation, and the letter from Peterson. A week later he was arrested as a British spy and packed off to Siberia. My mother lined up once a week for six years to send him whatever she could scrape together—tobacco, warm socks, lard. When she came home, her lips were blue with cold and fear. She never knew if he received the packages. She never saw him again, and was only permitted to receive one letter a year. One day one of the packages came back stamped 'Deceased.'" Katushka smiles sadly. "Here we never weep at sadness, only at happiness. That way we cry less."

There is a school of thought, backed up by a good deal of on-the-job experience, that holds that an agent operating in the field shouldn't trust his own mother. There is another school, to which Stone has always been committed in principle, that claims you get just as many good breaks as bad ones, and you'd be a fool not to take advantage of them. Stone, concentrating so hard he forgets the cold and Katushka's hand on his sexual organ, contemplates his "break": he has gone to ground, as planned, with a prostitute who—and here is the bonus—who claims to be secretly anti-Soviet and has a cat she calls Thermidor. If he could believe her, it would open all sorts of operating possibilities.

"If only I could believe you," Stone says carefully.

"I'll take you to meet my mother," Katushka whispers eagerly. "Then you'll tell me what I can do to help you, my beautiful circumcised foreigner."

The morning rushes at Stone with a cold, sunny suddenness; streams of light flow through the double windows with the cotton and moss between them, washing out the apricot cushions to the point where they look like bleached sand. Katushka is nowhere to be seen, though she has left traces behind her: an almost imperceptible impression in the pillow next to Stone; pleated trousers, an army web belt, scattered where she tossed them the night before; and Katushka's shadow, the cat called Thermidor, sulking on the washed-out apricot pillows, observing with a kind of bored detachment the latest in the long line of visitors to his lady's bed.

"Katushka," Stone calls. He hurriedly checks his shoulder bag and the lining in his jacket, finds both untouched, dresses quickly, slips in stockinged feet into the hallway, listens. There is the sound of dishes being noisily set out on a table, of breakfast being produced. Normal sounds, not alarming. Stone, cautious, tiptoes to the kitchen door and opens it a crack. "It'll send a shiver up your spine," Clandestine Residences said, "even though I'm warning you. He's the spitting image, a perfect double. He even keeps the mustache trimmed, though he seldom goes out because of the danger of being roughed up. My air attaché suspects he is stark raving, but harmless."

And there he is in the flesh, Joseph Dzugashvili, better known as Stalin, eighty years old if he is a day and still going strong, patiently turning the toast in the old-fashioned toaster and piling the finished slices on a serving plate. "What a book *he* could write," Clandestine Residences marveled. "Imagine being the stand-in for Stalin during all those years. Appearing at the Bolshoi while the great man locked himself behind the Kremlin walls and ran the war. Taking the salute of the soldiers trooping sixty abreast through Red Square. Shaking all those hands on the receiving line. During the war, Stalin used to stay up every night until dawn with his generals, moving his units around on a giant battle map. He was too tired to appear in public in the morning. So his double became known in the inner circle as the Morning Stalin." Clandestine Residences winked. "He's gay, of course, our Morning Stalin. Fluffy robes. Eye makeup. Dyes his gray hairs. And just wait until you see the other half of the couple!"

The other half of the couple, as Clandestine Residences called it, is a transvestite who turns up as a he sometimes (who goes by the name of Ilyador Aleksandrovich), and sometimes as a she (Isadora Aleksandrovna). Ilyador (he is going through a male phase now) is a puffy, out-of-shape fifty-year-old, with one sparkling gold tooth and a permanent depression, the way a woman is after childbirth or before her period. Now, meticulously folding paper napkins into triangles, he catches sight of Stone at the door, nudges Morning Stalin with an elbow.

"It's here, dear," he says. They both stop what they're doing to size up Stone.

"Toast's burning," says Stone. "Where Katushka?" He stares again at Stalin's double, unable to believe his eyes.

Morning Stalin slowly elevates his chin toward the roof. "She's puttering," he says loftily. After all those years of impersonating the great man, some of it has obviously rubbed off. His gaze is cool and confident. He speaks the way people do who expect others, as a matter of course, to hang on their every word. "I told her she was planting the begonias too early, but she's an independent fig; she does what she feels like doing."

Stone finds the door leading to the ladder and the roof. Katushka's greenhouse postdates her brief but well-documented affair with the American air attaché. Clandestine Residences knew that it was her dream to have one; knew, too, that she was already "bartering" her services for the raw materials she needed. And here it is, a *fait accompli*, double panels of glass enclosed in a thick wooden frame, a kind of lean-to greenhouse built against the side wall of the apartment building next door, which rises three stories higher than the one Katushka lives in.

"Come on in," she calls cheerily from inside the greenhouse, "—if you don't suffer from allergies, that is—and visit my act of defiance."

"What are you defying?"

"Winter!"

Stone leans against one of the greenhouse radiators, which has been hooked up to the building's central heating system, watching her as she cleans the sickly leaves of a *Medinilla magnifica* with a bit of moist cotton, murmuring words of encouragement all the while to the plant, which has survived a Moscow winter. "I feel like one of my plants after winter," Katushka tells Stone, looking up, smiling in a sad, distant way. "I need to be scrubbed and coaxed back to life."

"Nobody," comments Stone, "likes winter very much."

"It isn't only winter I don't like," reflects Katushka. "I don't like summer too. I prefer transitional seasons." She angles her head, peers myopically at him between the leaves, whispers conspiratorially: "I also would rather be en route than arrive." Suddenly she brightens. "Would you be interested to know what my ambition in life is? My ambition is to give my name to a rose. I've never told that to anyone before." She spoons fertilizer into a flowerpot, then gently waters it as she tests the sponginess of the earth with her thumb. "You will find, when you know me better, that I am the type of person who rises to occasions." She looks into Stone's face, and he feels the almost magnetic pull of her large pupils. "I only need someone to supply the occasion. I am pleased with you because you look like an occasion."

Morning Stalin systematically butters a slice of toast. "Excuse my hands," he says as he passes it to Ilyador, who spreads a coating of honey across it and offers it to Katushka. Morning Stalin tells Ilyador, "I always knew you had it in for the old cheese."

"Contrary to what you think"—Ilyador yawns, reaching for another slice of toast—"I have nothing personal against Karl Marx. I find it rather endearing that at the overripe age of eighty he learned to read Russian to get at Pushkin in the original."

"You're inventing again," accuses Morning Stalin, agitatedly stirring a spoonful of strawberry jam into his tea. "I can tell from your lips. They give you away every time. They are always thin when you invent."

Ilyador's feelings are hurt. "Every time I come up with something he doesn't know"—he appeals to Katushka—"he says I'm making it up."

"You missed your calling," Morning Stalin harasses Ilyador with glee. "You should be writing novels instead of installing telephones. Lot of good you do installing telephones anyhow. Half the people in the country are waiting for a phone, the other half are waiting for a dial tone. Ha! That's rather humorous, if I do say so myself."

Everyone laughs except Ilyador, who concentrates on his toast, chewing tiny mouthfuls with his lips delicately pressed together, his eyebrows elevated.

Katushka takes Ilyador's hand in hers, leans over and kisses him on the cheek. "You have the soul of an artist," she whispers in his ear.

"Artist!" Morning Stalin almost chokes on his tea. "Some artist he is. He's neither socialist nor realist." And in the bored voice of a university lecturer, he adds: "There are two kinds of artists in this world—the innovators, and the finders and users. If this mushroom here is an artist, he falls into the second category. Something like a garbage collector."

"It's not fair," shrieks Ilyador, scraping back his chair from the table. "One minute he accuses me of inventing. The next he says I'm a finder and user."

Katushka turns to Stone, "Which group do you fall into? The innovators, or the finders and users?"

Stone says, "I keep a foot in each camp."

"That's a bright reply," says Morning Stalin. He points to Stone with his chin. "Where did you find it?" he asks Katushka.

"It found me," she says with a laugh. "In the underground passageway."

"Typical," sneers Morning Stalin with an air of superiority. "Men generally go out in search of experience, but women always sit back and wait for it to come to them." He turns to

Stone and explains with elaborate politeness. "That, in my humble opinion, is the essential difference between the male of the species and the female—the way they experience experience."

"Another theory!" snorts Ilyador.

This time it's Morning Stalin whose feathers are ruffled. "And just what do you mean by 'another theory'? I read it in an article by none other than honored academician Anatol Jeliznia-kov." Morning Stalin wags his butter knife at Ilyador. "You're afraid of theories like this because it'll show you up for what you are."

"And what, in your warped view, am I?" demands Ilyador.

Morning Stalin pounces cruelly. "A male of the species is what you are! And the proof is that you don't wait for experience to come to you; you go out in search of it"—his voice rises to a hysterical pitch—"seven days a week, prowling the corridors of dilapidated tenements with *anybody* who jingles some kopecks in his pocket."

Ilyador's nostrils flare. "I keep a foot in each camp," he observes coquettishly.

Katushka intervenes. "The difference between the sexes isn't the way they experience experience," she tells Morning Stalin, "but in the fact that women"—she looks pointedly at Stone—"commit themselves to a thing, to a cause, to a person, before they really know anything about it. Men must see a baby first before they'll love it."

Stone takes the metro to Kutuzovsky Prospekt, wanders around looking in store windows, then doubles back in his own tracks. When he is sure he isn't being followed, he flags down a taxi heading back toward the center of the city. In a small park near the Kremlin, he stops to rest on the third bench from the end, and absently scratches the initials "DR" on the wood with the blade of a small pocket knife (manufactured in Russia, supplied by Clothing and Accessories). A solid grandmother with an overstuffed child in tow sails by, clucking her tongue at the sight of Stone defacing proletarian property. After a while Stone strolls over to a street wagon and waits his turn for a glass of kvass, then makes his way to a pay phone. A young woman is just finishing her call. "Genuine mohair," she tells someone happily. "No, I asked for red, but they gave me the next color that came up, which was green. Green's not the end of the world, is it? All right. All right. Don't panic. If you really can't support green, I'll sell it for twice what I paid. No. You get the bread; I have to see about repairing the iron."

The girl hangs up, spots Stone waiting patiently, smiles enticingly. "You wouldn't be interested in some fantastic green mohair, would you?" He shakes his head; inserts a two-kopeck coin in the phone, dials 291-78-15. The phone rings twice, then a third time. A woman answers. "Please?" she says in memorized Russian. Stone coughs twice into the receiver, then severs the connection and turns back in the direction of the zoo. In an hour or so the American naval attaché (the one who supplies the admiral with Havanas) will break for lunch and wander through the small Kremlin park searching for the carved initials that will confirm that the strange bird from Topology has nested in Moscow.

Katushka is silent most of the way out to the dacha, intent on her driving, glancing only occasionally out of the corners of her dark eyes at Stone. She leans on her horn, ignores a double white line and shoots past a black Zil with a chauffeur at the wheel and two stout women in the back seat. "Central Committee whores," she mutters under her breath. "Their husbands all have chauffered Zils and dachas out here."

They pass through a series of small villages full of mud paths and neat wooden houses painted dark green, with hand-carved shutters and tended vegetable gardens. Near Nikolina Gora, they speed past a single-lane macadam road that angles off into a forest of white birches.

"Did you see that?" says Stone, twisting in his seat to look out the back window. "There's a no-entrance sign at the turnoff. I wonder where it goes to, that road?"

"I had a client once who went there from time to time," says Katushka. "He repaired code machines in the Ministry of Defense. I used to drop him at the turnoff on my way out to visit my mother at the dacha, and pick him up again on the way back to Moscow."

They pass a young policeman who peers at the car, recognizes it and the driver, and waves them on. Katushka waves back. "Over there—that one was Prokofiev's dacha," she tells Stone, pointing at a large wooden building set back from the road. "And that one's Kapitsa's." She concentrates on her driving for a while, then asks suddenly: "Do people have dachas in England?"

Stone says, "How would I know?"

Katushka smiles at him knowingly. "We're almost there," she says. "You'll like my mother. She only reads thin books because she thinks they're more sensitive. She plants medicinal herbs as soon as the ground thaws, but nothing ever comes of it. She wears white lace gloves all the time so she won't be obliged to touch anything Soviet. The dacha's around the next bend."

"How is it," Stone asks, "that she has a dacha? They are usually reserved for very important people."

"She has been given permanent use of the dacha," Katushka explains distantly, "as a personal favor to me."

Katushka's mother, tall, brittle as a dried flower, with white lace gloves and an ancient fox fur drawn high up on her thin neck, is hovering over a gardener who is hacking away at the just thawed earth with an old hoe. "Straight rows," she instructs him, "are absolutely essential for medicinal plants. You're weaving all over the map as if—" She turns at the sound of the car pulling in, starts in surprise, rushes forward to embrace Katushka, who falls into her outstretched arms. "I had a premonition you would come earlier than usual this month," she tells her daughter. She catches sight of Stone emerging from the car and regards him with obvious curiosity. "You must have been born in a good year," she says, offering a gloved hand. "Katushka has never brought a man friend here before. Greetings to you. I'm the prototype, which is to say I am the mother."

Stone accepts her hand, which is extended to him in a way that gives him no choice but to kiss the back of it. Bending, he touches his lips to the lace—a gesture his father made him master on the day of his thirteenth birthday.

Katushka laughs, whispers in her mother's ear. "He is something special. He's a foreigner!"

Her mother, whose name is Tanya, observes Stone in this new light. "Oh, dear, how very original. He looks normal enough." She turns brightly to Katushka. "Let's decide not to hold it against him."

"Where did you find the gardener?" Katushka asks her mother as they start toward the dacha. Stone, forgotten, trails along behind.

Tanya wipes her shoes vigorously on the mat before the wooden door, surveys the others to make sure they follow suit, heads for the kitchen to put up water to boil. "I heard about the gardener from the cousin of the ridiculous woman who runs the bread shop in Nikolina Gora. He had just moved in with a sister of his there, and was rumored to be looking for work. He has a fantastic story," she says, licking her lips. And she sets about telling it: "Apparently the amount of lumber a log will yield is determined by the placement of the first cut in the log. A misjudgment of half a centimeter can reduce the yield by as much as a third. My man—you will have guessed it by now—was packed off to Siberia because he didn't get the first cut right. They called it sabotage and gave him a tenner. He was released six months ago and went back to work as a first-cutter. He was making splendid cuts, but was replaced by a computer that scans the log with an electric eye and automatically positions the saw. Well, their loss is my gain! We've organized to grow medicinal plants together. With my know-how and his brawn, we'll make a fortune. Oh, it's so thrilling, private enterprise. I adore it, don't you?" She smiles politely at Stone. "But then, you will have had a great deal of experience with private enterprise."

Stone says, "Katushka brought me all the way here so you could tell me about her father."

Tanya looks innocently at Katushka. "Which version am I to give him?"

"The real one, mother. Tell him the truth, and for God's sake, tell it so he'll believe it. It's important."

They settle into wooden chairs drawn up around the old tiled stove, which is still warm to the touch from the fire the night before. Katushka pours tea; her mother takes hers with slices of green apple in the glass. White lace curtains on the double windows filter the light, soften it. The voices too.

When they leave, two hours later, the sun has set and the air is sharp. The first-cutter is still hoeing; he has set stakes in the ground and tied lines between them to keep his rows straight. From behind a double window, Tanya raises a white-gloved hand; her breath has fogged the window in front of her face, and the fogged window blurs her features. Katushka waves back from the car as they set out in the twilight for Moscow.

"Well?"

Stone, still undecided, watches the birch trees slip past. "Well, what?"

Katushka says, "We have the possibility of a perfect relationship, you and I. You'll think you are using me. I'll think I am using you."

"I still don't understand," Stone says, "why you want to help me."

Katushka looks at him in the darkness. "I don't want to *help you*," she explains. "I want to *hurt them*."

Katushka and Stone join the queue for the sausages, which is moving at a painfully slow pace. Muttering about being a seven-month baby who can't support long periods on his feet, a frail man with a facial tic tries to cut into the line. Stone shrugs and steps back to make room, but Katushka delivers a healthy kick to the man's shins and pushes him from the line. "The best thing for you, comrade line-jumper"—she laughs good-naturedly—"is to return to the womb for two months!"

Outside the store, the sausages safely tucked into her handbag, Katushka looks triumphantly at Stone. "That proves you're a foreigner beyond any possible doubt," she says. "A real Russian would never let someone cut into line ahead of him!"

In a spacious corner office on the fourth floor of the KGB complex on Dzerzhinsky Square, a quiet, pipe-smoking man of about sixty studies a dossier open on his desk. Finally he looks up at the two young men.

"The name is obviously false," he says. "How did he get the magazines out of the hotel?"

"He had a shoulder sack."

The man with the pipe shakes his head in annoyance. "Have the photography lab work up some composites of him without the mustache and eyeglasses, and pass them around to the units assigned to the A-list dissidents. There's always a chance he'll try to contact one of them."

One of the young men says, "You'd think they'd get tired of their little game," and his companion laughs and says, "They certainly go to a lot of trouble to bring in a few dozen pamphlets."

The man with the pipe sucks it back into life. "The thing . . . that bothers . . . me is that he . . . left one copy of . . . Grani behind in the lining." The tobacco has caught, and he draws on it thoughtfully. "Almost as if he wanted to make sure we knew he was a Grani courier. Well"—he slides the dossier across the desk and waves impatiently at the two men—"what else do you have for me?"

CHAPTER

7

Stone is having second thoughts, and they keep him up most of the night. Occasionally he drifts off into a troubled sleep, only to be woken by the braying of a zebra in the zoo below, and toward dawn by a taunting argument between Morning Stalin and Ilyador, whispering feverishly to each other in the hallway. A toilet flushes in another part of the building, setting up a rattle of pipes in the walls. Stone, once again trapped on the surface of things, sits up with a start. The strange girl with the enormous dark eyes stirs; the blanket falls away, revealing a thin shoulder, a pale breast. Stone covers her, then lets the cold air bathe his skin for a long moment, thinking of things a world away: of Thro, of his daughter, of the lady lawyer who promised him what he promised Kulakov—that everything would work out in the end.

In the morning Katushka comes awake with a start, leaps lightly from the bed and, braced by the cold air which she draws in deep gulps, goes through her ritual: she peers at her body in the mirror, trying to see it as she thinks others see it. "When I was a small girl," she tells Stone, "my mother always told me that somewhere in the world there is someone living the same life as you—a kind of mirror image, the only difference being her hair is parted on the other side." She looks across at Stone. "You will come to understand that such things can be true," she announces, and before he can comment either way she asks,

137

"Have you decided to admit what I already know—that you are not Russian? Have you decided to let me help you?"

Stone makes up his mind on the spot. "I'm not the occasion you've been waiting for," he says. "What I have to do in Moscow, I'll do by myself. You can help me by staying out of it."

"Have it your way," Katushka says icily. "Don't forget the twenty-five rubles are payable in advance."

At breakfast, Ilyador Aleksandrovich turns up as Isadora Aleksandrovna, wearing a fluffy dressing gown and polish on his nails.

Morning Stalin paces back and forth behind Ilyador's chair and talks to the back of his neck. "You are the most naïve fig I have ever laid eyes on," he says, apparently picking up where they left off the night before.

"I'm delighted you think so." Ilyador refuses to rise to the bait. "Naïveté is something I try to cultivate. It's a quality, when all is said and done, that comes *after* sophistication."

Katushka swallows a spoonful of foul-smelling lavender pollen (supplied, in return for services rendered, by an acquaintance at the free market), taps Stone on the wrist with her spoon. "You should know that I'm not at all pleased with you." And she adds hopefully, "You can still change your mind."

"Change his mind about what?" demands Morning Stalin.

"I'll be gone most of the day," Stone announces.

Ilyador holds his fingernails to the light and admires them. "Naïveté"—he talks to nobody in particular—"is intoxicating."

Stone gets up to leave. Katushka, angry now, watches him go, then flings her teacup against the wall, plastering it with tea leaves, shattering the cup to bits. Ilyador cringes against Morning Stalin. "What did we do?" he asks in a weak voice.

Stone spends the better part of the morning doing some fairly elementary street work. He lingers at a kiosk studying the headlines in *Pravda*, suddenly glances at his watch and sprints across a street just as the light changes. No one sprints across behind him. He dashes through an underground passageway, late for an appointment (he doesn't have), and stops at the far end to look at East German radios in a store window. He leaps from a subway car just as the doors start to close, crosses over and crowds into a train going in the other direction. When he is absolutely sure he isn't being followed, he enters a sporting goods store on Arbat Street to buy a cheap leather briefcase, then ducks into the men's room in the Stalin Gothic at the foot of the Arbat to empty the contents of his shoulder bag into the briefcase. On his way out he casually discards the bag (in a very public wastebasket; whoever finds it will keep it). That done, he sets out on foot for the Ministry of Defense canteen, on a side street not far from the Kremlin.

Moscow is a sprawling scar; people who aren't used to it tend to hold their breath so they won't catch whatever it has. Crusts of soot cling to massive buildings like sediment. Stalin Gothics, seven show skyscrapers in all, brutalize the horizon. Twelve-lane boulevards cut through the city like geological faults.

Stone knows Moscow as well as he knows the back of his hand: its alleyways and boulevards, its bus routes and subway lines, its parks and playgrounds, its garbage collection system, its sewer system, its public steam baths and soccer stadiums, its central markets and railroad stations. It was Stone, in fact, who—just starting out in Topology in the early fifties—organized what became known as the Moscow Project. After he was promoted, he handed it on to one of his juniors, but he kept in touch the way someone does with an alma mater—out of a vague feeling that one ought to be nostalgic. But knowing Moscow's idiosyncrasies—knowing, for instance, that the stores stay open on the last Sunday of every month to fulfill their selling plans—is not the same as knowing its mood or its pulse. And its mood is gray and its pulse is slow; people move as if they have all the time in the world to get where they are going, as if the getting there won't change anything.

But Stone makes his way through the streets with a purposefulness that sets him apart. At the ministry canteen he gives the guard at the door a discreet glimpse of his KGB identification card, then lines up to check his coat in the cloakroom.

"Have you ever been unfaithful to your wife?" the colonel in front of Stone asks his companion, who is in civilian clothes.

"No. Never."

The colonel is incredulous. "You never slept with another woman?"

The man in civilian clothes says, "Sleeping with another woman has nothing to do with being unfaithful to your wife."

Stone checks his overcoat and hat, but keeps his briefcase tucked under his arm as he heads for the dining room. At the entrance, he presses a ruble note into the headwaiter's hand and tells him, "I'm looking for an old comrade, name of Aksenov. He's a diplomatic courier with the ministry."

"The one on crutches." The headwaiter nods, rising on his toes to survey the room. "Ah, he's over there, the second table from the end, next to the bleached blonde."

Stone makes his way to the table. "Comrade Major Aksenov?"

Aksenov looks up from his soup and studies Stone's face, trying to place it. Puzzled, he asks politely, "Do we know each other?"

Stone flashes his KGB card at the bleached blonde. "Why don't you find another table," he orders her without a trace of politeness. She quickly gathers up her plate, napkin and pocketbook and goes off, with a backward glance, in search of a vacant seat.

"You must have quite a calling card to send her scurrying like that," Aksenov comments good-naturedly. "Can I get a look at it too?"

Stone shows it to him, and Aksenov says, "So that's how it is. If it's about Kulakov, I've already told the ministry investigators everything I know. Which is nothing."

The waiter, an elderly man in an ill-fitting black jacket with food stains on the lapels, offers Stone a menu, but he waves him away. "I'm not eating," he says, playing the KGB role to the hilt. "I'm asking." To Aksenov he says, "You were supposed to be on duty the day Kulakov was sent out of the country."

Aksenov jerks his head toward his crutches, which are leaning against the wall next to the table. "I was indisposed," he says sarcastically. "Listen, I went all through this with the military intelligence people. If you got along better with each other you wouldn't have to go over the same ground a second time."

Stone lets the silence build up until it is uncomfortable; Aksenov looks around nervously. Stone, toying with a fork, says quietly, "When we need instructions on how to conduct our investigations, we will come to you for advice. For now, simply tell me how, and where, and when, and under what circumstances, you broke your leg."

"I was hit by a jeep as I went out for my morning bread. One second there was no car there, the next it was bearing down on me. I couldn't get out of the way. The bastard driver never stopped."

"Did anybody see the accident? Did anybody note the jeep's number?"

"A teen-age girl, a neighbor of mine, thought she did, but she must have got it wrong in the excitement, because it turned out there was no jeep with that number on its plates. And the local militia never found out who it was either." Aksenov smiles grimly. "If I ever get my hands on the driver—"

Stone asks, "Who reported you sick?"

"My wife phoned in from the hospital. They told her not to worry, that nothing was scheduled, and in any case they would find a substitute if a run came up over the weekend."

Stone looks hard at Aksenov. "Who was 'they'?"

"The duty officer," explains Aksenov. "I've already told all this to the military intelligence cleanup team. Why are you coming back to it now?"

A very old man at the next table, obviously drunk, taps a scallion against an empty glass. "The cosmonauts go to the moon," he tells his equally aged, equally drunk, companion, "and everyone pees in their pants in excitement. Here I am about to em-

141

bark on a voyage to eternity, and nobody takes the slightest notice."

The other old man meticulously measures out another vodka from the almost empty bottle. "Departures," he comforts his friend, "have to be scheduled in order to be interesting."

Stone asks Aksenov, "Who was the duty officer?"

"It was Dedov," he replies.

Stone shakes his head. "Gamov was the duty officer who sent Kulakov to Cairo. He has one arm missing, and wears the Order of Stalin on his breast."

"Dedov was on duty until nine A.M. Saturday," Aksenov insists. "I don't know who came after him. And I never heard of your one-armed Gamov."

Stone knocks softly on the polished oak door with the simple porcelain plaque bearing the number 666.

After a moment a muffled voice calls, "Come."

Stone turns the knob, pushes open the door with his left hand. The décor that confronts him is Ministry of Defense Cubbyhole Office, brown, with the only touch of color coming from the bright-red background in the obligatory portrait of Lenin behind the desk. The room itself is long and narrow—it has the atmosphere of a corridor—with shelves full of lawbooks on one wall, and not so much as a picture on the other. A kindly man, fiftyish, balding, wearing the insignias of a colonel on his pressed uniform, looks up from the dossier he has been studying.

Stone closes the door behind him, slips into the seat across from the colonel without being invited, lays his KGB card face down on the edge of the desk nearest him. The colonel stares at the card for a long moment through narrowed eyes, then breathes deeply and reaches for it. He studies the photograph and compares it to the original across the desk. "What can I do for you?" he inquires finally.

"You are the Colonel Koptin who conducted the investigation of the defector Kulakov," Stone announces; it is not put in the form of a question.

Koptin says, "I've already submitted a full report to—"

Stone stops him with a raised finger. "Comrade Koptin"—he purposefully addresses him by his name and omits his rank—"we will cover the ground again. Now. Verbally."

Koptin purses his lips, controls his temper. "I am at your disposal," he says coldly; there is no love lost between the military prosecutor and a representative of the civilian KGB.

"You are invited to begin at the beginning," Stone instructs him. "Why did you reopen Kulakov's dossier, and what led you to conclude that he had lied about his father being a war hero?"

Koptin leans back in his chair, taps two fingernails on the dossier open on his desk. "The dossier was reopened routinely," he explains. "It is our habit to conduct routine background investigations every three years on officers with access to very secret material."

Stone asks, "The information that his father had been executed for collaboration with the Nazis turned up during this routine investigation?"

"Not exactly," says Koptin. "It turned up coincidentally to the background investigation. It was in the form of an unsigned letter which accused Kulakov of obscuring the truth about his father for careerist motives. The letter suggested that the officer who had actually executed Kulakov's father for collaboration might still be alive. We tracked him down. He is a retired major general named Denisov. You will want the address, I'm sure. He lives in Moscow." Koptin searches through the pages of a loose-leaf book. "Malaya Gruzinskaya 33, apartment 118. He remembered the incident, and showed us an entry in his war diary to confirm his version. There is no question that Kulakov's father was executed for collaborating with the invaders."

"Did Kulakov admit knowing this? Did he admit to falsifying his dossier?"

"As a matter of fact, he vigorously denied it," Koptin says. "He maintained that he had honestly thought his father died a war hero. I have had some experience in such matters, and I may say he appeared sincere—so much so that I asked him if he would be willing to submit to a lie detector test."

"What would it matter?" asks Stone. "If the father was executed for collaboration, the son would not be suitable for service as a diplomatic courier."

"That's true, of course," Koptin agrees. "But if he sincerely believed his father was a war hero, he would not have faced charges of falsifying his service record. He would not have been threatened with a sentence of ten years in prison. He would simply have lost his assignment, perhaps his rank even. But he wouldn't have gone to prison."

"And so you submitted him to a lie detector test?"

"I got into a bit of hot water for taking it upon myself to order the test," Koptin admits. "My superiors were very annoyed at first—"

"At first?"

"They were annoyed, until they heard the results of the test. It clearly indicated he was lying about his father. This reinforced our decision to bring him to trial. His name had already been stricken from the active courier list. I myself informed him of this, and advised him to retain a lawyer, as there was every chance he would be court-martialed. I advised him that a guilty verdict would probably bring him a sentence of ten years. Shortly after, to my astonishment, I learned he had been sent out of the country on a courier run, and had defected to the Americans with the contents of a courier pouch."

"Were you involved in the follow-up investigation?" Stone wants to know.

"I was part of a three-officer tribunal that prepared preliminary dossiers on several people involved, yes," says Koptin.

Stone waits patiently. Koptin shrugs and supplies the details. "The case involved two embassy guards who were escorting Kulakov in Athens when he defected. In addition, there was a young second secretary in the car with them at the time."

"What was the disposition of these cases?"

"The two guards were tried by court-martial, convicted of dereliction of duty and sentenced to ten years at a strict regime labor camp. The second secretary, who was actually a military intelligence captain operating under cover out of the Athens embassy, was arraigned on similar charges, but one of his superiors interceded—it was said that the young man came from a family of influence—and the case was shelved."

"And what happened to the man who made the mistake of dispatching Kulakov abroad? What happened to the duty officer Gamov?"

Koptin becomes aware of his fingernails drumming on the dossier, and stops abruptly. "The dossier on the duty officer—you say his name was Gamov, but this is the first time I've heard it—was handled on a very high level. I have no idea as to the disposition of the case. I assume he was shot."

The street in front of Malaya Gruzinskaya 33 has been torn up to make way for new sewage pipes that have, so far, not even been delivered. During the thaw, the trench has turned into a moat, giving to the sturdy building a fortresslike atmosphere. Stone crosses the moat on one of the dozen or so wooden boards placed there for that purpose, takes the lift to the sixth floor, hunts from door to door until he finds number 118 and a small scrap of paper taped over the bell that reads, "Denisov, V. M."

An old man, shabbily dressed in a frayed military jacket, opens the door. "Ah, you came very fast," he says excitedly, pushing up with his forefinger the bifocals that keep sliding down his long nose. "I only wrote the letter two weeks ago. Come in. Come in. Don't stand there like a statue. I'll show you where I calculate the lake is." The old man limps down the narrow hallway toward the small living room–bedroom that appears, to Stone's eye, to have been furnished with items that came from a much larger apartment.

"You're Major General Denisov?" Stone inquires.

"Denisov, that's right," the old man says. He rolls open a large map of Central Asia on the dining table and starts to weight down the corners with whatever comes to hand—a Soviet encyclopedia, a shoe, a wooden cane, a pitcher of water. "I was flying from Tashkent to Bukhara, to visit my son and his wife. . . . My son is in the Army—like father, like son. He's stationed in Bukhara, but expects to be transferred to Lvov. . . . As I said, I was flying to Bukhara over the Kara-Kum desert when I spotted this lake that wasn't on my map. Imagine! An entire lake—not a small lake, mind you—that isn't on any map—"

Stone interrupts. "I'm not here about the lake you discovered." He shows his KGB card to the retired major general.

The old man is puzzled. "You're not here about the lake, then?"

"No. Not about the lake. I want to ask you some questions about the Kulakov affair. I understand you provided evidence that his father had been executed for collaborating with the enemy."

The old man sinks slowly into a chair and regards Stone suspiciously. "The collaborator Kulakov was executed," he says. "I should know. It was me that had him executed."

"Do you have the court-martial record—" Stone starts to ask, but the old man wags his finger impatiently.

"Was no court-martial. No time for legal trappings. He was caught red-handed. Wearing a German uniform. We were moving through the Ukraine at the time. Racing for the Dnieper, spearheading for Konev's Second Ukrainian. Noted his name in the war diary. Show it to you if you like. Listened to his pleas, gave him a cigarette, stood him up against a wall. That was how it went in those days."

"You shot a great many collaborators?" Stone asks.

The old man nods. "They knew what was waiting for them. Mostly wanted to get it over with as quick as possible. So did we." He laughs viciously, then has a coughing spell; his thin frame shakes as he buries his face in an enormous white handkerchief. Gasping for breath, he adds, "We had a common interest, you might say."

Stone asks, "Do you personally remember the execution of the collaborator Kulakov?"

Denisov avoids Stone's eye, busies himself folding his handkerchief and stuffing it back in his hip pocket. "Shot too many to remember every single one of them."

"Then aside from the entry in your war diary, you have no evidence that you shot a collaborator named Kulakov?"

"Diary doesn't lie," the old man insists stubbornly. "You can see for yourself if you got eyes."

Stone picks up the book, which is yellow with age, and reads the entry. It is written in longhand and dated September 4, 1943. "Near the village of Bilyansk, seven collaborators, caught the previous day wearing Wehrmacht uniforms, summarily executed." There follows a list of names and, in three cases, serial numbers. Kulakov's name is the last on the list. There is a serial number after it.

"No doubt about it being the right Kulakov," snorts Denisov. "Serial number matched."

Stone returns the diary. "What made you bring this affair up after all these years?"

"Wasn't me that brought it up," snaps the old man. He reaches toward his hip pocket for the handkerchief, changes his mind. "Ministry people showed up at the door one day. Spent the morning skimming through the diary till they came to the Kulakov entry. They took the book with them when they left. Very efficient. Gave me a receipt. Got the book back in the mail a month or so later. Don't know why they were so damn interested in a dead man, do you?"

Stone knocks on the door of Kulakov's old apartment just off Volgagrad Boulevard. After a while the door is opened to the limit of the chain, and a woman's eye peers out. "I don't care who you are," she croaks. She sizes up Stone, makes no secret that she doesn't particularly like what she sees. "You've got dirty shoes, and you look like you could be a germ carrier. You want to ask questions, ask. The answers don't get any better if I let you in."

Stone tries a different tack. "You were treated badly by people you shared the apartment with," he says soothingly. "It's a question of compensation."

"Compensation?" The widow closes the door, removes the safety chain, opens it to let Stone in, glancing all the while at his

147

shoes. "Compensation, as in money?" she asks, and when Stone nods encouragingly, she says (in a voice that has no relation at all to the one she used before), "I didn't know this was something you could get compensation for. Oh, dear, wait until my sister hears about this."

The widow offers Stone tea, refuses to take no for an answer, refuses to talk until he drinks. Once she starts, though, she doesn't stop. "My late lamented knew Oleg during the war, which I found out after I moved in, not before. A coincidence is what it was. We were looking at some of my old photographs and Oleg said, 'Who's that?' and I said it was my late lamented, and he said he knew him during the war, which is why I put up with as much as I put up with before I decided enough was enough and phoned the militia—"

"What exactly did you put up with?" Stone asks, priming the pump.

It gushes. Hardly pausing to come up for air, the widow describes wild family scenes with the father shouting, the daughter screaming hysterically, the wife collapsing in sobs, people stamping off in all directions, doors slamming behind them. "It got so disgusting, I finally called the militia, but Oleg took them outside and bribed them with some vodka. I swear to you, I only slept during the day, when they were all off somewhere. The girl, Nadia"—the widow smirks—"she was funny, you know."

"How funny?" Stones asks. "Funny how?"

"Funny," the widow repeats, "as in weird." And she whispers, "She liked girls more than she liked boys. It quieted down for a while when she went off to the hospital, but then the boy of theirs got into trouble at the university—he was expelled for taking drugs—and they started in on one another again. No wonder his wife upped and left him. She was a genuine hero for staying around as long as she did, if you ask me."

"Did you meet the actress who moved in with him later?" Stone wants to know.

The widow snickers. "Actress, my foot! If she ever set foot in a theater, she would have been the usher. If you want my opinion, she was a whore straight off the street, is what she was. She turned up once with one of her boyfriends in tow. That was too much even for Oleg, and he threw her out, but not before they each had their say. Another row!"

Stone asks her what happened to Kulakov.

"Disappeared." She snaps her fingers. "Like that. One day he was here. Next he wasn't. Don't have the vaguest idea where he went. Don't care either. Good riddance. He was gone two, maybe three days when some Army people with fairly clean shoes knocked at the door. They packed up everything that belonged to Oleg—books, papers, clothes, everything—and carted it off." The widow's face brightens with a sudden thought. "If you're calculating compensation," she tells Stone, "there are things I could tell you about the couple that moved in afterwards."

Stone, dog tired, sits on the edge of the bed, removes his shoes, massages his calves. Katushka, dressed in faded jeans and an old Eisenhower jacket with a black armband on the sleeve, is talking on the telephone. "Have you tried a spoonful of brown sugar?" she asks. She shakes her head vigorously. "No, no, holding your breath never works. The same for drinking water. No, the thing to do is to have someone rub the bone on the back of your neck in small circular motions. Clockwise is better than counter. Ah, you're alone. No, it won't work if you do it yourself. Someone has to do it for you." Katushka reflects a moment, staring thoughtfully at Stone. "Well, you can always cross the fingers of both hands, and if that doesn't do it, try hopping on your left foot and drawing circles with a finger around your belly button. Clockwise, yes. Ring me back if that doesn't work."

Katushka breaks the connection with a finger, furiously dials another number. "It's me," she tells someone on the other end. "I'm having trouble starting the car again." She listens for a moment, covers the mouthpiece with her palm and whispers to Stone, "Have you ever heard of something called spark plug?" To the phone she says, "If I have a choice, I prefer West German to Czech, and Czech to Russian. Yes. Okay. If I'm not here,

I'll leave the keys with Morning Stalin. Thanks. I owe you a favor." She listens for a moment, laughs. "You always want the same thing, don't you?"

Stone, leaning back against the cushions, asks, "Who died?"

Katushka looks back blankly until he points to the black band on her arm. "Oh, that. I lost a *Ficus benjamina* this morning. It's very upsetting really. I had it for almost two years. You become attached to a plant, you know. It struggled through the winter, only to give up at the first sign of spring. If only it had hung on for a bit, I would have nursed it back." She flings a magazine across the room in disgust. "It's the damn electricity," she mutters.

Stone, amused, asks, "What's wrong with the electricity?"

Katushka pours herself a glass of celery juice from a pitcher. "Has it ever occurred to you there is a direct relationship between electricity and sex? The question astonishes you, I can see. It's like this: the network of wires running through the walls sets up electric fields—poles of attraction and repulsion. That's why there's so much frigidity in the world!" She sinks onto the bed alongside Stone. "Think of it this way: we live on a kind of concrete platform, suspended in space over a maze of subway tunnels and sanitation pipes and water mains, surrounded on all sides by a mesh of electric wires. The rhythm of our lives is imposed on us by the pulsating of currents, the flushing of toilets, the dripping of faucets, the vibrations of trains passing underneath. We are cut off from the earth. We are cut off from its seasons." She catches Stone starting to smile, and says harshly, "You have the habit of mocking things you don't understand. It is a fault that you should work to overcome." Katushka changes the subject abruptly. "Morning Stalin, who is a fairly good judge of character, is positive you're not Latin. He says your polite aggressiveness is a disguise for anger, and the anger is the leading edge of sadness. In his experience, Latins are never sad. He says if he has to guess, he'd guess you're German. He says you're too methodical for a Frenchman or an American. As for Ilyador, he thinks you're Bulgarian because you remind him of a Bulgarian lover he once had. Something about the shape of the mouth. I suspect Ilyador is attracted to you. I advise you to watch out when the lights go out for the séance."

"What séance?" Stone wants to know.

The séance, a regular monthly event in the apartment, gets under way as soon as Morning Stalin clears away the dinner dishes. There are five of them seated around the kitchen table: Morning Stalin, Ilyador (dressed again as Ilyador), Katushka (wearing a long Uzbek robe), Stone, and the ancient woman who claims to be Assyrian, has a thick mustache on her upper lip, reads entrails and treats sexual problems with acupuncture. Now, in the flickering light of a single candle, she moistens her forefinger, which has no nail, and rubs the tip around the edge of a brandy glass until it starts to hum. The black cat, Thermidor, observing the proceedings from a kitchen counter, arches its back and bares its fangs in a silent snarl.

"I hear voices," the old woman mutters, still producing the hum from the glass. Her head falls back like a rag doll's, her lips move like a ventriloquist's—and a voice, vague, high-pitched, drifts above her head.

At first it is garbled and it is impossible to make out the words. Gradually the voice becomes more distinct. "I warned them . . . what would happen . . . if I was shòt," it says. "It wasn't a question of saving my skin. It was a question of the officer corps disintegrating. I told them the war would come and we wouldn't be ready. But they instructed me to confess, so I confessed. When they shot me, in the basement with a smooth-bore naval pistol, I looked my executioner in the eye, and he looked away before he pulled the trigger."

Ilyador, thoroughly frightened, turns to Morning Stalin, who whispers, "It's Marshal Tukhachevsky. He used to stand beside me for military reviews. He never knew I wasn't the real mushroom, and treated me with great deference."

"We paid in blood for—" Tukhachevsky's voice disappears, as if a needle has been suddenly lifted from a record. The humming grows louder. Thermidor hisses. Another voice, that of a feeble old man speaking with great effort, can be heard. It says again and again, "Stalin is too rude. Stalin is too rude. Stalin is too rude."

Tears stream down Morning Stalin's cheeks, soaking into his mustache. "It's Comrade Lenin," he sobs, "composing his last testament."

Lenin's voice fades, and another voice comes surging through it. "I always thought they were guilty," the voice says casually, "though not necessarily of the crime they were charged with. But someone in my position mustn't quibble. In my defense, it must be noted that they all *acted* guilty."

Ilyador, terrified now, whispers, "Do you recognize him?"

Morning Stalin, puzzled, asks the voice, "How did they act?"

The hum from the rim of the brandy snifter rises and falls in a curious pulsating rhythm. From above, the voice replies, "They acted as if they had something to be afraid of. It goes without saying, those who were innocent had nothing to be afraid of. They were all wreckers in their hearts, and what was hidden in their hearts was written on their faces, and they knew this and so they were afraid."

"I've got it," Morning Stalin announces triumphantly. "It's Stalin's hatchet man during the '36 purge. It's Gamov!"

"Gamov!" Stone lunges for the light switch, flicks on the overhead, grabs the woman who claims to be Assyrian by her shawl, shakes her back into consciousness. She comes awake reluctantly, blinking in confusion, a startled expression on her wrinkled features.

"What do you know about Gamov?" cries Stone.

Katushka pulls him off the woman and Morning Stalin says softly, "For the love of God, she knows nothing. I am the only one who recognizes the voices."

Stone turns on Morning Stalin. "Who is Gamov?"

Thermidor screeches and leaps in panic from the counter, knocking over a glass, which shatters on the floor. Morning Stalin's eyes open wide in fright. "Gamov," he whispers—he looks at Katushka inquiringly, but she only shrugs—"Gamov was the fig Stalin sent to investigate the Kirov murder in '34. In '36 and '37, he was the principal interrogator of Zinoviev, Kamenev, Bukharin, Rykov, Yakir and Tukhachevsky. He used to boast that he never lost a client until they confessed. When they confessed, they were shot. Vishinsky was the star of the show trials, but the mushroom behind the scenes was Gamov. That wasn't his real name. That was his *nom de guerre* he took during the revolution. I don't remember his real name."

"Where can I find him?" Stone's tone is urgent.

Morning Stalin cackles nervously. "In some cemetery," he says. "His turn came in '53. As soon as Stalin breathed his last, Gamov was put up against a wall."

The zebra in heat is strangely quiet during the night. Also Stalin and Ilyador, who squabble earlier than usual and, exhausted, are heard no more. Katushka has difficulty sleeping because of the lack of noise. She sits in a perfect lotus position reading and rereading her favorite "inner émigré"—Akhmatova—into the early hours of the morning. At one point she looks up to find Stone studying her. "I realize you're not asking me," she says as if she is simply continuing a conversation that has been going on for some time, "but if you want my opinion, the only thing that will bring a change is if women take over. Men who represent radically different political parties, or radically different points of view, wind up tinkering with the status quo, but they leave things essentially the way they found them. Women, on the other hand, tend to be less corrupted by power, and therefore—"

"I accept," Stone says abruptly.

Katushka stops in midsentence. "Accept what?" she asks suspiciously.

"I accept being the occasion to which you rise. I accept your help."

In a bound, Katushka is across the room. "I am extremely pleased with you," she says. And curling herself into the angles

153

of his body, pressing her lips to his nipple, she adds in a whisper, "I will demonstrate to you just how pleased I am."

For a long time no one speaks. The room is afloat in drifting shadows. Outside, a stiff wind whips through the antennas on the roof. Eventually one of the officers shakes his head and says, "Where did we go wrong?"

The senior officer doesn't look up from the handwritten report on his desk. "You're ahead of the game," he quietly chastises the officer. "It's not clear that anything's wrong."

"But one of their people got onto Denisov," another of the officers says. "The devil only knows what the old fool told him."

The senior officer produces a cigarette. One of the officers quickly supplies a light. "The old fool"—the senior officer sucks on his cigarette until it is glowing—"told him what he was supposed to tell him. That we turned up at his door one day and borrowed his war diary."

"How did they get onto Denisov?" the third officer asks.

"They got Denisov's name from the prosecutor Koptin," the senior officer explains. "They've also been to see Aksenov."

"Koptin's not a weak line," one of the officers says reassuringly. "Remember, Kulakov really was lying about his father."

"Which one's Aksenov?" someone asks.

"Aksenov's the one with the broken leg," the first officer explains.

"Ah, yes, the one who walked in front of a jeep." The senior officer's upper lip curls into a suggestion of a sneer. "The question is, why is the KGB suddenly interested in Kulakov at this late date."

"It can't be a coincidence," one of the officers says. "They must be onto something."

"If they're onto something," suggests another, "we're in water over our heads."

The three officers look at the senior officer, who turns in his chair to stare broodingly at a wall calendar. "I have a contact in the KGB," he says finally. "I'll sound him out tomorrow. If the KGB's onto something, he'll know about it. For now, the most important thing is not to lose our nerve." He laughs huskily—a laughter totally without mirth. "They can backtrack from now to eternity. What will they find? We've been over every detail a thousand times."

CHAPTER

"I don't mind your asking, not at all," Morning Stalin tells Stone politely. He stops peeling his orange, stares off into space with a sudden watery look. "I came face to face with him once, yes. It was in 1931, just after I had the plastic surgery. He was curious to see if we really looked alike. He circled around me as if he were measuring me for a coffin. Then he smiled that cold smile which I had mastered with some difficulty, and offered me his hand. 'Stalin,' he said, as if I didn't know who he was."

Ilyador, polishing a fingernail, guffaws. Stone asks, "And that was all?"

"Not quite," Morning Stalin explains. "A sly expression crept into his eye. He rang up Molotov and told him to drop what he was doing and come right down. Molotov came on the run, knocked once, opened the door and stopped dead in his tracks, staring from one to the other. I understood that Stalin was testing to see if it would really work, so I casually turned to Molotov, smiled that cold smile and said, 'It's incredible, isn't it? He could be my twin.' Molotov immediately assumed I was the real egg, and replied to me with great courtesy. Stalin's eyes flickered angrily—he must have sensed we were playing a potentially dangerous game—and he dismissed me with a wave of his hand. As I left, I saw Molotov collapsing in a chair in a state of shock."

Shaking his head nostalgically, Morning Stalin goes back to

his orange and Ilyador, waving his fingernails in the air to dry them, comments, "What an idiot you were. You could have kept up the pretense, shot the other as an impostor, and taken over the country."

"I would have lost World War Two," Morning Stalin says morosely. "I simply can't support explosions." He smiles at Stone apologetically. "To this day, there are people who think Stalin panicked and fled Moscow for ten days when the Teutonic cows invaded. Ha! It was me who panicked and skipped town. He never set foot outside the Kremlin."

Ilyador, pleased with his nails, says, "I spent the war in Siberia. Conditions were primitive. If we had milk, we kept it outside the window and chipped off pieces when we were thirsty."

Katushka returns with a paper and pencil. "I'm ready if you are," she tells Stone.

Stone stares for a long moment at the pencil poised over the paper. "I'm trying to find four people. The first is a major attached to the Ministry of Defense courier service in the capacity of a duty officer. His name is Gamov—"

"Ah, Gamov—that's why you got excited at the séance," says Morning Stalin.

"My Gamov is about sixty," Stone continues, "is missing his left arm, wears the Order of Stalin on his chest, has dandruff on his shoulders, wears his wrist watch on the inside of his wrist, and has long, delicate fingers like a woman's." He pauses to let Katushka, who is scribbling furiously, catch up with him. "The second person I'm looking for is a Jew named Leon Davidov. He works as a combination janitor-handyman for the Ministry of Defense. For reasons I'd rather not go into, I want to meet him outside the ministry building. His home would be ideal. The third is a lesbian named Lina. She may be Polish." He fishes Kulakov's photograph from his pocket. "This is what she looks like. The fourth is an actress. All I know about her is that her first name is Galya, she is supposed to be beautiful, she worked for a theater company in Leningrad but came to Moscow about five months ago to try and get a job in one of the theater or movie companies here. She has been described by someone who knew her as being very demanding."

Ilyador snickers and says, "That doesn't narrow it down at all."

Katushka asks, "What do you mean, demanding?"

"She tends to make sexual demands on a man that he can't fulfill, and then ridicules him for not satisfying her," Stone says.

Morning Stalin is very superior. "A man," he says, looking at Ilyador for confirmation, "would never do that to another man."

Stone holds the fort. The others scramble from the apartment after breakfast, reappear to leave urgent notes to each other, then disappear on the run once again. Ilyador phones in and leaves a number where he can be reached for the next half hour and Stone passes the message on to Katushka when she calls in shortly afterward. Toward noon Morning Stalin turns up, collapses into a kitchen chair massaging his feet (he wears the same size shoe Stalin wore, which is one size too small for him), gasping for air. For a moment Stone is afraid he is having a heart attack. When Morning Stalin can speak he says, "The actress's name is Borisova. Galya Borisova. I got it from the brother of a man who committed suicide over her. She's back in Leningrad, at the Pushkin Theater." Morning Stalin holds up a palm as Stone starts to thank him. Tears brim in his eyes. "No one has found me useful in twenty years," he says. "I'm very grateful to you."

Stone, flashing the credentials of an Aeroflot official, bumps a passenger and catches an early-afternoon flight to Leningrad. Driving into the city from the airport in a taxi, he suddenly remembers some lines Mandelstam wrote before he was packed off to Siberia—and his death—with a copy of Pushkin in one pocket and Dante in another. Stone's mother, who was born in Leningrad when it was still called Saint Petersburg, used to quote them over and over:

158

We'll meet again in Petersburg
As if we'd buried the sun there, . . .
In the black velvet of Soviet night
In the velvet of universal emptiness.

Despite the black velvet of Soviet night, Leningrad is still a northern beauty. Peter's proud window on the West, never quite opened, never quite closed, is colder and calmer than Moscow. The light slanting in from the sun hanging low over the rooftops sucks the orange out of the ocher façades. Mists rise from the canals that lace the city, or drift in from the Neva, where the battleship that really fired a shot heard 'round the world rides at anchor. Youngsters with their arms gaily linked swarm down Nevsky Prospekt, past an ornate cinema showing a Western starring Gregory Peck. Stone pays off the taxi several blocks from the Pushkin Theater, wanders through some side streets, crosses one of the imperial bridges and follows the canal to the next bridge. When he is certain he is clean, he makes his way to the stage entrance of the Pushkin, gently shakes awake the man with the hearing aid dozing in the chair just inside the door.

"I'm looking for Galya Borisova," he says loudly, presenting his KGB card.

The man turns up his hearing aid, squints at the card for a moment, trying to decipher the letters, shakes his head in frustration. "Reading provokes headaches," he says. Stone nods sympathetically, presses a five-ruble note into his fist. He glances at it, manages without difficulty to make out the number 5, smiles a toothless smile. "She lives in the Haymarket," he says immediately, waving with his hand in the general direction. He mutters the name of a street, then a number, pockets the fiver, sinks back into the considerable comfort of his afternoon nap.

It takes Stone a while to find the house in the Haymarket, a neighborhood made famous by Dostoevsky in *Crime and Punishment;* the number is missing from the façade and he has to interpolate. The building must have been the city residence of a member of the imperial court; the windows are large, the ceilings are high, the general atmosphere is one of faded elegance. Inside, the banister is made of mahogany, the steps are paved with cracked tiles and covered with a threadbare rug to keep people from slipping. A man in an undershirt answers the plastic bell on the top floor, left apartment. He studies Stone's KGB card with an absolute minimum of interest, steps back without a word to let him enter. The one room that forms the apartment was once the house's library; one whole wall is made up of floor-to-ceiling shelves, but instead of books, they are stacked with folded shirts, scarves, winter boots, canned goods and wineglasses (no two of which match). Washing hangs from a line strung between two unlit crystal chandeliers. Galya, looking worn and tired, lounges in a hideous modern easy chair, her legs spread wide, her shirt hanging between her thighs in a way that outlines them. She nibbles absently on dried sunflower seeds, spitting the husks into her palm and depositing them in a dinner plate that has served as an ashtray for several days. Stone glances at the man in the T-shirt, who is leaning against the wall near the door. "You can disappear," Stone instructs him. The man doesn't move a muscle until Galya motions with her chin for him to leave.

Stone gives her a glimpse of his identification card, but she ignores it. "Who you are is written all over you." She smiles belligerently.

"I want to know about Oleg Kulakov," says Stone.

"What makes you think I know anyone by that name?"

Now it is Stone's turn to smile. "You met him at the Actors Union buffet. You kissed him on the lips. Later you moved in with him. If you're not willing to discuss this now, and here, we can organize to discuss it at another time, and in another place."

Galya takes the hint. "You don't have to throw your weight around. What do you want to know?"

Stone puts Galya through the paces, checking Kulakov's version of the story detail by detail. Yes, she says, they met again by accident in a record store on Gorky street. Yes, she knows that Kulakov defected to America; she was questioned by someone from the Ministry of Defense just afterward. Yes, it was Galya who asked Kulakov if she could move in with him; she was shopping around for a job in Moscow and needed a place to stay, since she didn't have a Moscow residence permit. "He was very preoccupied," she explains, "with certain problems he had—something to do with his daughter and his boy. He didn't pay much attention to me. Sometimes I had the feeling I could have died in bed alongside him and he wouldn't have noticed." Yes, she once brought a man back to the apartment, an actor from Leningrad she had run into. If she kissed him on the lips in front of Kulakov, it was in the spirit of playfulness. "I like to keep my men nervous," she admits, and she adds with a provocative smile, "Nervous men make better lovers." Galya moistens her lips, leans toward Stone, looks at him in a new light. "You, for instance, look reasonably nervous. What are you doing tonight?"

Katushka says, "You don't look nervous to me. If I had to describe you, I'd say you were . . . alert. Yes. Alert."

Stone smirks. "I was lucky to get out of there alive."

"You could always have cried rape," teases Katushka. "The man with the undershirt might have rushed in to save you." She absently strokes Thermidor, coiled in her lap. "I can see you are disappointed," she says suddenly. "Things are not working out the way you thought they would."

Things are not working out at all the way Stone thought they would. The more people he talks to, the more it seems as if Kulakov's story is true. *And Stone doesn't want Kulakov's story to be true.* Because if it is true, he will have to go crawling back to Washington with empty hands. But if Kulakov is a Soviet operation, and Stone can find the key to prove it—to prove false a story that everyone in Washington has accepted—he will return home to a whole new ball game. Topology budgets will increase, and the sky will be the limit for Stone. He glances across the

161

room at Katushka, who studies him with her dark eyes. Her face and her voice are expressionless as she asks in a low voice, "And will you go away when you have finished whatever it is you are doing here?"

There is no expression on Stone's face either as he answers. "Yes," he tells her. "I will leave. I will not come back."

The next several days are so hectic that Stone loses track of time. He leaves a midmission message with the embassy (a phone call to the naval attaché asking, in a broad American accent, if he is the Bolster who graduated from Cornell in 1956) indicating he is alive and well, and has turned up nothing so far to prove that Kulakov is a fraud. While Katushka, Morning Stalin and Ilyador are tracking down leads on the three missing links, Stone interviews the rector at Lomonosov University who expelled Kulakov's son, Gregori, for drug abuse, then the doctor who for a short time treated Gregori at a clinic, and finally the militia captain who discovered the needle marks in Gregori's arm and packed him off to Irkutsk. "His father was well connected," the militia captain remembers, glancing up from Gregori's dossier to reply to Stone's questions. "Involved in some kind of secret work for the Ministry of Defense. We see the same thing all the time these days—the sons and daughters of important comrades, raised with every advantage up to and including foreign travel, and they wind up with puncture holes in their arms. It's disgusting. Just yesterday we had the daughter of a Georgian Komsomol official in here—"

Stone interrupts briskly. "Who turned Gregori on to drugs?"

The militia captain, a tired time-server with an eye tic, shrugs. "He wouldn't say. During the withdrawal period, he was invited in for another round of questioning; they're usually more—how to put it?—cooperative when they're going through withdrawal. But this one, he kept crying over and over that it wasn't his fault, that they had obliged him to try the stuff." He smiles knowingly at Stone, one professional speaking to another. "That's what they all say, isn't it? It's never their fault, it's always someone else's."

On a rainy Wednesday, Stone goes through his usual routine of checking to see if he is being followed. He cuts through the almost deserted alleyway behind the house where Gorky once lived, rounds a corner, waits an instant, then doubles back in his tracks—*and spots something*. Even as he hurries away, his pulse racing, short of breath, he is not sure what has caught his eye. A shadow receding too rapidly from his field of vision? A flicker of motion where there should have been none? Whatever it was, it is enough to set Stone's nerves on edge, and he spends the rest of the morning ducking through back doors into obscure alleyways before he comes to the conclusion (tentative; once an alarm goes off, you can disconnect it but it still echoes) that he is jumping at shadows, which is something that occurs to almost everyone who has spent any time at all in the field.

After lunch, Stone—still keeping a wary eye on his trail—turns up at the Serbsky Institute for Forensic Psychiatry in Chernyakhovsk, a suburb of Moscow. "Are you expected?" demands the uniformed sentry at the end of the driveway.

Stone holds up his KGB identity card. "We have a standing invitation," he says with a wink, and the guard nods knowingly and swings back the heavy steel gate just enough to allow Stone to squeeze through. As he walks up the driveway toward the building, he hears the gate clang shut behind him, and he has to fight down the fear that surges to his throat.

"Kulakova, Nadia." Stone repeats the name to the overweight doctor as she flips with a thumb through a stack of file cards.

"Ah, Kulakova." She looks up at Stone with new interest, her head slanted to one side, a Bulgarian cigarette bobbing on her lips. "The daughter of the defector Kulakov. She's already been interrogated, you know."

"Not by me," Stone says with finality, and the overweight doctor has no choice but to lead Stone through the maze of corridors, with guarded iron doors at every turn, to the basement lunchroom, which has been converted into a theater in the round for the afternoon. Dozens of inmates of the institute, all wearing formless gray bathrobes that they clutch to their bodies in the absence of belts, are seated in the chairs that have been drawn up. Some slouch with their heads nodding on their chests, others lean forward following every word spoken by the actors, who are also clutching formless gray bathrobes to their taut bodies.

"Kulakova is the young one with the short hair," whispers the overweight doctor. "The play is the latest thing in the way of therapy," she says apologetically; she obviously expects him to disapprove. "It has only a vague form; a starting point, if you like. The actors make up their lines as they go along. Sometimes things come out, from one of the actors or even from one of the spectators, that are very helpful. . . ." Her voice starts to trail off. "All the bourgeois countries are doing this kind of . . ."

A young man, completely bald but running his fingers across his scalp as if he has a full head of hair, steps away from one of the two groups the actors have divided themselves into. "Every time my mind snares an event," he cries, backpedaling toward center stage, "my interest runs out like the string on a reel attached to a kite." He tries to lift off the ground, to fly, then sinks back dejectedly. "I need more wind," he sobs. "I need more wind."

Nadia Kulakova drifts away from the group she is with, starts to speak with excruciating slowness, as if each word will be the last. "They are making preparations for a birth. My birth. Warm water is brought. Clean sheets too. The midwife is prevailed upon to wash her hands, which is a concession she makes to the master of the house, who is a member of the party in more or less good standing. My mother, who is religious, secretly crosses herself as the ordeal begins. When it is over, the umbilical cord is cut and I am hung on a clothesline in the sun to dry. A neighbor, notified of the joyous event by word of mouth, throws handfuls of artificial snowflakes from the roof of our building. One flake lands in my tiny palm, and I burst into tears because it refuses to melt."

Nadia stares at her outstretched hand for a long moment, and then bursts into tears because the artificial snowflake will not melt.

164

Stone notices her nails, which are bitten to the quick, and her hair, which is uneven, as if someone had cut off handfuls with a sheep shears. Her voice is singularly without melody, without inflection, as if she is stuck on one wavelength. "They gave me haloperidol and triftazine, and once, after my father left the country, a treatment of sulfur. Sulfur raises the temperature— it's as if you had a very high fever. You lie in bed and search hour after hour for a position that doesn't hurt. But you never find one."

"What was the play about?" Stone asks.

"Which play are you speaking of? There are many here."

"The play you were performing downstairs," Stone says.

"It's thoughtful of you to ask," Nadia says. "It began as a story about two psychiatrists who run asylums with opposing points of view. One holds that we invent the problems we enjoy not coping with. The other believes we can trace all our problems back to the trauma of our birth, which is etched in our memories the way circuits are printed in transistor radios. The play is a confrontation between the patients of the two psychiatrists."

"Do you get to choose your camp, or are you assigned?"

"We are offered a choice," Nadia says, "but when we make one, it is usually not honored."

Stone is touched by the fragility of the girl sitting on the edge of her bunk. He remembers Kulakov's despair when he spoke about her; he thinks suddenly of his own daughter, and then finds himself cutting off the thought before it becomes too painful. "Have you seen your friend Lina?" he asks.

Nadia is jarred by the question. "How is it you know that name?" she demands. When Stone doesn't say anything, she shrugs. "I'm finished with all that," she says. "They've fixed it so I don't like girls anymore. I don't like boys either." She looks up with a pleading expression in her eyes. "I don't even like myself," she says softly.

Katushka is beaming with satisfaction. "I found her," she tells Stone triumphantly. "I went to see her—"

"Found whom?" Stone demands, but Katushka, flushed with excitement, rushes on.

"I thought that as long as I knew where she was, I might as well talk to her," she explains, sinking onto the cushions, stroking Thermidor.

"Talk to whom?" Stone asks in exasperation.

Katushka looks at Stone in bewilderment. "The girl in the photograph is whom," she says as if it is perfectly obvious. "The one named Lina is whom." She tosses the photograph onto the cushions. "She's Polish, all right. Even speaks with an accent. Her father is a big shot in Polish Army intelligence. Lina's a professional. You knew that already, didn't you? Does nicely for herself too, judging from the layout she has—three rooms on the outer circle, a Mercedes, a dacha."

"How's her technique?" Stone asks sarcastically, but Katushka takes the question at face value.

"She's good, but not great," she says seriously. "She's not spontaneous, not inventive. Just competent. She has a tendency to rely too much on paraphernalia." She adds teasingly, "All you need to make love well is what you began life with—two hands, a tongue . . ."

Stone is not amused. "How did you find out so much about her?"

The question seems to surprise Katushka. "Why, by making love with her. How else can you find out about someone?"

They argue through dinner and most of the evening, and Katushka, near tears, goes off to sleep on a cot in Morning Stalin's room. Stone waits a decent interval, then tiptoes down the hallway in bare feet, opens Morning Stalin's door, to find the three of them, Morning Stalin, Ilyador and Katushka, asleep in each other's arms.

It doesn't occur to Stone until he is four hours into the flight to Alma-Ata that what has taken place was a lovers' quarrel.

Stone is staring out the small oval window at the vast tracts of plowed land that stretch to the horizon—Khrushchev's virgin lands, with endless rows of trees to break the winds that threaten to turn the region into a huge dust bowl. "I'm jealous," Stone tells himself. "I'm actually jealous."

Lake Baikal glistens under the left wingtip. When the plane banks, Stone can make out far ahead the white crests of the mountains that back up to the frontier with China. Next to Stone, a very fat major general in the artillery is recounting the battle for Berlin to a young girl in a miniskirt. "I was nineteen at the time, and thin as your pinkie," he says. "We were crazy with excitement, you can imagine. They were fighting for every house on the street, and for every room in the house. Children, old men—that's all they had left. Decaying corpses hung from lampposts with cardboard signs on their chests saying they had been executed for desertion. Desertion! There was no place to desert to. What was hard was seeing the last comrades dying a few hours before the end. They fought across the Ukraine, across Poland and Czechoslovakia, across the Oder into Germany, across Germany, to die at the doorstep of the Reichstag." The general's double chins vibrate with emotion. He turns to Stone. "The young people today, they don't have the slightest idea of what it was like," he complains. "Everything comes too easily to them. Isn't it so, comrade? We sow and they reap."

Stone fixes the general with a serious look. "It is in the nature of things that one generation always constructs for the next," he lectures. "Lenin illustrated the formula when he instructed us to break down the wall between generations and become, all of us, simple builders of Communism."

The girl in the miniskirt rolls her eyes in her sockets and turns back to her book. The major general nods vigorously in agreement. "Just so," he says, squirming uncomfortably in his seat belt. "What a pleasure to come across someone who knows his Lenin. I take it you are a member of the party? I, too, have the honor." He offers his hand. "Petrov, Nikolai. Major general of the artillery. Currently on an inspection tour of our frontier."

167

From the way Major General Petrov smiles into Stone's face, it is obvious he expects the same amount of information back— and once again a shadow of danger flickers across Stone's field of vision. He remembers the three-quarter-hour wait before the passengers were allowed to board the plane to Alma-Ata. He remembers also that the major general took the seat next to him, not vice versa. Still, the idea that the other side—in training, the Russians were always referred to as "the other side"—has latched on to him, has then managed to plant one of their people next to him, is too far-fetched for Stone to accept.

"I am . . ." Stone gives him one of the names he hasn't used before. "I am an assistant editor of children's stories at the Central Publishing Combine in Moscow. I am going to Alma-Ata to meet with members of the Kazak Writers Union."

The major general beams good-naturedly. "You might say we have something in common, you and I. I have edited for publication a manual on spotting the fall of cannon shot from the air. It is not as easy as you would suppose, because the point of view of the spotter is seldom the same as the point of view of the shooter, which is another way of saying that what looks short to the spotter can be long and to the right for the shooter."

The major general is still trying to explain the intricacies of spotting when Alma-Ata looms out of the snow-covered mountains. In short order the Ilyushin is taxiing past rows of khaki-colored biplanes used by the collective farms for crop dusting. The terminal, a prewar poured-cement structure, seethes with people coming or going—Stone is not sure which. Long lines of Kazaks, pushing cardboard suitcases or burlap bags ahead of them, file past a harried official who barely glances at the documents waved in his face. Stone catches a glimpse of the fat major general ducking into a military limousine. With no taxi in sight, he regrets he hasn't stuck closer to the author of the book on spotting; the worst that would have happened is he would have had another earful of technical jargon. Eventually Stone manages to bribe the chauffeur of a car belonging to the local cotton combine, and he heads into the city along broad boulevards lined with budding apple trees.

Alma-Ata is half city, half oasis. Shadows of leafy trees fall across the sidewalks. Miniature canals carry ice water (drawn from the melting snows of the nearby mountains) through the streets, giving to the atmosphere the freshness of a racing brook. Sidewalk vendors do a brisk business in vegetables grown on private plots. Stone, suddenly famished, pays off his driver, treats himself to a quick lunch at a workers' canteen and a glass of kvass from a street wagon, then slowly wends his way toward the complex of prefabricated apartment buildings behind the party building in the center of town. At building number four, he checks the mailboxes in the lobby, finds the name he is looking for, mounts the stairs to the third floor, waits a long while in the stairwell as a precaution, then climbs one more flight to the fourth floor and buzzes once.

Someone in slippers shuffles toward the door. "Leave the lamp and slip the bill underneath," a tired voice says. Stone pushes his KGB identity card under the door, and an instant later it opens and he finds himself face to face with Kulakov's wife. She is very much thinner than Stone imagined her, thinner and tougher and angrier too. Her eyes have hollows under them from lack of sleep. Her mouth is grim. There is nothing soft or feminine or pretty about her. She looks at Stone and returns his card. "I prefer to speak to you when a third person is present," she announces.

"I will note your preference in my report," Stone replies. "For the moment, you are not being offered a choice."

Kulakov's wife controls her temper, steps back reluctantly to let Stone enter, indicates with her chin which room the interview will take place in.

Stone enters a combination bedroom–living room filled with modern plasticized furniture, a sideboard with glass doors, a small table with the dirty breakfast dishes still on it, a television with a magnifying lens clamped in front of it to enlarge the screen.

"Where is your tank commander?" Stone inquires politely.

"My tank commander," says Kulakov's wife, "ran off with his tank."

169

Stone says, "What does that mean?"

Kulakov's wife laughs without humor. "My tank commander disappeared just about the time Oleg disappeared. I haven't heard from either one of them since." A thought occurs to her. "Maybe they defected together. Maybe they're sharing an apartment in Washington—the bastards, both of them!"

She turns away to struggle with the bitterness that rises in her like sap. When she turns back, Stone gestures to a chair and says, "May I?" Without waiting for permission, he sits down. Kulakov's wife runs her fingers through her uncombed hair, leans back against the sideboard, lights a cigarette without offering one to Stone. She looks up at him through a cloud of smoke.

"I want to ask you," Stone begins, "about various problems in your family life that may have influenced the defection of your husband." And then, patiently and meticulously, he leads Kulakov's wife over painfully familiar ground: the daughter's lesbian love affair, the son's arrest and expulsion from Moscow for using drugs, her own affair with the tank commander, which ended soon after she came to live with him in Alma-Ata. "I have given it a great deal of thought," she tells Stone. "I am of the opinion that my husband didn't defect because of the breakdown of his personal life. No. He defected to get even with me for leaving him. You people"—her tone drips with venom—"have deprived me of his pension rights, his medical rights. Even the apartment in Moscow was taken away. I couldn't go back if I wanted to—I have no place to go to. After twenty years of marriage"—she is shrill now, and close to hysteria—"I have nothing to show for it. Nothing. No daughter. No son. No husband. No home. No money. Nothing. It wasn't me that defected. But it's me that suffers."

At the door, Stone turns back to ask a last question. "Where can I find your son? Where is Gregori?"

A cloud of cigarette smoke separates them, and Stone has a sudden vision of her living in hell. Her voice, strangely distant, says, "You seem to know all the answers. You want to speak to Gregori, you go and find him."

170

Finding Gregori is not difficult. Like all addicts who have been expelled from Moscow, he is registered with the local militia. "Sign here," the militia captain instructs Stone, spinning the log around and holding out a cheap ballpoint pen. Stone is not happy about having to sign for the receipt of information; this is the first tangible record he has left of his presence. But once the militia captain—impressed with anybody who comes from Moscow, not to mention a member of the KGB—passes him the slip of paper with Gregori's address on it, he can't very well refuse to sign for it without arousing suspicion.

Gregori, it turns out, lives on the other side of the tracks—tracks made by trucks going to and from a suburban cement factory along a stretch of thin tarmac that has long since given way to dirt and crab grass. "Wait for me," Stone orders his taxi driver, who has already been primed with a glimpse of his KGB card and a ten-ruble note. He climbs the wooden steps of the run-down house and knocks loudly on the door. An arthritic man who tends the coal burner during the winter in exchange for a rent-free room comes up behind Stone. "Isn't home," he tells him matter-of-factly. "Hasn't been for days." He spits on the floor.

Stone starts to turn away when the arthritic man says, "I got a passkey if you got an official reason for using it." He smiles broadly, revealing tar-stained teeth.

Stone supplies the official reason, and the man produces a key ring, selects one, inserts it in the keyhole. The door clicks open. Stone indicates the man is to wait outside, and enters.

The shutters are nailed closed, and what light there is comes from cracks in the boarded-over skylight. The room reeks of dirt and decay. Clothes are strewn across chairs, a dresser drawer has been placed upside down next to the mattress and used as a table. The moldy remains of a meal—an empty sardine tin, crusts of bread—are on it. Tacked to the wall over the mattress, its edges curling with age, is a snapshot of Oleg Kulakov.

Stone has come to the right place.

He edges the bathroom door open with his toes, flicks on the overhead light with the back of his hand—and finds Gregori, naked, long dead from the look of him, stretched out in a waterless bathtub with rust streaks where the enamel has worn away. The cracked pieces of a syringe lie on the floor where it fell out of his outstretched hand. A necktie that has been tied around his arm and then loosened dangles from his left elbow.

"Looks like he might be dead!" The arthritic man has come up quietly and stares at the body in the bathtub.

Stone's mind is racing. The death of Gregori will be reported, and it won't take long for the local militia to zero in on the log with the name of the KGB man who came all the way from Moscow to see him. When they discover they can't put their hands on the KGB man, cables will go out to Moscow. An answer will come back asking them to verify the name. Soon it will become apparent to everyone—the local militia as well as the KGB people in Moscow—that someone has been impersonating a KGB man. All that should take not less than a day; with luck, it could take two or three.

Stone draws the arthritic man into the hallway, closes the door of the apartment. "You are to stand guard here," he orders him. "Nobody is to enter until I return with the militia."

The arthritic man straightens his rounded shoulders. "Count on me, comrade," he says. "I served in the Great Patriotic War."

And Stone, with one eye on his wrist watch, starts to put as much distance as he can between himself and the dingy wooden house on the other side of the tracks in Alma-Ata.

The marshal's lids hang like folds of skin over his angry eyes. He stabs with a stubby finger at the buttons on his desk intercom, and barks orders into the speaker in a gravelly voice. "No pictures. No Bulgarians. No journalists. No veterans. No visitors of any kind. No calls. Understand?" He removes what appears to be a small black portable radio from his desk drawer, sets it on the blotter, raises the antenna and switches it on. A barely audible high-pitched squeal comes from the box. "So much for any microphones," says the marshal. He turns to his visitor, who is fumbling for a cigarette with his only hand. "No cigarettes," he snaps. "Too much smoke, my eyes start to sting. You've got ten minutes. What are we dealing with?"

"It's definitely not our friends over at the KGB," says the one-armed officer. His upper lip curls into a suggestion of a sneer as he pronounces "KGB." "I have a pipeline into the KGB. Well placed. If they were backtracking, he would know about it."

The marshal nods. "At least that's something to be thankful for," he says grudgingly. "But if it's not the KGB, who is it?"

The one-armed officer shifts uncomfortably in his chair. "My personal guess is it's the Americans," he says quietly. "When he questioned the actress in Leningrad, he revealed details—how she met Kulakov, for instance—that could only have come from the defector himself after the defection."

"The Americans!" The marshal's fist comes smashing down on the desk, causing everything on it to jump. "You assured me—" He tries to control his temper; excitement is not good for his blood pressure. "You assured me that the Americans would limit their attentions to the defector and the papers he took with him."

"It was a miscalculation," the one-armed officer admits. "We looked at it from every point of view, and concluded that the CIA would never authorize a penetration. They already have enough embarrassing things on their plate without getting into a penetration." He shakes his head. "I don't understand the logic of it. . . ."

The marshal places a small pill on his tongue and downs it with a gulp of mineral water. Calmer now, he asks, "What makes you so sure the man checking up on Kulakov is American? Even if the CIA is behind it, they'd be more likely to farm this kind of thing out to the French or Germans."

"We managed to place one of our language specialists next to him on the plane to Alma-Ata—"

"He didn't get suspicious, I hope?"

173

"No, no," the one-armed officer assures him. "Our man posed as an artillery expert on an inspection tour. He says the suspect speaks letter-perfect Russian—too perfect, if anything. But he had the impression—I must stress that it was only an impression—that the suspect might have been raised in the White Russian community in China. Something about the way he flattened his a's when he pronounced certain words."

"How do we get from China to America?" the marshal demands.

"If he was raised in a Russian-speaking family in China, nine chances out of ten they were White Russian Jews who fled during or after the Revolution. Almost all the Jews among the Russians in China wound up in America after 1949, and during the fifties many of them drifted into anti-Soviet organizations. It was a natural marriage. They spoke Russian, and they hated Communism."

"This American—assuming he is, as you speculate, an American—has he been here under deep cover and is just now surfacing, or . . ."

The one-armed officer absently brushes dandruff from his left shoulder. "I suspect he came in on a one-time assignment," he explains. "Remember the Grani courier who disappeared from his hotel without a trace? Change the part in his hair, add a mustache and eyeglasses, and the description more or less matches our man."

The marshal takes this all in. "You're absolutely certain there's no possibility it's a KGB operation?"

"None. I'd stake my reputation on it."

The marshal laughs softly. "You're staking more than your reputation, Comrade Volkov." He reflects a moment. "If it is an American, that means the Americans haven't bought the defection?"

"Not at all," says the one-armed officer. "If they weren't buying it, they wouldn't bother checking it out. No. There may be one faction, or even one man, who hasn't entirely bought it, *and they're backtracking, as a routine precaution, to see if they can come up with something to indicate Kulakov wasn't genuine."*

"And will they?" The marshal glances at his appointment calendar, scribbles a note to himself in the margin. "Will they come up with anything?"

"We've been over the ground many times," says the one-armed Volkov. "He can nose around from now to doomsday. There's nothing to come up with. There was only one weak link—the boy Gregori. We arranged that he will never talk to anyone."

"I still don't like it," says the marshal. "I don't like the idea of an American digging in our yard. What would happen if he simply disappeared?"

"With all respect, Marshal, that's the last thing in the world to do at this stage."

The marshal nods thoughtfully. "If their man disappears," he thinks aloud, "it will indicate to those in the American establishment who already suspect Kulakov that their field man must have come up with something to support their suspicions."

"Worse than that, Marshal," says Volkov. "The Americans won't take the disappearance of a field operative sitting down. They will raise a very quiet but very efficient storm in intelligence circles. Our KGB friends will be contacted by the Americans and accused of terminating a field man. The KGB will investigate, find that they had nothing to do with it—and turn to us for an explanation. They will want to know why an American agent backtracking on Kulakov disappeared. The answer that will offer itself to their small minds is that Kulakov was, in fact, a fraud; that the American agent discovered this. We must remember, Marshal, that the KGB thinks Kulakov was a genuine defector because we backtracked on him after the defection and assured them he was genuine. No; the disappearance of the American agent will only lead the KGB to our door. The best thing we can do is permit this American field man to

check out Kulakov's story until he is satisfied it is all true, and then let him go quietly back home and convince anyone there who still has doubts."

There is a soft knock at the door, and a colonel pops his head in.

"I thought I told you no interruptions," explodes the marshal. "No interruptions means no knocks at the door."

"I beg your pardon, Marshal." The colonel stands his ground. "I have an 'Eyes Urgent' for General Volkov that I thought he would want to see. Now." He stresses the "Now."

The marshal consents with a toss of his head. The colonel hands the metal clipboard to the one-armed officer and leaves the room. Volkov opens the cover and scans the message. His brow furrows. His eyes are grim as he looks up. "I must report to you that the body of Kulakov's son, Gregori, has been discovered by someone pretending to be an agent of the KGB. The man who found the body used the name and identification number of a retired KGB agent when he signed a receipt for Gregori's address at the local militia headquarters in Alma-Ata. The KGB assumes that a Grani agent, probably of German nationality, was attempting to locate the son of the defector in order to publish a story on the mistreatment of relatives of a defector."

The marshal pulls a colorful silk handkerchief from his pocket and mops his brow. When he finally speaks, his voice is not much above a hoarse whisper. "Whatever happens, your American must not be allowed to fall into KGB hands."

Volkov understands that his ten minutes with the marshal in charge of the Soviet Armed Forces is up. "That doesn't leave us much room to maneuver in," he says, rising to his feet.

"Comrade General Volkov." The marshal looks him in the eyes. "I had your personal assurances, when we went ahead with this thing, that we were operating under conditions that left absolutely no room for failure. If anyone becomes suspicious now"—the marshal's tone is even; he is merely noting the obvious—"it will, of course, be you they become suspicious of."

176

CHAPTER

Lounging against the side of a kiosk in the underground passage that runs between Gorky Street and Red Square, Katushka still stands out in the crowd. She is wearing an ankle-length printed skirt and an off-white silk shirt (tied, Cossack-style, around her waist with a belt made of braided horsehair) through which her nipples are clearly visible. And almost everyone who passes looks. Stone, watching from behind another kiosk farther along the tunnel, sees her size up a prospective customer who plants his bulky body before her, throws out his barrel chest as he gives her all the reasons (money aside) why she should sleep with him. She listens politely, her head cocked to one side, then says, "No, thank you," in a way that leaves no room for argument. The barrel-chested hero scowls, makes an unflattering comment on the size of her breasts and stalks off.

Stone has been keeping an eye on Katushka long enough to be certain that no one else is keeping an eye on her. He steps into the flow of Muscovites and drifts down on her. Unaccountably, he finds his pulse racing. When he is close enough to see her eyes, they widen with unconcealed delight.

"Aren't you worried about the world ending?" Stone asks, pointing to a poster on the kiosk that says the Americans have enough nuclear warheads to destroy the entire population of the planet several times over.

Katushka smiles warmly, links her arm through his. "The

world will end," she says happily, "when the people in it stop making love. Where have you been? You disappeared like a cloud. I looked up and you weren't there. To tell you the truth, I thought I would never see you again." In a surprisingly shy voice, she adds, "I am pleased with you for coming back."

Stone starts to explain that he has come back to say goodbye to her, but before he can get the words sorted out she bubbles over with news. "Ilyador went through some old phone directories in the post office basement and found a listing for the Jew you're looking for—Leon Davidov. I called the number, but Davidov had moved out several years ago."

"So that's the end of that," Stone comments.

"Not quite," says Katushka. "The man who answered the phone gave me the name of an old Jew who might know where Davidov is."

"Did you speak to him too?"

"I tried to," Katushka explains, "but the moment he saw what I wanted, he closed up like a clam. He refused to have anything to do with me. He was very insulting, actually. He accused me of being unclean. I take a bath at least twice a week!"

"Come on," says Stone. "Let's see what I can get out of him."

They cut through a courtyard not far from the Hotel Rossiya and come out on Arkhipova Street, just down from the only active synagogue in Moscow. In the entrance, two old Jews in black fedoras are bickering politely. They stop talking as Stone and the girl enter, stare at Katushka's nipples, then look at each other with wide eyes and shrug.

"That's him," whispers Katushka, indicating an old Jew dovening in the back row of the almost empty synagogue. He wears a black suit that has seen better days, a black yarmulke on his bald head and a tefillin wrapped around his forehead. Stone places his handkerchief over his own head in place of a yarmulke, and slides in alongside the old man, who is talking, his eyes half closed, with God. Once again, Stone feels the sweet nostalgia for things he barely remembers. His own father, and his father's father, might have sat on this very same bench talking with this very same God, whom they blamed for everything, and still honored.

Slowly the old man turns toward Stone, sizes him up, makes no effort to hide that he is not overly impressed with what he sees.

Stone speaks in Yiddish. "Excuse me for interrupting," he says. "I'm looking for someone, and I was told you could help me find him."

"You're looking for someone," the old man repeats belligerently, "and you were told I would help you find him. Maybe yes, maybe no. The man you're looking for, he maybe has a name?"

Stone says, "I'm trying to find Leon Davidov."

The old man studies Stone for a long moment, then mutters in an undertone, presumably so that God won't hear, "Go get murdered!" With an innocent look on his face, he turns back to resume his conversation with God.

"It's very important," insists Stone. Three rows in front, a middle-aged man turns and glares angrily at the intruder. "It's important," Stone repeats in a whisper. "I don't want to hurt him. I only want to speak to him."

The old Jew looks at Stone out of the corner of his bloodshot eyes. "The why is what you haven't explained."

Stone measures his man for a fraction of a second. "I want to tell him what happened to his son."

The old man mumbles the word "son" several times, starts to tremble. Tears well in his eyes. "It's me, Davidov," he mutters. "So where is the good-for-nothing? So what trouble is he in that he admits after all these years he has a father?"

The old man's pain stirs Stone, and he reaches out awkwardly to touch his elbow. Davidov shrinks back, looking at the hand that almost touched him as if it could contaminate him. "If you have things to tell me, tell them and leave me in relative peace," he says.

"I have things to tell you," Stone says, "and I have things to ask you."

Davidov shakes his head stubbornly. "Nothing is what I'll tell you," he whispers dramatically. "People like you is whom I don't talk to." He leans toward Stone, his eyes gleaming, his sour breath coming out in excited little gasps; he looks like an emaciated bird about to pounce on a worm. "I was a loyal Stalinist when you were sucking on a tit. I worked in the Ministry of Defense. Stalin once passed within an arm's reach of me. I could have reached out and touched him, that's how close he was. It's the fashion not to talk like this these days, but old clothes are what I feel comfortable in. So you want to tell me news, sonny, so tell it. Me, I'm clean as a whistle!"

In the lobby, Stone tells Katushka, "It's like talking to a wall."

"I told you," she says.

"He's half mad," Stone says. "He claims he's an old Stalinist and has nothing to be afraid of." Suddenly Stone and Katushka stop in their tracks and look at one another. "Why not?" Stone asks.

"It's a crazy idea," Katushka says, "but what do you have to lose?"

"Do you think he'll do it?" Stone wants to know.

"If it's me that asks," Katushka tells him, "he'll do it."

Morning Stalin brushes back his mustache with the tips of his index fingers. "I picked the gesture up from the original mushroom," he says proudly. "I was letter perfect. I once played with Svetlana for an afternoon, and she didn't suspect I wasn't the real fig."

"Maybe she suspected," says Stone, "and was grateful for the change."

"Not funny," snaps Morning Stalin. "Not funny at all."

"Don't be nervous," Stone soothes Morning Stalin. "He's an old man. Nothing can go wrong." Stone signals for silence, then knocks gently on the door.

After a moment Davidov calls through the closed door, "So who is knocking?"

"Leon Isayevich Davidov?" Morning Stalin asks. His voice is deep and filled with its own importance.

The door opens as far as the chain will allow. A watery eye stares out into the dimly lit landing. The eye widens. There is a distant choking, a half cry of astonishment. The old man fumbles with the lock, opens the door, sways against the wall for support as he stares at Morning Stalin. "It's Malechamovitz—it's the angel of death," he whispers, backing away from his visitors, sinking weakly onto an unmade bed in the corner of the small dark room.

"Not to panic," Morning Stalin instructs Davidov in a strong voice. "You are not on any of my lists. I need your help. I need information."

"Dead is what you are," Davidov wails, but Morning Stalin silences him with a gesture, walks over to where he is sitting. "Touch," he orders him.

The old man does as he is told. He reaches out with shaking fingers and touches the back of Morning Stalin's wrist. The skin is soft with age and moves easily over the bones. Davidov says in a weak voice, "You want to know what? Only ask."

Stone comes up behind Morning Stalin. "During the war your son, Oleg, took another identity?"

"I had a friend in the Army named Kulakov," the old man explains, talking to Morning Stalin. "He died a hero's death. Oleg paid someone at the registry office to file him under *K*." Davidov is beginning to enjoy the experience of talking to Stalin. His eyes twinkle. "He was entering the military academy. He thought he stood a better chance with a name like Kulakov than Davidov, if you don't mind my saying it." The old man stares up into Morning Stalin's face. "By any chance, you don't remember me? In the hall of the Ministry of Defense you once passed me. It was during the Great Patriotic War. Nineteen forty-four. Five at the outside. I was putting new bulbs in old sockets. You passed so close, I could have touched you."

Morning Stalin glances uneasily at Stone for a cue; Stone nods and Morning Stalin turns cheerfully to Davidov. "Now that you mention it . . . light bulbs ring a bell . . ."

"Gray overalls is what I was wearing," the old man says eagerly.

"Gray overalls; of course," says Morning Stalin.

"Where is Oleg?" Davidov suddenly asks Morning Stalin.

Again Morning Stalin looks at Stone, who says, "Oleg is in America."

"On a mission?" the old man asks.

Morning Stalin coughs and clears his throat, and then acknowledges that Oleg is, indeed, on an important mission for the Politburo.

Davidov explodes off the bed. "Ah, I knew it in my heart of hearts," he tells Morning Stalin. "When that one-armed bandit Volkov came out of the room after Oleg—"

Stone pushes Morning Stalin aside, grabs the old man by his lapels. "Say that again," he says softly.

Davidov looks Stone full in the face for the first time. "I know you—you're the Jew with the handkerchief instead of a yarmulke." He asks Morning Stalin, "Is he one of us?"

Stone lifts Davidov off the ground and gently shakes him. "Say what you said again," he orders.

Thoroughly intimidated, the old man cackles weakly. "I knew Oleg was going on a mission when I saw that one-armed bandit Volkov come out of the room after him. Volkov is a big cheese in military intelligence. Not many people know that. But I know it. I used to clean fifteen years ago his toilet."

Stone relaxes his grip, and Davidov sinks back onto the bed. "That's what I thought you said," Stone tells nobody in particular.

Morning Stalin snaps his fingers excitedly. "Of course," he tells Stone. "Now I remember. Volkov. Ha! Volkov was the real name of the mushroom who conducted the investigations for Vishinsky in the thirties. What was the name he used?"

Stone, smiling broadly, says, "It was Gamov. Gamov was the name."

"Gamov, yes," says Morning Stalin. "Gamov's real name was Volkov. I knew I'd get it eventually."

182

"Me too," exults Stone. "I also knew I'd get it eventually."

"So you're leaving," Morning Stalin says glumly. "I'll admit it to you frankly: I'm sorry to see you go. You're an interesting fig. You made me ... forget for a few days ..." And he adds, "Katushka, too, will be sorry to see you go."

They pass the zoo park and turn into Katushka's building. The night watchman, eating cheese off a page of *Pravda* spread on the desk, salutes Morning Stalin—a bit stiffly, it seems to Stone. He rings for the elevator. "I'm sorry to go," he tells Morning Stalin as the elevator arrives. He hears himself say it, and realizes how profoundly true it is; deep down he is very sorry to leave.

Morning Stalin is silent for a moment, lost in thought. Then he sighs and shakes his head. The elevator door jars open and they head down the dimly lit hallway toward the apartment. "The world has changed in my time," says Morning Stalin. "When I was a boy, I worked for a dentist. I pedaled his drill. The patients used to tip me to pedal as fast as I could so that the drill would turn rapidly. Nowadays"—he inserts his key in the lock; the door clicks open—"nowadays—"

Morning Stalin never finishes the thought. As he steps across the threshold, he is grabbed on either side by strong arms and pinned against the wall. Stone, all nerve ends, spins away from the arms that reach for him—only to find two heavies blocking the corridor behind him. Now Stone, too, is pinned against the wall and frisked. One of the men cries excitedly when he feels the passports and money in the lining of Stone's jacket. Stone is thrust, along with Morning Stalin, down the hallway into Katushka's room. Katushka stands near the window, her thin wrists handcuffed in front of her, a faint mocking smile on her lips. The broken, lifeless body of a cat lies in a corner, and Stone has to stare at it for a long moment before he realizes that it is Thermidor.

Ilyador, without handcuffs, sits on a cushion whimpering hysterically. "I had to do it," he pleads with Katushka. "They threatened to put me away in one of those asylums." The words

183

come between gasps for air. "They said ... I was schizophrenic ... that I had two personalities ... that I was a transvestite. ... God help me ... I had to do it ... I had to do it...."

Far away, from a saner world, comes the braying sound of a zebra in heat.

They come at Stone in relays, two to a team, patiently posing questions as he sits in a straight-backed wooden chair, his wrists handcuffed behind him, a spotlight trained on his face, the voices coming out of the impenetrable blackness around it.

"What is your real name?"

"What is your nationality?"

"What is your parent organization?"

"Only admit you are the *Grani* courier and we will switch off the light and let you sleep."

"Your name?"

"Your nationality?"

"Your organization?"

Stone struggles desperately to keep hold of certain threads. He has been arrested by the KGB, of that much he is sure; he recognized Lubyanka Prison, the headquarters of the KGB, as the car into which all three had been bundled drove through the gate. His inquisitors realize he is a foreigner; Stone caught a glimpse of his phony passports and his money piled on the desk just before the spotlight was trained on his face. From the questions thrown at him, he understands that they are convinced that he is the *Grani* courier who disappeared ten days before from the Hotel Rossiya, leaving behind a single copy of *Grani* in his valise lining. Which means they don't know he is American. Stone means to keep it that way.

"I've told you again and again," he says tiredly—his head is spinning with fatigue, and he has to struggle to organize his sentences sequentially—"my name is ..." He gives them the identity of an engineer in a remote Georgian city on the theory that it will take at least a day for them to track down the man who really goes by that name. Buy time, Stone keeps repeating to himself. The only thing that counts now is to buy time.

184

One of the interrogators, a young man by the sound of his voice, laughs wickedly, and the other moves behind Stone and whispers in his ear: "If you don't cooperate, it will go hard on you. We know you work for the anti-Soviet émigré groups. We know you were tracking down the relatives of the defector Kulakov to write a story on how they were made to suffer."

"You will be charged with the murder of the boy Gregori," sneers the younger man.

"Save yourself," coaxes the man behind Stone.

"What is your name?"

"What is your nationality?"

"What is your parent organization?"

Somewhere in the building, a woman screams; Stone convinces himself it is Katushka, and he strains against the handcuffs until they cut into the flesh on his wrists. "You're making a mistake," he says weakly. "You're making a terrible mistake."

"You are without hope," the man behind Stone whispers. "Think of yourself. What is your name? Only tell us your real name and you will be permitted to sleep."

Dazed, his head drooping onto his chest, Stone is half dragged, half marched through an endless corridor, down a narrow back staircase to a waiting van. Katushka and Morning Stalin are already inside. They reach down and help him climb in. The metal door is slammed shut, bolted on the outside, and the van lurches forward.

"Are you all right?" Stone asks Katushka. "I thought I heard you scream."

"They never questioned us," she explains. "They said we would be charged with harboring an agent sent in by one of the anti-Soviet exile groups. They said they would get back to us when they finished with you. Then some others came and whisked us down the stairs to the van. Then you came. Where are they taking us?"

Stone can tell from her voice that she is very frightened, though she is trying hard not to show it. "How long ago did they arrest us?" he asks.

"Forty hours," Morning Stalin tells him. "They fed us twice—a breakfast, a lunch." He grimaces. "My face made them very nervous. You should have seen the heads turn as I walked down the hall. Didn't I make them nervous, Katushka?"

"They thought you were a ghost who had come to haunt them," Katushka agrees. To Stone she says softly, "Are you really an anti-Soviet agent?"

There is no answer. His head bobbing on his chest, Stone has fallen into a deep sleep.

Stone surfaces slowly. The first thing he sees when he finally manages to open an eye are the shoulder boards of the young Army officer standing alongside the bed. The bed! Stone jerks upright, blinks several times, looks around. The small room is as neat as a pin. The cot he is lying on is Army-style, with khaki blankets and a footlocker next to it that serves as a night table.

"You can shave if you like," says the Army officer. "You'll find an electric razor in the bathroom. After which you are invited to take breakfast with the officer in charge."

The young officer watches in a noncommittal way as Stone gets out of bed and pads across on bare feet to the window. There are no bars on it. Stone looks out at the compound, which is bathed in bright sunlight. There are several small wooden buildings. Smoke rises from chimneys. At the center of the compound is a two-story cement structure with a forest of antennas on the roof. Two or three soldiers can be seen walking around the compound. Stone turns back to the young officer, puzzled. "Where are the others? Where is Katushka and Morning Stalin?"

But the officer only repeats, "You are invited to take breakfast with the officer in charge."

Stone showers and shaves, finds his clothes (cleaned and pressed) on a hanger in the closet, and dresses. The young officer motions with his head, and leads Stone out of the building and across the compound toward the two-story cement building with the antennas on the roof. Inside, the officer indicates the staircase and says, "Upstairs, first door on your right."

186

Stone hesitates before the door, wonders if he has any alternatives, decides he hasn't and goes in without knocking. The officer eating breakfast at a small table in front of the window turns, rises politely, motions with his only hand for Stone to take the seat across from him.

The one-armed officer, who is wearing the uniform of a lieutenant general with the Order of Stalin conspicuous on his tunic, pours a cup of coffee for Stone. "So you are the famous Stone we've heard so much about. Sugar? Cream?" He pushes the two bowls across the table, and Stone notices his fingers— long and thin and graceful, the fingers of a woman on the hands of a man.

Stone's thoughts race as he tries to figure out how the one-armed officer learned who he was. "My name is . . . " Again he supplies the Russian identity that he gave to the KGB.

The one-armed officer smiles grimly. "It is a little late to start playing games with each other," he says. "We have identified you through your left thumbprint as the Stone, first name unknown, who is in charge of a small group that works exclusively for the chairman of the Joint Chiefs and goes by the relatively innocent though poetic name Topology. Curious choice of names: Topology—the study of surfaces! Actually, we have followed your career with interest ever since you devised that very original gambit in the early 1960s of watching us to see if we were mobilizing for war. It was about that time that we purchased an envelope with your thumbprint on it—you will bear with me if I don't mention the identity of the seller—for the tidy sum, as I remember it, of three thousand American dollars. Until yesterday, we had no idea what you looked like. You will be interested to know that your great idea of watching us for mobilization didn't work quite the way you thought it would. Instead of asking ourselves: 'What are the Americans developing which would cause us to mobilize if we found out about it?' we instead posed the somewhat more intelligent question: "Why do the Americans want us to *think* they are watching us for mobilization?' The answer was relatively simple once we asked the right question. You wanted us to think you were developing

187

weapon systems which you weren't developing. To match weapon systems you thought we had *already* developed. And you thought we had developed them because we wanted you to think we had developed them. Well"—the general uses his one hand to brush away the past—"all that's water under the bridge. Do you have the same expression in English? Water under the bridge?"

It seems like an innocent question, but Stone understands that the general is asking him if he is ready to stop pretending he is Russian. And Stone is ready; something, he is not sure what, is in the air. He was arrested by the KGB, but now finds himself calmly taking breakfast across the table from none other than Comrade Volkov, the head of Soviet military intelligence, who happens by coincidence to be the duty officer Gamov who sent Kulakov on his way to America. And so Stone says simply. "Yes, General Volkov, we have the same expression in English."

"Ah," sighs Volkov, "that's what I call progress. Well done, Mr. Stone. Yes, indeed, that was very well done. I take it you put the Gamov-Volkov puzzle together after you talked to the old man Davidov. The one you call Morning Stalin told us all about it while you were sleeping. It's curious, isn't it, how you plan an operation down to the smallest detail, and then something unforeseen trips you up."

"How long were you working on the Kulakov operation?" Stone asks conversationally.

Now it is Volkov's turn to smile at the innocence of the question. "We devised the general idea about two years ago. It took us a while to come up with the right man, and then develop the various teams to deal with his daughter and son and wife. Speaking as one professional to another, the whole operation was incredibly complicated, you can imagine. The thing nearly fell through when the military prosecutor, acting on his own initiative, decided to give Kulakov a lie detector test. If he had passed that, it would have all gone down the drain. Fortunately for us, Kulakov was lying about his father, though it wasn't the lie we accused him of. But no matter. One lie was as good as another."

"It was a spectacular operation," Stone agrees.

Volkov smiles at the memory. "We even had some of our people stop the laundry van in Athens, knowing the defector wasn't in it. We calculated you would be impressed by our efforts to get back the pouch."

"The defection of Kulakov," says Stone, "is probably one of the great intelligence operations of our time."

Volkov accepts the compliment gracefully. "It wasn't an intelligence operation," he says mildly. "It was a *military* intelligence operation."

Stone says, "Excuse me. Military intelligence operation." And suddenly he begins to see some light. "Of course. A *military* intelligence operation. In which your civilian counterparts, the KGB, played no role."

"Our civilian counterparts don't know, even now, that Kulakov was an operation."

Stone, tingling down to his fingertips, is one small jump ahead of Volkov. "And now you are about to break every rule in the book and tell me *why* you organized the defection of Kulakov."

Volkov nods. "You are very quick, Mr. Stone. I am going to tell you why because only by telling you why will the operation stand a chance of success." And Volkov, speaking in a low voice, occasionally flicking dandruff off his shoulder boards, tells Stone what the military hoped to gain by the defection of the diplomatic courier Kulakov.

Stone is silent for a long while after the general finishes. Finally he shakes his head in admiration. "It's really incredible. All that effort to make us swallow the contents of one small scrap of paper. And the only mistake you made was to play the role of the duty officer yourself."

Volkov purses his lips. "I was curious to see the face of the man whose life I had manipulated—"

Stone remembers his own curiosity to see the face of the Russian diplomat in Paris. "Ruined," he corrects Volkov.

Volkov accepts the correction. "Ruined."

"And Kulakov's Jewish father, who you didn't know existed, happened to work as a janitor in the ministry building and saw you come out after him," says Stone.

"He saw me come out, and knew who I was," agrees Volkov. "And told you about it. Which is why we're having our little breakfast this morning."

Stone stares out the window; they are changing the guards posted at various points along the electrified fence that surrounds the compound. "What do you expect me to do now?" he asks Volkov.

"Assuming you could leave the country and return to Washington," says the general, "what would you normally do?"

"I'd report directly to my boss, the chairman of the Joint Chiefs. I'd tell him Kulakov was an intelligence—I mean, a *military* intelligence operation. And he'd blow the whistle on you." And Stone adds sweetly, "We have the same expression in English—blow the whistle on someone."

Volkov drums his long, delicate fingers against the side of a glass. "I'm arranging for you to return to Washington on the condition that you do precisely what you said you would do—report directly to the admiral who is chairman of the Joint Chiefs. No one else. Only him. And let him make the decision what to do with the information you give him."

Stone is still feeling his way. "What if I skywrite?" He traces a message in the air with his index finger. "Kulakov is a phony."

"We will salvage what we can," Volkov says evenly. "We will claim that it is a Topology operation designed to turn us against each other. Of course, the girl will be dead; you must understand this. We are after all in the same line of work. . . ."

"We may be in the same line of work, General," Stone tells him with sudden passion, "but we're still on different sides of the fence."

Volkov glances at his watch, which he wears on the inside of his wrist, then looks at Stone with unconcealed contempt. "It is my understanding that the various sides more or less resemble each other."

"Oh, no, they don't, General. My side would never do to someone what you did to Kulakov—ruin a man's life like that, ruin the lives of the people around him. That's the basic difference between our systems. On my side, there are limits. You crossed. We wouldn't."

"You are dead wrong, Mr. Stone," says Volkov. "There are no limits. During the Great Patriotic War, I spent fourteen months in a German concentration camp. Once we locked ourselves in our barracks. The guard cut off our food to starve us out. After a while they grew impatient and sent in dogs. We ate them and threw out the bones. And then we ate each other." Volkov's upper lip curls into a suggestion of a sneer. "We are still eating each other."

"So you got what you came for," says Katushka. "And now you're going home . . . wherever that is."

They are talking quietly, the midday sun playing on their heads, in the middle of the compound. Stone sees the general looking down at them from the second-floor window. Just outside the main gate of the compound, a black limousine and an Army jeep wait, their engines idling. The young officer who woke Stone that morning stands next to the limousine, looking impatiently in his direction.

"I must go now," Stone says.

"Will we be all right—me, Morning Stalin? Will we be . . . taken care of?"

Stone looks Katushka in the eyes. "You'll be taken care of. Not to worry."

Katushka looks back with her enormous eyes, mulling over what hasn't been said. Then she starts to walk with him toward the limousine. At the gate, she puts a hand on Stone's arm. "I'll get news of you by opening a book at random." They stand in silence for a long, long moment. "It is a tradition," she explains, "to wait quietly on the threshold of a home before going on a journey."

Stone nods and turns away, and then turns back to look at her a last time. And he hears her say, very softly, her lips barely

191

moving, "You came into our lives as casually as a raindrop. All things considered, I am very pleased with you."

The marshal leans forward and taps the driver on the shoulder. "Slow down. I don't want to get there until I've finished this conversation." To Volkov he says, "What about our friends over at Lubyanka? What about the KGB?"

Volkov absently watches a burly woman push her way into a queue outside a toy store. "They think it's a Grani operation," he says. "They're looking under the sheets for a team of émigrés. And they're doing all the looking quietly; they're not too proud about having had a Grani courier lifted from under their noses, so they're not advertising."

The marshal takes this in. "You're sure he'll go directly to the admiral? He won't take it to some congressman, or the White House?"

"He's been in the game a long time," Volkov assures him. "He'll go up the chain of command. It's a big decision, what with the girl and everything. He'll let the admiral make it."

The marshal turns toward Volkov and asks bitterly, "And what will the admiral do?"

Volkov avoids the marshal's eyes. "I wish I knew," is all he can bring himself to say.

CHAPTER
10

The admiral punches the button on his intercom. "Only interrupt me if war is declared." He thinks a moment, adds, "No half wars either." He switches on the black box with the small circular antenna, then swivels back toward Stone and observes him through the dark haze of Havana cigar smoke hanging like a rain cloud over his enormous desk. "All right. In ten words or less, what did you find when you looked under the rock?"

"I was right," Stone tells him. There is no trace of smugness in his voice. "The defection of Kulakov was an intelligence operation mounted by the Soviet military establishment. They required a genuine defector to plant information on us that we would swallow. So they created the defector. They drugged his son and turned his daughter on to girls and seduced his wife and framed him with some trumped-up charges. They did it all so he'd run when he got the chance, and then they gave him the chance. And he ran. The poor son of a bitch who had lost everything ran just the way he was supposed to."

"Where'd they go wrong?" the admiral wants to know. "Where'd they trip up?"

"Volkov himself mounted the operation," explains Stone.

"The faceless Volkov who runs their military intelligence show?"

"One and the same. In the end, he wanted to take a look at the man he ruined. So he played the role of the duty officer. He

193

used the name Gamov because that was the pseudonym his father used in the thirties while interrogating suspects for Stalin. What Volkov didn't know was that Kulakov's real father worked as a janitor in the Ministry of Defense. He's been there thirty years. The father recognized Volkov coming out of the duty office after his son. And he told me about it."

The admiral grinds out his cigar in an ashtray, then empties the ashtray into his wastepaper basket. "Hate butts accumulating," he explains, his brow furrowed, his mind obviously elsewhere. "All right, let's get down to the nitty-gritty. You've explained how they did it. But not, why? What's the piece of paper they wanted us to swallow?"

Stone says, "The one that reads: 'You owe me a hundred rubles.'" He glances at the clipping that says: "The fact that the situation is desperate doesn't make it any more interesting," then looks back at the admiral, who is lighting another cigar. "They counted on our breaking into the safe of the diplomat in Geneva who wrote the note. They wanted us to think that all we had to do was hang tough at the disarmament talks and the Russians would give in." Stone is suddenly very tired; his mind wanders. He thinks of Katushka defying moral conventions by playing the whore, defying fashion with her boyish clothes, defying winter with her greenhouse. "They wanted us to think that, Admiral, because the military knows that the party people, which is to say the civilians, have no intention of making concessions. And the military wanted to make sure we wouldn't make concessions either. They want a standoff at Geneva. They don't want a disarmament agreement. They like things just the way they are, with each side chasing the tail of the other."

"I've known you a long time, Stone," the admiral muses. "This is the first time I've ever heard you sound . . . judgmental. I can appreciate this hasn't been easy for you. Hmm. How many people on our side are in on all this?"

"I know it, Admiral. Now you know it. That makes two."

The admiral swivels a hundred and eighty degrees and stares out the window. A gray dusk, with traces of blue in it, is beginning to settle over the city like soot. Silhouettes are softening.

The admiral's voice drifts back over his shoulder to Stone. "How do you see our options?"

"You can blow the whistle on the operation," Stone says. "Charlie Evans and the CIA will wind up with egg on their faces; they bought Kulakov, and they were dead wrong. Evans would probably end up job-hunting, but I doubt if he'd find anything in Washington. In Moscow, the penalty for being wrong is more serious. If we handle the whistle-blowing right, Volkov and several others will be put up against a wall and shot for defying party authority. The most repressive group in Russia, the KGB, will use the affair as an excuse to cut into the power of the military establishment, which is the one institution in the Soviet Union that stands as a counterbalance to the party. What else? The President will be very pleased with you; he'll invite you to breakfast in the Oval Office and pat you on the back before the cameras and offer you a second term as chairman of the Joint Chiefs. He'll undoubtedly authorize his negotiators at Geneva to make the necessary concessions, because he's counting on a disarmament agreement with the Soviets for domestic political reasons. That'll be the big gain; we'll wind up signing a disarmament agreement with the Russians."

"On their terms," notes the admiral. "What if I don't blow the whistle?" He is speaking very carefully, weighing the possibilities. "What if I forget the whole thing?"

"Volkov's counting on you to do just that, Admiral."

"I asked you to explore options," the admiral snaps, "not make judgments."

"If you don't blow the whistle," Stone says, "our side will hang tough in Geneva and wait for the Russians to make the concessions that Charlie Evans said they would make. The Russians won't make concessions, and there won't be a disarmament agreement."

"If there's no disarmament agreement"—the admiral is talking to himself now—"Charlie Evans will have a bit of explaining to do anyway. He'll have to answer for the fact that things didn't work out the way he said they would."

"He can always claim the Russians, under heavy pressure

195

le military people, simply changed their minds," suggests

e admiral absently picks up his pocket calculator and
s squaring numbers. "Some things puzzle me. For starters,
didn't Volkov simply kill you and dump your body in a very
p Siberian lake?"

"Volkov assumed I went in on a formal penetration," Stone
plains. "If I had disappeared, the people who sent me in
vould presumably have begun asking questions. Agents aren't
killed these days; they're traded. Volkov reasoned that you
would have held the KGB responsible for my disappearance.
The KGB would know they had nothing to do with it, so they'd
start to wonder what an American agent checking on Kulakov
found that caused him to disappear. The whole plot would unra-
vel. Remember, Volkov had to keep the real reason for the defection secret not only from us, but from the KGB, which is to
say the civilians, who very much want a disarmament agreement
if they can get it on what they consider reasonable terms."

"Hmm. It bothers me," says the admiral, "that they gave
away so many secrets to make us swallow one piece of paper."

"They gave away some little fishes for a big one," says Stone.
"When it comes right down to it, they didn't give *that* much
away anyhow. The night sight on their T-62 was bound to fall
into our hands as soon as the Israelis captured one of the Egyptian tanks. The fact that Moscow got NATO code Alpha Delta
from a code clerk in Germany won't change very much. The
clerk who gave it to them is in jail, but the Russians may have a
dozen more sources, for all we know. And we seldom put priority
material into NATO codes because we assume the system's rid-
dled with leaks. Then there's the defect of the low-level parallax
input on the SAM tracking system. By now the defect's probably been corrected. They could afford to give it away."

"What about the man they planted in the Egyptian cabinet
secretariat?"

Stone shrugs. "They may have wanted to write him off for
any one of a dozen reasons." A sudden thought comes to him.

"He may even be innocent. The trail of money that leads to him may be a plant to keep us away from someone else in the cabinet secretariat who really works for them. Who knows? What does that leave? Some letters about bread riots or someone's sex life. Lists of spare parts for Egyptian MIGs. What does it really amount to?"

The admiral focuses on his Havana. "What would prevent us from sitting on what we know and blackmailing Volkov at some future date?"

"Won't work," Stone says flatly. "The fact that you didn't blow the whistle when you could have—that you let the disarmament talks go down the drain—can be turned against you. No. It would be a standoff."

The printout on the admiral's calculator is beginning to get dimmer. "Goddamn contraption needs new batteries," he mutters absently. "The girl—she must be important to you?"

"She's important, yes."

"If I blow the whistle on Volkov, what happens to her?"

"He'll get rid of the evidence," Stone says. "She's evidence."

"If she's important to you," the admiral wants to know, "why didn't you just report back that you didn't find anything to indicate Kulakov is a phony?"

"We're talking about the disarmament talks," Stone says softly. "We're talking about the arms race going on and on. I don't make decisions like that. You do."

The admiral snickers. "You're like everyone else, Stone. You pass the buck. You want me to do what you haven't the guts to do. You want me to forget the whole thing to save the girl—"

"You've got it backwards, Admiral. I want you to blow the whistle on them even if it kills the girl! I can't do it, but you can. You must."

The admiral's voice is hard now. "I don't give a damn about the girl. What I care about are all the civilian know-it-alls who are trying to take from us the weapons we need to guarantee victory in the next war."

"That's exactly Volkov's view," Stone says wearily. And from

197

of a long tunnel, he hears his own voice coming almost
is an echo: "The victor, Admiral, belongs to the spoils."

ro's heart just isn't in it. "Do you know that every time it
,," she says vaguely, "it rains acid rain, polluting lakes, wip-
out fish life, stunting forest growth, penetrating the soil to
ack . . . Stone, you're not listening."

"The world will end," he says quietly, "when people in it stop
aking love."

Thro turns toward him so that the length of her body is
stretched out along the length of his. "What happened to you
over there, Stone? You're not the same."

Stone shuts his eyes tightly. "I'm nostalgic for things I never
experienced," he says. He makes an effort to explain: to her, also
to himself. "All my life I've hated Communist Russia and loved
America the way only an immigrant loves America. This was the
promised land for me. But too many promises have been
broken." He shakes his head in confusion. "I don't know heads
from tails anymore. Both sides of the coin look the same to me."

At the last moment, Mozart remembers protocol: juniors enter first and leave last. He squeezes his bulk into the back of the
Buick and slides across the seat to make room for the admiral,
who asks, "How do you like Topology now that it's your shop?"

Mozart glances uncomfortably at the cigar protruding from
the admiral's mouth. "I waited for it a long time, Admiral. It's
my cup of tea."

The chairman of the Joint Chiefs lights up and relishes the
first drag on the cigar. "Stone said it would be when he recom-
mended you," he says.

The Buick is caught in bumper-to-bumper traffic going down
Pennsylvania Avenue. The driver, an army corporal, asks over
his shoulder, "Want me to use the siren, Admiral, sir?"

"Better not," snaps the admiral. "Some wise ass on the *Washington Post* will accuse the Joint Chiefs of misusing the siren to
attend a cocktail party."

Mozart says, "Too bad about Geneva," and when he gets no

reaction from the admiral, he adds, "Funny how everyone assumed an agreement was in the bag. I hear scuttlebutt that Charlie Evans has been on the carpet all morning over at the Oval Office trying to explain where the CIA went wrong. Claims the intelligence estimates were correct, but that the Russians changed their minds about wanting an agreement. Word is that Evans's lease on his job has just about expired, that he'll wind up as ambassador to India in his next incarnation."

"Couldn't happen to a nicer guy," says the admiral with a straight face. They pass a group of fifty or so women, some carrying signs that read "Disarmament Now," on their way to demonstrate in front of the White House. "What do you have for me this week?" the admiral asks Mozart.

Mozart extracts a Manila folder from his briefcase. "The congressman we talked about last week, the one making all the fuss about the cost overruns in the shipbuilding program—well, it turns out he's got himself a mistress over in Georgetown. We've got footage on him going in and out, and ticket stubs when he passed her off as his secretary on a junket to London last fall."

"Hm. I'll have one of Stone's people over at the Defense Intelligence Agency drop around to his office and ask some routine questions about her as part of a security clearance," says the admiral. "He'll get the point."

"We've got the suicide of the defector Kulakov on our hands," continues Mozart. "You remember, the courier with the diplomatic pouch full of goodies. Hanged himself with some picture wire in an art gallery. Funny part is he left a note addressed to Stone. Something about how things like this don't happen in real life."

"Things like what?" the admiral asks.

"He didn't specify," says Mozart. "It required a bit of doing, but we managed to keep the story out of the papers." He looks up. "Wouldn't want to do anything to discourage future defectors."

"No, we wouldn't," agrees the admiral. "Have you given any thought to the matter I mentioned last week?"

"I put an ad hoc team onto it, and I think we've come up with something," says Mozart. "As I understand it, the Joint Chiefs want to build a new generation of mobile intercontinental ballistic missiles deployed in long trenches so the Russians could never pinpoint their location and destroy them in a preemptive first strike."

"The problem," says the admiral, "is to get Congress to spring for the thirty billion to fund the project."

"I think we've come up with a workable scenario," says Mozart, toying with his Phi Beta Kappa key. "In my opinion, we can get Congress to come up with the money if we can offer them evidence that the Russians are developing a new generation of missiles accurate enough to threaten our existing force of nonmobile missiles."

The admiral doesn't follow Mozart's drift. "But the Russians *aren't* developing a new generation of superaccurate missiles."

Mozart has arrived at his point. "But they will," he says triumphantly, "if they can somehow be made to believe that we are secretly developing a new generation of missiles accurate up to one yard at six thousand miles!"

The admiral is intrigued. "And how can we make the Russkies believe we are secretly developing a new missile system?"

"All we have to do," Mozart explains, as if it is as plain as the nose on his face, "is have someone carrying the right bit of information defect."

He seems at loose ends, half-hearted, polite but distant, vaguely disreputable with his crosscurrents of thick hair spilling off in several directions. He stares vacantly over the shoulders of people and tends to become aware of their voices when they stop talking.

"Did you hear what I said?" asks Kiick, the balding man who runs the Paris shop for Topology. He is hot and perspiring and mops the back of his neck with an oversized handkerchief. He stares at Stone, then catches himself staring and looks elsewhere.

"I'm sorry," says Stone. "I was thinking about greenhouses."

He checks his watch, and then studies the departure board. "There it is—Air France 613 to Istanbul, gate six."

They start down one of the wings of Orly toward the departure gate. Stone's mind wanders—to the telegram from the lady lawyer who puts an "Ms." before her name, telling him the judge has ruled against him; to her defensive letter that followed, claiming that some kind of scandal was brewing around Stone and the hint of it had undermined his case; to the long, almost incoherent letter from Thro, admitting (in a rambling parenthesis) that the scratching incident had not been an accident after all, and announcing (in a brutal P.S.) the end of their little world.

Kiick has trouble keeping up with Stone. "I never got to congratulate you on the new post. Defense Intelligence is a bigger canvas than Topology—more room to be creative, if you know what I mean."

"It's nice not to have Mozart breathing down my neck," Stone admits.

Kiick laughs uneasily, looks nervously around at the passengers behind them. "Listen, Stone, you did me a good turn once"—Kiick is speaking quickly now, almost as if he wants to get it over with as soon as he can—"and I owe you one."

Stone glances at Kiick, only mildly interested.

"It's like this," says Kiick. "Someone's after your scalp. They're putting together a dossier—they've got film, they've got tapes—of you selling NATO stuff to that Russian in the Grand Vefour."

Stone stops in his tracks. "But you know that was an operation."

"I have your word for it," Kiick says, "and I believe you." He mops his neck again. "You got the authorization in writing?"

They both know the answer; authorizations of this kind are always verbal.

"You were in on it," says Stone, starting to walk again. "You can prove it was an operation—you can tell them what happened to the money."

201

"They found the money, Stone," Kiick says. "In Zurich. In a numbered account that's been traced back to you."

Over the loudspeaker system, a female voice announces in French, English and Turkish the imminent departure of Air France flight 613 to Istanbul. Stone looks at Kiick without seeing him, then turns toward the desk to present his ticket.

Kiick says, "I almost forgot why I came here. The embassy heard you were going to check out the lay of the land in Istanbul. They asked, as long as you were going, would you mind taking this along with you." Kiick unlocks the thin gold-colored bracelet around his wrist and offers Stone the diplomatic pouch. "Save them a courier run, if you know what I mean."

To Stone, it is suddenly just another solution. *"On my side, there are limits."* An echo of his own voice comes back to mock him, to haunt him. *"You crossed. We wouldn't."* Frowning as if he has confirmed the absence of a great scheme of things, he snaps the bracelet onto his wrist and turns his back on Kiick.

The Sisters

Centering on Francis and Carroll, two enigmatic and extremely dangerous CIA legends dubbed "the Sisters Death and Night," *The Sisters* masterfully unveils an abyss of artful deception. By luring a former head of the KGB sleeper school into betraying his last and best assassin, Francis and Carroll set off a desperate race against time as he tries to stop his protégé from committing the Sisters' world-shattering crime.   ISBN 978-0-14-303821-4

Legends

Martin Odum is a one-time CIA field agent turned private detective in Brooklyn, struggling his way through a labyrinth of memories and past identities—"legends" in Agency parlance. But who is Martin Odum? Is he a creation of the Legend Committee at the CIA's Langley headquarters? Is he suffering from multiple personality disorder, brainwashing, or simply exhaustion?   ISBN 978-0-14-303703-3

An Agent in Place

Deep in the vastness of the Pentagon and the bowels of the massive KGB center in Moscow are old Cold Warriors who refuse to fade away. Yet how can they wage their battles when there are no enemies anymore? Their answer is Ben Bassett. Sent to Moscow as a lowly embassy "housekeeper," Bassett meets a fiercely independent, passionate Russian poet, Aïda Zavaskaya, and falls under her spell. Together they become pawns in a dreadful game that leads to the clandestine heart of the Soviet system itself.   ISBN 978-0-14-303564-0

The Once and Future Spy

When "the Weeder," an operative at work on a highly sensitive project for the Company, encounters an elite group of specialists and a clandestine plan within the innermost core of the CIA, disturbing moral choices must be weighed against a shining patriotic dream.
                                                   ISBN 978-0-14-200405-0

The Defection of A.J. Lewinter

For years an insignificant cog in America's complex defense machinery, A.J. Lewinter, a scientist, is now playing both sides against the middle. As Russia and America struggle to anticipate its opponent's next move, Lewinter is swept up in a terrifying web of deceit and treachery.
                                                   ISBN 978-0-14-200346-6